CELIA BUC

FAMIL

CELIA Buckmaster was born on 28 November 1914, and her youth was spent in London and Buckinghamshire.

In September 1937 she married Robert Gibson-Fleming, but they divorced two years later. Around this time Celia Buckmaster moved in the London literary circles centring on Dylan Thomas, publishing work in progressive literary magazines. She was also close to poet Lynette Roberts, with whom she worked as a professional flower arranger.

In late 1939 Celia Buckmaster travelled to Burma and married Edmund Leach there in February 1940. In 1942, after the Japanese invasion of Burma, Celia returned to England with her new-born baby Loulou, and bought a house in the Hertfordshire village of Holwell. Celia and Edmund later had a son, Alexander, in 1946. The family moved to Cambridge in 1953 where Edmund Leach was a university lecturer. At Holwell Celia wrote her only two published novels, *Village Story* (1951) and *Family Ties* (1952).

Edmund Leach was knighted in 1975 and after his retirement the couple lived at Barrington, outside Cambridge. Lady Celia Leach died in 2005.

FICTION BY CELIA BUCKMASTER

Village Story (1951)

Family Ties (1952)

CELIA BUCKMASTER

FAMILY TIES

With an introduction by
Elizabeth Crawford

DEAN STREET PRESS

A Furrowed Middlebrow Book
FM52

Published by Dean Street Press 2020

First published in 1952 by Hogarth Press

Cover by DSP

ISBN 978 1 913527 31 0

www.deanstreetpress.co.uk

Introduction

'No one was more important to both my wife and myself than Celia Leach, wife of the Provost, Professor Edmund Leach', wrote Michael Craig-Martin of his time in the early 1970s as artist-in-residence at King's College, Cambridge (*On Being An Artist*, 2015). He remembered that 'Celia was a strikingly handsome woman, tall and thin, sharply observant and good humoured. She was a fine painter and writer. . . .', a comment suggesting that he knew of Celia Leach's previous incarnation as Celia Buckmaster, author of two novels published twenty years earlier, *Village Story* (1951) and *Family Ties* (1952). Both had been issued by the Hogarth Press, the publishing house created by Leonard and Virginia Woolf, by then subsumed into Chatto and Windus. Although Celia Buckmaster did write at least one further novel, her career as a published author came to an abrupt halt after *Family Ties*, her existence as an author all but forgotten, even by those researching women authors of the period. Craig-Martin remarks that Celia was 'fundamentally out of sorts with what she felt was the philistine and intellectually pretentious academic world surrounding her', a view confirmed by her daughter, Loulou Brown, who remembers that, during the period when her father was provost of King's (1966-1979), her mother 'loathed' the social duties it was necessary for her to perform.

Celia Buckmaster was born on 28 November 1914, the eldest child of Guy Buckmaster (1886-1937) and his wife Barbara (*née* Geidt, 1888-1975). Her grandfather, Henry Buckmaster, was a brewer and at the time of his marriage Guy Buckmaster was a manager in the family business. This was, however, not a station in society favoured by his wife's family and by 1915 he had qualified as a barrister. The change of career could have been prompted by a desire to remove the taint of trade, anathema to the Geidts, but, more practically, was probably taken in the knowledge that the future of the family business was insecure; his father was made bankrupt in 1921. Celia's mother had been born and brought up in Germany, of British/Tasmanian parentage, very conscious of the wealth and social position that previous generations of the family had enjoyed.

Details of Celia's childhood and youth are shrouded in mystery; for instance, she never revealed to her daughter where and how she was educated nor, in detail, where she had lived. Research shows that in the 1920s and 1930s the Buckmasters occupied a succession of houses, first in Northwood, on the northern fringes of London, and then in Buckinghamshire. For many years they also had a London apartment in New Court, Carey Street, and, after Guy's death, his widow and children occupied a flat in King's Bench Walk, in the Temple.

Reviewing *Family Ties* in the *Daily Telegraph* (26 September 1952), John Betjeman wrote 'There are families which can only converse in terms of bickering. This authoress knows exactly how they do it. The characters are all in the same walk of life, the impoverished semi-gentry of a country village, consisting of cantankerous parents and frustrated adult children, married and unmarried. Each family quarrels with itself in the same laconic and polite way'. Personal experience is likely to have honed Celia's skill in this sphere, the relationship between the four Buckmaster siblings being, as her daughter remembers, far from harmonious.

Guy Buckmaster died in March 1937 and in August Celia's engagement was announced to Robert Gibson-Fleming, a solicitor. The wedding took place in Kensington the following month. The marriage, however, proved disastrous and two years later Celia, still only 24 years old, emerged from it, a divorced woman. As such she incurred severe disapproval from some family members and in later years knowledge of this first marriage was firmly suppressed. The episode is, perhaps, echoed in *Family Ties* when Amy Monsoon's erst-while father-in-law is relieved when she remarries because, although very fond of her, he had thought of her, 'after George divorced her, as a social outcast'. After the real-life marriage breakdown Celia, traumatised, took to her bed, only emerging after treatment, found for her by her mother, from Kilton Stewart, an unconventional US psychotherapist.

In the late 1930s Celia Buckmaster moved in the London circle that centred on Dylan Thomas, publishing work in a handful of progressive literary magazines, such as *Wales*, *Seven*, *Twentieth Century Verse*, and *Poetry: London*. She was particularly close to the poet Lynette Roberts, acting as bridesmaid at her wedding to Keidrych Rhys in October 1939, her beauty remarked by the best man, Dylan Thomas. A few days earlier, when supplying information to the enumerator of the 1939 Register, Celia had described herself as a 'Flower Decorator', for she worked with Lynette Roberts buying flowers from Covent Garden and arranging them in the homes of the wealthy. 'Bruska', as this rather bohemian little business was known, fitted neatly into the daily social whirl. In late 1938 and early 1939 the two young women had spent a couple of months in Madeira, their journey home enlivened by a near shipwreck. Celia, described as 'poet and authoress', was reported by the *Daily Mail* (10 April 1939) to be worried about the fate of 'the novel she was writing [and] pictures she had painted'. For Celia was indeed an artist, painting throughout her life. She appears to have had no formal training, other than, in the post-war period, that gained in annual visits to the Suffolk art school run by Cedric Morris and Arthur Lett-Haines at Benton End. These visits gave her the utmost pleasure.

In late 1939 Celia Buckmaster travelled to Burma to marry Edmund Leach, later an eminent anthropologist, the wedding taking place in Rangoon (Yangon) the day after her arrival in February 1940. They had been introduced by Kilton

Stewart, with whom Leach had a few years earlier undertaken his first, still amateur, fieldwork on an island off the coast of Formosa [Taiwan]. Their daughter acknowledges that, as in *Family Ties* 'Mr Swan' had returned from the East with the idea of finding a wife, so a faint parallel could be drawn with the inception of her parent's marriage. In 1942, after the Japanese invasion of Burma, Celia, carrying her new-born baby, Loulou, made a hazardous journey back to England, where she eventually bought a dilapidated, part-Elizabethan house, 'Gurneys', in the Hertfordshire village of Holwell. After Leach's return from Burma, the family, augmented by the birth of a son, Alexander, in 1946, continued living at Holwell until moving to Cambridge in 1953 following Leach's appointment as a university lecturer. It was while living at Holwell that Celia wrote her two published novels. Leach was knighted in 1975 and after his retirement as provost of King's College the couple lived at Barrington, outside Cambridge. Lady Celia Leach died in 2005.

Elizabeth Crawford

CHAPTER ONE

MR. MONSOON was known in the village as "the old gentleman," and nobody minded when he said, "Amen, Amen, Amen," when the prayers got too long on Sunday morning; people knew he had rheumatism, and in any case the Vicar was apt to ramble on and on. He kept the sermons short too by sighing and clearing his throat after a certain time. But when the old Vicar died and a new one came, all this was changed. The old Vicar had always chosen something out of the Old Testament as a text for his sermon, and generally preached about woe and destruction. This was comforting for his congregation, who knew what to expect, and it had suited the tone of his voice, which had been low and quivering and full of poetic emotion. The new Vicar was quite different and spoke about "Conditions in the modern world" in his sermons (with a text taken from the New Testament) and nobody knew what he was driving at. Besides which, he used his normal everyday tone of voice in the pulpit and was apt to say—"And that means You and You and You" (pointing)—which made everyone nervous.

The village church was ancient. It had a Norman tower and Saxon remains. Oliver Cromwell's men had removed all the heads of the statues from it, and the Victorian lord of the manor had added chancel rails, an organ loft and an organ and put in some hefty mahogany stalls for his family. Various other people had put up plaques, windows, and bits of statuary. But otherwise the church remained the same through the ages. There was also an effigy of some nameless Crusader (feet crossed at the ankles). Legend had it that he was the first Tyce to be lord of the manor, and, as such, Mr. Tyce all through his life had done honour to that Crusader by laying a bunch of flowers near the feet, on his own birthday.

But Mr. Tyce is dead. He lies outside in the graveyard among the yew trees where the rooks caw and the cats sleep;

his home is sold, and his children are dispersed; and his wife, living on in the Dower House, gets more and more difficult and dotty as time goes by. Mr. Tyce was the last of the squires. He had started drinking seriously in 1918 when hard times forced him to part with a great deal of his land, and just about a year before my story begins he collapsed and died—officially of pneumonia; really it was drink. Parting with his land, bit by bit, had broken him. It was sad, but also it was history coming round full circle, because it had been by enclosing land that the Tyces had first become rich.

On coming to this rather remote little village, Mr. Ashe, the new Vicar, had thought that here, where men lived close to the soil, the bitterness and discontent which marred the urban scene would be unknown, and life would focus, with a little help from him, around the church. He was a good soul, the Vicar, full of ideas for helping people on, getting them going, and setting them up on their feet. But as it happened, no one in the village was in need of having these things done; they were enjoying a bit of prosperity for once.

The end of the Tyces at Hereward Hall (their ancestral home) had been accomplished quietly, and because the old lady retained her rights over the Dower House until she died (when it would revert to the rest of the property) nothing seemed to have changed. Mr. Ashe liked to be thought of as a modern up-to-date sort of chap, so he didn't talk much about the sadness of the Old Order passing; but when fewer and fewer people came to his church he began to feel the need of expressing his sentiments about village folk, who, he now saw, were after all a pretty hopeless Godless lot. Turning towards the gentry, he found them pretty Godless too. Having rebuked Mr. Monsoon sharply about the Amens and sighings and shushings, he didn't feel like visiting him again socially; Mrs. Tyce lived like a recluse and hardly ever went out, much less came to church, and Mr. Rockaby, a retired business man who dabbled in archaeology, didn't count for much one way or the other, and his wife made herself ridiculous wearing nylons in the country, Mrs. Ashe said; and the daughter never went to church. So that left Mr. Swan. But Mr. Swan was one of those people who keep themselves to themselves, very much so. The new people at Hereward Hall (which was now a girls' school) went by bus every Sunday to the town eight miles away where there was a Cathedral. The Vicar was feeling cut off. It was fortunate then, in one respect at least, that Mrs. Tyce started writing anonymous letters. Mr. Rockaby was the first to receive one of these, and complained to the Vicar at once. Mr. Ashe, recognising the handwriting, found out the address of the old lady's nearest relative, and, waving aside all offers of help from his wife, said with feeling, "Leave this to me."

Now Mrs. Tyce, although she has no vestige of power left, is still, in the hierarchy of village society, first lady; so I think I ought to describe her first before Mr. Monsoon. She is past eighty and so is able to look back on a long life more than half of which she has spent being horribly bored. You see, her husband was definitely County, but she was Society. Her father had been a banker and made pots of money, and was accepted at Court, and Mr. Tyce married the daughter for money. All this was in order; but unfortunately, soon after the marriage, Mrs. Tyce's father lost all his money and the whole structure of this excellent alliance collapsed. However, Mrs. Tyce did her duty and lived in the country and bore seven children, all of them boys. Every single one of the boys had a proper education, and now they have all settled down with dull jobs and boring wives (common girls Mrs. Tyce called them, but it couldn't be helped)—except the youngest.

This boy, a man now of thirty-eight, is called Rupert. He travels about. He has been to Lhasa, Pekin and all those far-away places that one reads about in expensive books with colour plates; but, as his brothers say, he always turns up in the end like a bad penny. He is a worry. His family won't lend him any more money, so at the moment he is stuck in London in a small mews flat, writing articles on Chinese painting and boring all his friends by pointing out the decadence of modern art. He collects jade and Chinese bowls and has love affairs but isn't married yet. Mrs. Tyce never cared much for any of her children, and unless she had to, never met them, as they were looked after by governesses and nurses; but now Rupert is grown up, she rather likes him. He is on friendly terms with his mother and takes her part when she irritates the rest of the family as she sometimes does by interfering with their private affairs. "Mother is all right" he says when his brothers complain that the old lady has become a menace. But when he gets the Vicar's letter he says "Blast!"

The Vicar has just returned from an afternoon visit to Mrs. Tyce. It is over a week now since he wrote a letter asking Rupert to communicate with him at once, or, better still, to come down and see him to talk over the distressing affair of that anonymous letter. He still hasn't had a reply and is getting nervous. He had hoped to find out whether Mrs. Tyce had heard from her son, or if she were expecting him to come down to stay some time soon. He has walked pretty fast all the way back from the Dower House to the Vicarage and is still out of breath.

"Well, Helen," he says, "they're quite right, the poor old thing is potty. Clean off her head."

The kettle, which was fitted with one of those gadgets which scream at the boil, now let off this dreadful noise. Mrs. Ashe rushed off into the kitchen to stop it, while the Vicar called out after her, "It's all right, dear, I only want a cup"— which she couldn't hear. They had both supposed Mrs. Tyce would ask the Vicar to stay to tea, so Mrs. Ashe hadn't bothered about the kettle or the table-cloth and was just eating an apple when her husband came back, very cross, and grumbling about, "Good heavens, a man did want something more than an apple when he came home fagged out." The visit had been a failure. In fact, Mrs. Tyce had talked so much the Vicar had hardly been able to get in a word; and when Mrs. Tyce had suddenly said, "Well, it has been most pleasant, Mr. Ashe, this unexpected visit. But I am sure your wife expects you for tea, so I won't detain you"—he had been taken by surprise and had quite forgotten to ask about Rupert. But he needn't have worried because Mrs. Tyce was expecting Rupert. She was much too polite to have mentioned this as it might have seemed that she was shooing the Vicar away. And, otherwise, had she not been expecting her son, she would have asked the Vicar to share her tea; only of course she would have been most annoyed had he accepted.

Directly the Vicar had gone Mrs. Tyce looked him up in Burke's *Landed Gentry*. He wasn't there, but then she hadn't expected he would be. It was a habit of hers to look people up after they called. She also had the *Parish Registry* handy with which to refresh her memory, because, although she so seldom went out, she believed in keeping in touch. Smyly, Mrs. Tyce's faithful old slave, who smelt of mint drops and always looked quite uninterested, brought in tea, and Mrs. Tyce said, "Um. Crumpets. Good." She loved her food.

Meanwhile Rupert is being driven along through the countryside in a taxi which he can't afford, but considering there is only one bus a day and that in the morning, what else could he have done arriving at four o'clock at the station eight miles away? He was lucky to have found that taxi. Rupert hasn't been home for a very long time. His excuse is, he is either just back, or just going to go away, or else he is away. He hates sentiment, family reunions, rows and those sort of things, and he puts on a stern expression because he thinks he is doing his duty. Out of the corner of his eye, though, he is watching the countryside and recognising places. He passes by the Monsoons' rather grand gateway (the gate is permanently open because it is broken) and he knows he will be home in a few minutes. His mother will have to pay for that taxi.

Because Rupert is young and handsome and at times quite gay, it would be natural to assume that he is the hero of this story. But really my hero is Mr. Monsoon. It is very easy to laugh at the Monsoons. For instance, Mrs. Rockaby (the one who wears nylons) writes to her London friends that the Monsoons really are incredible. "Poor as church mice, my dear," she says, "and fearfully upstage. The old man is huntin', shootin' and fishin' and the old girl goes about with a nasty smell under her nose. George, the eldest son, is solid bone from the neck up, and the other son, Stephen, is the back-slapping type—fearfully hearty and fellow-well-met. The back-slapper's wife is the pick of the bunch. Honestly, my dear, she wears woollen ribbed stockings, has her hair screwed up in a bun at the back of her neck, and her face shines like a beacon and is covered with freckles. Amy, George's wife, is a bit of a mystery . . ." and then Mrs. Rockaby goes on to wonder about Amy.

In a way the Monsoons are like this, but to understand Mrs. Rockaby's attitude towards that family, I should explain here that Lavinia, Mrs. Rockaby's daughter, does typing sometimes for George; it puts her in an awkward position socially, she feels, to be thus linked by way of her daughter's employment to the Monsoons, who, no great shakes from a cosmopolitan point of view perhaps, are, definitely, gentry.

Mr. Monsoon, though an active man in the past—he had run through the family fortune, made another, and lost that—has now, at the time of my story, reached that stage in life when one falls back on one's hobbies (fishing and shooting and enjoying the garden in his case) and as for the rest, well, it's up to one's family. His house, which was called the Grange, was not very old, and had it not been covered with creepers would have been rather ugly. But the garden was nice. There had once been a model farm attached to the property. This had been sold. For some reason Mr. Monsoon had always hoped that one or both of his sons would be farmers.

"The point is," he used to tell them, "you have both had a public-school education, without which no one can be a gentleman. And to be a good farmer one must be a gentleman; the other sort are only interested in making money and ruin the land and don't count." These words had no effect. Stephen made friends with a local young man and got himself taken on as an ordinary hand at market gardening. He learned the ropes, saved up, and said he looked forward one day to setting up on his own not too far away. But somehow, even when he became his own master, and having made the thing pay, that day never came. His wife, Vivienne, a thrifty gentlewoman whose people lived in a nearby village, would have liked to have had a home of her own. But, as her husband said, he travelled about so much because of his job (he drove one of the lorries sometimes as well as rushing around in a shooting brake looking for contracts with shops)—really, the expense of a separate establishment wasn't worth it. If Vivienne persisted he always said, "Well, if we had a houseful of kids . . . Thank God, though, we haven't." Which clinched the argument. Vivienne suffered a lot being childless. She knitted thick useful socks for Amy's two sons because Amy always bought clothes and wasn't much good with the needle, and the things she bought didn't last.

"Poor George, such an expense," Vivienne would often say to her husband.

George, now a solicitor with an office in the town which he reached every morning by car, wasn't very well off. Having an energetic partner, and not being a demon for work like his brother, he rather neglected his office, returning home early, especially in summer. Unlike his father, he didn't go in for shooting or fishing, and the only things he had ever killed intentionally were butterflies—for collecting, not for sport. But this had been in his youth. He had quite a large collection of butterflies, and now that he no longer hunted them, he was trying to write a book about them. This book of George's (it was always the same one) had been twice refused for publication. He used to read parts of it out to his family sometimes on winter evenings. Mr. Monsoon went straight off to sleep at such times, his mother generally played Bezique with Vivienne, so it was left to Amy to listen. But he never asked her opinion, and when he stopped reading, it was Mrs. Monsoon who said, "Oh, George dear, how nice." Amy said nothing. The last time the book had come back from the publishers, George had asked for an interview, which had been granted. He had learned then that his book was much too heavy going for the General Public. He asked Amy what she thought this meant, and she had suggested making the book a bit more light-hearted.

"How do you mean?" he said.

"Well, put in a few jokes, for instance," Amy had said.

So now he was putting in jokes. Anyone who has ever tried to be funny will know how hard this is.

The Monsoons as a family were all enormous. George and his brother were over six foot, the old man not much less, and Mrs. Monsoon was five foot eight. Vivienne looked taller than she was because she was thin and wore pipe-like skirts, and so Amy, who was of medium height, seemed small. She had brown eyes and fair hair and was intelligent, but this didn't show, and men liked her at once. Her real name was Aimée; not that she was French, her parents just lived in France where her father wrote novels. Even to George Aimée had sounded queer, so when his mother had made a terrible fuss about having a foreign girl to live in the house and he had made it clear at last that his bride was as English as he was, he had given way when Mrs. Monsoon said, "Very well. But if she's English she must be called Amy." It was a thoroughly suitable name, as George explained, and so ever afterwards Aimée was known as Amy.

Not being interested in butterflies really, Amy had tried to be interested in her children when they arrived. Now that they had gone to school she found life rather pointless. She read French books to keep up her French, helped with the housework, and then in the afternoons, either wrote letters or went for long walks. But not being a countrywoman, the number of partridges in a covey, or seeing a fox, didn't really excite her imagination, and she still disliked mud and getting her feet wet. As the gentry were getting poorer and poorer and selling up their estates, there were few amusements; no point to points and no hunting, and of course no more entertainments at Hereward Hall; so that it was a dull world because even though Amy had never been very enthusiastic about these things, she had met people in the old days, and in her own way had enjoyed such gatherings.

The boredom she felt must have crept into her letters, for her father, not usually unsympathetic, wrote back rather sharply, saying, "Cultivate your garden, Aimée!" While her mother wrote (in a separate letter), "You have made your bed and must lie on it. I warned you about the frightful dullness of being respectable and living in the country. But you wouldn't listen. It's too late now to complain."

George couldn't understand anyone being bored. "Collect something," he said. "Or you could go visiting. You ought to go out more. There's that new Mrs. Ashe, or there's Mrs. Rockaby. Pay them a visit and see." Mrs. Monsoon suggested Amy should join a library, and Mr. Monsoon thought (privately) that the solution was more children. He also thought that teasing was a good remedy for gloominess or distress. So because Mr. Swan, a neighbour who long ago had made sheep's eyes at Amy, had just come home from the East, he said things like, "Better tell George to look out now. That old beau of yours will be prowling round—you wait!" It was maddening. Mr. Monsoon was very fond of Amy.

"I hate to see an unhappy woman about the place," he said to his wife one day. They were walking in the garden.

"If you worried a little more about other things, and not always about Amy," Mrs. Monsoon said, "then, you know, Charlie, things might get done."

"But this really does worry me," Mr. Monsoon said. "I can't stand unhappy women. Men can always do something like big-game hunting when the worst comes to the worst. Or take up politics. But it's different for your sex. They grieve. And I can't stand it. When women get really unhappy I always feel that, like animals, they should be put out of their misery."

"What on earth do you mean?" his wife said.

But Mr. Monsoon avoided answering and said he must speak to George, seriously.

"And I hope, in future, you will consult George before spending any more money," Mrs. Monsoon said.

Now old Mr. Monsoon had just lately, and against Mrs. Monsoon's wishes—he understood finance, she knew they were very hard up—restocked the river with trout. This river ran past the garden and on through the village. Mr. Monsoon was a keen fisherman, but so were other people in the village. When she pointed this out, Mr. Monsoon told his wife to mind her own business. Women didn't understand sport. So Mrs. Monsoon had retired. However, with the advent of the new stock of trout, a heron had put in its appearance. It perched on an overhanging branch of the cedar tree some distance from the house, down by the river where it was very quiet. Nevertheless Mr. Monsoon had spotted it, and, worried about the fate of his trout, had decided that at all costs the heron must be done away with. So every morning early when it appeared, he would dodge out along the path through the wood with his gun, in order to surprise and shoot the bird when he came out, very carefully, at the far side by the river. But always when he got there, the heron had disappeared. To attack it frontally from the house was no good because directly the bird saw anyone coming through the garden it lifted its enormous wings and flapped off.

"The damn thing must have a sixth sense," Mr. Monsoon would say, very saddened when time after time he had made his manoeuvre through the wood to no purpose. But in fact it was Mrs. Monsoon who saw to it that the bird disappeared before destruction could overtake it. As soon as her husband left the house and was safely among the trees, she grabbed hold of a table-cloth or an apron or whatever was handy and waved it vigorously out of the dining-room window.

"Just shaking out crumbs, dear," she said when George asked once what on earth she was up to. Although she ate trout and birds and anything else that came to the table and wasn't a bit peculiar about food, even so Mrs. Monsoon had never believed in the wanton destruction of life. She said that the animal creation had as much right to live in the world as humans, and the world was there to be shared. It was a spiritual conviction, but it made life difficult none the less. There was the matter of the pigeons for instance.

For as long as anyone could remember there had been pigeons in the dovecote over the stables; but all of a sudden in the spring of the year I am talking about they had begun to increase out of all proportion. This was a nuisance because Mrs. Smith, the cook, had taken a sharp and revengeful dislike to the birds when they started flying about in the yard and making a mess of her washing.

"Isn't that sort of thing supposed to be lucky?" Mrs. Monsoon had said vaguely when accosted with the results.

"Yes, on your head," cook said, holding out a sheet for inspection, "but not on my washing."

Mrs. Smith and her husband are the only servants left now in the Monsoons' house. Mrs. Smith does the cooking and the washing and a bit of the housework, and Mr. Smith, who is much the same age as his master, does things like stoking the boiler, bringing in coal and cleaning shoes. But his usefulness in these matters is offset by his habit of quarrelling with any outside help such as girls from the village his wife introduces, or used to, in order to train them up as she said. He is not on very good terms with William the gardener, and is thoroughly disliked by Stephen, whom he once caught as a child catapulting a cow, and later watched being punished (Mr. Monsoon had no qualms about beating his children). Mr. Smith is religious. Also he is sentimental and talks a good deal about Nature in an old-fashioned way. He used to drink but got Saved and is rather pompous because of this, and tells little children about the Devil and idle hands. He likes to watch his wife work, but when she gets in a temper goes and sits at the end of the garden reading his Bible by the beehives. Seeing him there one afternoon, as it seemed to her doing nothing, Mrs. Monsoon reproved him. Without looking up, Mr. Smith began reading aloud.

"He saith among the trumpets, ha, ha," he read.

"That'll do, Mr. Smith," she said.

He looked up then and told Mrs. Monsoon that she too would be called to judgment, and wasn't it high time she ceased being concerned so much with the frivolous affairs of the world?

"He's perfectly right," Mr. Monsoon said when the conversation was repeated to him afterwards.

"Very well," Mrs. Monsoon said. "Then that means, Charlie, there won't be any more meals, no one's going to see about the house—and you'll have to make your own bed."

"It's all lost on a woman who can't see things in proportion," Mr. Monsoon said as she walked out.

George was reading the paper and said nothing. But Vivienne, who was knitting, said, "A woman's work is never done!"

"You don't know what you are talking about," Mr. Monsoon said. And Amy, sewing on name-tapes very badly, for she hated sewing, looked up and said, "Oh well, it's no good quarrelling about the day of judgment. Perhaps father will put in a good word for us when the time comes."

Mr. Monsoon leaned forward and patted her hand and said, "Dear Amy."

Afterwards he must have made it up with his wife, for the meals appeared as usual, the house got looked after in a mild way as it always had; and of course Mr. Monsoon did not have to make his own bed. All the same Mr. Monsoon made it quite clear that he was not going to have any nonsense about those pigeons and he took no notice whatsoever when his wife said, "Charlie, Mrs. Tyce's remarks were uncalled for, but she is perfectly right. You are not safe with a gun."

This was an allusion to Mrs. Tyce's anonymous letter, received four days ago. It had been easily identified as she had not bothered to disguise her flowing italianate hand.

"Old men should not be allowed to handle guns," it read. Which was rude. But worse, it was perfectly true, because not very long ago Mr. Monsoon had taken a shot at a sitting bird (one of the pigeons) at such an angle that, missing their target, the bullets went straight through the bathroom window, ricochetted off the bathroom tiles, and narrowly missed Mrs. Smith, who was having a bath at the time.

And now Mr. Monsoon is at it again. He lies flat on his belly in the wet grass taking careful aim at the decoy pigeon. Mrs. Monsoon, who was just coming out of the house with her gardening gloves and a pair of scissors and a basket, was terribly startled by the bang, and two upstair windows opened almost immediately.

"Father, do be careful!" Amy called down. She could see her father-in-law from the nursery window, but couldn't quite make out what he was up to. The other window, farther along to the right of the house, belonged to George's study. He shut it now, having heard his wife call out, because obviously the situation was in hand. He hated interruptions and said, "Oh!

Damn!" and then went back, through a haze of pipe smoke, to get on with his work. The jokes were getting him down.

This time the bullets had found their mark and the decoy pigeon was all over the place in bits.

"Whatever did you do that for?" Amy said. She had come down, and was standing looking reproachfully at her father-in-law, who was still lying on the grass.

"It wasn't any good, that's why," Mr. Monsoon said. "The pigeons never took the slightest notice of it. Why should they? And in any case, it wasn't sporting. But you wouldn't understand that." He got up as his wife came down the path towards him. She had her gloves on by this time and was just off to pick a few roses before it got damp.

"Missed, I suppose," Mrs. Monsoon said as she passed by.

"Not at all," Mr. Monsoon said.

"That means pigeon pie again. Oh dear," his wife said. She wandered off without looking back. Mr. Monsoon was rather annoyed, so didn't correct her any further. From the corner of his eye he had seen Mrs. Smith come creeping round the side of the house. She was not pretending, she really was frightened after what had happened in the bathroom. She had heard the gun go off, and had feared the worst. Now when she saw that there was no fuss and that therefore no one was dead, she came along faster, calling out, "It's no good, Sir, it really isn't any good. All this shooting only makes us all nervous."

Mrs. Smith had her own ideas on how to keep pigeons down. She climbed up into the pigeon loft when they were nesting (which they did right up till winter-time), took down their eggs, boiled them hard, and put them back. This way the pigeons didn't lay again immediately and sat sometimes for weeks, on hard-boiled eggs. Naturally when she got hold of them she wrung the pigeons' necks, and just lately the Monsoons had eaten practically nothing else except pigeon pie. And when Mr. Monsoon said, "Oh, get away with you, woman!" she went off to put yet another in the oven for dinner that night.

CHAPTER TWO

MR. SWAN really had been in love with Amy once in a negative dreamy way before going off to take up his job. Now he lives all alone in his father's house. He has been in the East; but he got black-water fever and came home on leave. Then his father died, and he sent for his things, gave up his job, and decided to settle down and make the best of the small property which his father, being a doctor and very busy, had allowed to go to bits. Mr. Swan is always tidying up things, putting things in order and saying, "Where there's a will there's a way," though really he doesn't believe this. He has that puzzled, melancholy look common to many Englishmen who, believing in Justice as something Absolute, get broken-hearted living in the East. Unlike Rupert Tyce, who is sometimes consoled and even reconciled to the many difficulties of life through Art, he cannot tell the difference between one bowl and another and collects things to remind himself he's been about the world, not because he likes them or can't do without them. Thus in his sitting-room on the mantelpiece a large Buddha—so large that it is apt to intimidate his guests—stares over the top of people's heads with wide metallic eyes on to the far wall where spears and battle ornaments are hung. Deities with too many arms stand about on little tables next to ashtrays which belonged to Temples once, and sometimes when nostalgic and remembering the magic of the East, Mr. Swan even lights joss sticks. This makes the place smell odd, and his housekeeper, Mrs. Henlow, who comes in every day from the village, sniffs and starts a search behind the sofa and in all the corners; but Ting the Siamese cat is neutered and perfectly clean.

One day Mr. Swan got an unsigned letter which read: "Young man, you ought to get married." He thought this very extraordinary. Having no real contacts with the village, he didn't know about Mrs. Tyce's activities. It was not a thing about which he cared to start enquiries. He noticed the post-mark and came to the conclusion that the letter must be a leg-pull, a joke in very bad taste. He had, as a matter of fact, often thought about marriage, and supposing himself to be free of illusions concerning love after that long stay in the East, had already begun looking around for a decent girl who would care for him and his house, bear him a child or two, darn his socks and be there if he wanted to talk in the evenings. This girl, and there wasn't another of his own class in the village, turned out to be Lavinia Rockaby, the Rockabys' only daughter. Mr. Swan has just recently asked her to marry him and has been accepted, but made her promise not to say anything about it yet to her parents. He likes things done in his own good time and doesn't want to feel rushed.

Mr. Swan came out of his lonely house with a gun, intending to shoot some rabbits. It was evening and the long warm twilight of summer had begun. After a while, having wandered about, keeping his eyes open for rabbits but at the same time noticing weeds and checking up on the number of trees already marked to be cut down, he approached the hedge at the end of his garden. Mr. Monsoon's garden was on the other side of the hedge, and a ditch running parallel with the hedge smelled very badly. Mr. Swan had already complained about this.

"Must get a move on with that ditch," he said now. "Those Monsoons want waking up. Insanitary. Never could get on with them." He has forgotten all about being in love with Amy. But of course that was calf love.

A loud voice said suddenly from beyond the hedge, "It's no good you going off like this in a fit of sulks." Mr. Swan craned his neck and saw George and Amy.

"I want to go for a walk in the fields by myself," Amy was saying.

"But that's just ridiculous," George said. "You know you are afraid of the dark."

"I shall be back before that."

"All right. Have it your own way."

Mr. Swan coughed and called out, "Good evening." George bent down to examine the ditch and Amy fled.

"Evening," George said.

Mr. Swan smiled. "Sorry if I'm being a nuisance, but you do see, don't you, what I mean about the mess. It smells."

George looked up. "Yes," he said, "it has always been like that. Bad drainage."

"Where there's a will there's a way," Mr. Swan said. "I daresay it'll be quite a job. But perhaps you'll be able to repair it. Still having trouble with your pigeons?"

"Oh yes," George said. "I took some away by bike last week, but they got back before I did."

Mr. Swan frowned. "But, my dear chap," he said, "whatever's the point of that? If you really wanted to be rid of them, why didn't you wring their necks?"

"I know, I know," George said. "The whole thing is quite ridiculous. You'd have to be one of the family to understand. Look here, what exactly do you want me to do about this ditch?"

"Well, it's insanitary, isn't it."

"The smell is a bit of a nuisance in hot weather. But smell never killed anybody."

"It's a question of getting things straight."

"Quite. But there are so many other things beside the ditch."

"I agree. For instance, this hedge is full of holes. Haven't you noticed it? And as it happens, it's a party hedge. So it's up to both of us to keep it in good repair. But it's getting late now. How about meeting some time to discuss things? By the way, care for a rabbit?"

"No, thanks."

"Getting a bit dark now to shoot any more, so I'll be turning in. Good night. See you perhaps in the morning."

"Good night," George said.

Mr. Swan thought afterwards he might have asked George round for a drink and got the thing settled.

"A matter of organisation," he said to himself, pouring out whisky. On the other hand, it was getting late.

"Cheers!" he said automatically, raising his glass. "Well, I'd better make this my night-cap." He drank it and went to bed.

Left alone after Amy and George had gone, Mr. Monsoon had fallen asleep that evening. Suddenly he woke up and couldn't think where he was. After a bit he recognised the verandah arches and said, "Fancy leaving me all alone like this!"

He began to get up, but was very stiff. "They shouldn't have left me alone," he said. He listened to hear whether anyone was about in the house, but all was silent. He looked out into the garden, but it was dark there. A bit of jasmine tickled his ear. He picked it and then, liking the scent, snapped off a few more branches. Going indoors, he turned the lights on and began searching about in the bottom of the dining-room cupboard for a vase. And finding one behind cartons of breakfast food and jars of malt left unfinished by Amy's children, he made his way upstairs and along the landing to the nursery, where, now that the children had gone to school, Amy sewed and wrote letters and read. He knocked on the door. There was no answer. So he went in and put the flowers down on the table nearest the door. Then he sighed and walked slowly off to his bedroom down the landing.

Very soon after this George came back. He had put a lot of slug death down after his talk with Mr. Swan, having noticed the sad state of the irises which grew near the ditch. He came in by the verandah and called out softly, "Amy?" He saw that his father had left two cushions and a rug out and put these away.

He decided Amy must have got home and called her name again gently, and then in a louder voice. Not getting an answer, he switched the lights on in the hall and looked about him. But obviously, Amy wasn't there. So he went upstairs. When he found that she was not in the nursery or their bedroom, he became annoyed and began shouting "Amy! Amy!" at the top of the stairs with one hand holding on to the banisters.

Shut up in his room with his warm purple dressing-gown on over his clothes, old Mr. Monsoon could hear this, but he took no notice. He was patiently constructing bait for his trout from a number of bright small feathers. He always made his own dry flies. Afterwards he would read either a page or two of the *Financial Times* or a book by Zane Grey—(preferably the one about Lassiter)—or *Hamlet*; these two being his favourites—and after that, something from the Old Testament. Finally he would finish *The Times* crossword puzzle which he had purposefully left unfinished during the day (nobody else was allowed to complete it). Last of all he would say a prayer, kneeling down on a footstool at the side of his four-poster bed. And then for the rest of the night he would toss about trying to sleep. Because although for some reason it was easy enough to fall asleep directly after a meal, once he got into bed really tired and bored, sleep often evaded him until the small hours. And he always got up at six. Mrs. Monsoon, who slept in a room beyond the dressing-room, complained about this early rising habit of his. But it was no good; and possibly he made such a fearful noise about getting up just because he wanted to wake his wife, being certain, as he said so often, that early rising predisposed one to live a long life.

George, who also believed in getting up early, but not at six, was now thoroughly angry. He spoke sharply to Mr. Smith, who was hanging about in the kitchen looking for something to give the cats, and told him to stoke the boiler. Then, making a good deal of noise, he went from room to room downstairs turning all the lights on and off, wound up the grandfather clock (which was unnecessary, it went for eight days and had been wound two days before), and finally, having come to the conclusion that Amy was perverse and in one of her tempers and wouldn't come in till he fetched her, pulled his mackintosh off the coat-rack with a jerk. It was one of those coat-racks which need attention and careful treatment. He himself had been at pains just lately to fix it up when, overloaded, the nails had given way and it had come apart from the wall. With the jerk he gave it, and because his mackintosh was hung up and kept fast on its peg by the loop of Mrs. Monsoon's garden hat—which he hadn't noticed—the coat-rack once again gave way, depositing coats, hats, umbrellas, scarves and lots of other things like binoculars and baskets, which shouldn't have been there, all over his feet. For a moment George stood looking at the mess. Then he said "Damn!" disengaged himself and went off to fetch his tools. Coming back, he had just started repairs when Amy came rushing in leaving the front door open and crying out, "George! Oh George!"

"What on earth's the matter?" George said.

She looked as though she might throw her arms round him, but he didn't want this. He put a nail in his mouth, and taking a hammer from the tool bag, turned his back on her to consider the wall.

"I've been so terribly frightened," Amy said.

He made a soothing noise through his teeth.

"George," Amy said.

"Shut that door," George said, taking the nail out.

Amy did. "You might say something, you haven't even looked at me," she said.

"You shouldn't go out alone if it makes you frightened," George said. "You know you are frightened of the dark. Anyway you didn't do what you said. Why didn't you come home when you said you would? How was I to know where you were? I haven't got second sight. And what do you think it was like for me? Nobody here, the lights all left on. I looked all over the place, I couldn't find you. Amy, sometimes you are rather selfish."

"And you are getting more and more unkind to me," Amy said.

George looked very unhappy. He put one hand in his pocket and swung the hammer to and fro with the other. Then he started to pace up and down on the hall carpet. He never went over the edge on to the floorboards, but always turned round sharply where the fringe began. He didn't look up at Amy, though she stood close by, following him with her eyes.

"Things are going from bad to worse," he said. "I don't know what's the matter with everybody. First father, then you. It's too much. And then that fellow Swan. I know father's too old now to be responsible for this place and its upkeep. I know I agreed to take over. It's only right I should. But it's all very well for father to make a fuss and say how much he dislikes Swan; I've got to deal with him. How on earth does he think I can afford to get that ditch done? And, anyway, what's the matter with it? Of course it's choked up. It's been like that for years. I can't see that it matters. And then he wants me to help with the hedge. I can't afford it. He says it's a party hedge. I don't know whether it is or not. The old Doctor never bothered about such things. Why should I? The trouble is, the fellow's come home with a swollen head. Well, he'll damn soon find out we're not one of his Tribes. That's what comes of administering natives. Poor devils. Well, I'm not going to put up with it. I shall have to have a proper talk to father."

He sighed very heavily and went on walking up and down, but a bit more slowly now. He also jingled some keys in his pocket; a thing Amy could not stand. She said nothing, however, but began picking up the coats. Seeing this as he made a turn at the edge of the carpet, George walked forward, and breaking the spell or whatever it was that kept him off the floorboards, he walked over them now and started once more on repairs. Amy knew all about rawlplugs and such things and so was able to help. She handed him the right tools at the right moment. They worked in silence. It took some long time to get things in order. The wall looked terribly scarred. "Finish it in the morning," George said at last.

So they hung the coats and mackintoshes and hats up; Amy choosing them from the heap and George hanging them so that no one peg became overweighted.

"You see," he said in a patient voice, "it doesn't do to hang up too much. I know I keep on saying it. But nobody takes any notice. Don't let me have to say it again."

"No, George," Amy said.

"You're not cross with me, Amy, are you?"

"No."

"Good. Well, let's go to bed."

Amy liked to read a bit before going to sleep, so first she went into the nursery to fetch a book. On opening the nursery door she immediately noticed the jasmine stuck in the vase. She said "Oh!" with surprise.

George, who was in their bedroom next door, heard this and called out rather crossly, "*Not* mice again!"

"It's all right," Amy called back.

"Well, do come along, I'm dead tired," he said. Later, while she was doing her hair, she said over her shoulder, "You didn't put any flowers in the nursery, did you?"

And George, who was already half asleep, said, "No, no. Why ever should I?"

"Strange," Amy said, brushing her hair. "I suppose father must have put them there. I wonder why? Or do you think it was your mother?"

George did not answer, so she went on, speaking to herself, or rather, to her reflection in the looking-glass. "A long time since anyone's given me flowers," she said, "or perhaps they weren't really meant for me. They'd dropped off and someone just stuck them in a vase. Nice though, all the same. Yes, it's a very long time since anyone gave me flowers. Queer the way one lives. Red roses they used to give. And silly girls blushed. Jasmine, now what could jasmine mean? I've never heard of a girl being presented with jasmine! Don't they put it on corpses? No, that's stephanotis. George, do you remember . . . ?"

"Dear Amy," George said sleepily. "So like you to make a fuss about flowers at this time of night. Look here, if I'd known you'd been wanting flowers in the nursery, I'd have got them, you know I would. Why didn't you ask? Do stop being unhappy about it. And I'll pick you a whole great basket of flowers in the morning. And now I'm sorry, dear, I really must get some sleep."

He turned over. Amy watched him in the looking-glass. Then she looked at herself again, examining her face for wrinkles. But there were only a few. George groaned, so she went to bed.

CHAPTER THREE

MRS. Rockaby was less fortunate than Amy. She had rather a lot of wrinkles, but called them laughter lines. Whatever they were she put grease on them from a little jar every night. She believed in the grease. It was very expensive and smelt horrible and when it got in her eyes, as it sometimes did, it stung. So after putting it on she always tried to get to sleep as soon as possible. It was said of her in London, where she much preferred to live, that it was ridiculous to think of her as the mother of a grown-up son. And, going about arm-in-arm with Bertram as she frequently had, that they looked more like brother and sister than mother and son. This made it all the harder to leave London because nobody said things like that in the country and in this remote little village where she now lived it seemed hardly worth while to keep on being young. But it was so much part of her life at the age of forty that Mrs. Rockaby couldn't stop it. She went on bursting into fits of laughter, smiling dreamily and walking quickly, humming and tossing her head (she had her hair cut in the very latest style) all because in that way she felt she could keep herself young. And one day, somehow or other, she hoped to get back to London and hear her friends say, "Why, Evelyn, you haven't altered a bit."

The Rockabys had fallen on bad times. Indeed, they had come down in life, and instead of owning a house in town and a place in the country, they now lived in a small rather Gothic house covered with lots of ivy in the middle of the village. Mrs. Rockaby managed wonderfully. She cooked interesting meals on an oil stove, bottled masses of fruit in the summer and asked all her friends to send her recipes (French ones preferably) so that there would be something to think about in the winter. A woman came in from the village to do all the scrubbing and cleaning, so she kept her hands nice. It was a grind, though. No sooner had you finished with one meal than you had to begin on the next, which, if one wasn't used to it, was sheer slavery.

Lavinia tried all she could to help her mother. She did the washing up, made the beds, and being practical (which, alas, Mrs. Rockaby wasn't) was able to deal with things like blocked sinks, lamps which refused to light or even exploded, and the lavatory when it refused to flush. Really Lavinia was interested in the garden. Which was queer because she hadn't been brought up in the country. After a bit Mrs. Rockaby stopped telling the girl how untidy she was and tried not to notice the dirt under her nails. It was sad how she didn't get married. Lavinia was the eldest, twenty-four. Bertram was twenty-two. Mrs. Rockaby herself had married when only seventeen; very young. And Mr. Rockaby had been old even then. Now he was very old, and pottered. Ever since they married Mr. Rockaby had talked about giving up his job, but Mrs. Rockaby had kept him to it as her friends told her it kept him in touch and he would lose interest altogether if he gave up. When the time came that because of money they had to sell their house in London, Mr. Rockaby had had to give up in the City too because it didn't bring in enough and it was so much cheaper to live in the country. They had often come down to the village in the summer for a bit of peace and a good rest away from it all, so they were not strangers. But, as they had foreseen in part, it was a very different matter living in the country; and cooking and housekeeping instead of being something one gave orders about or did joking when necessary, like washing one's hair when away from town on a visit, was a full-time job.

The sort of appearances that most people worry about such as having one tidy room, a parlour or a drawing-room, didn't worry Mrs. Rockaby. Her house was always untidy, and if it hadn't been for Mrs. Burt (the woman from the village) it would have been filthy. Before going to work at 'The Lodge' (as the Rockabys' house was called) Mrs. Burt had consulted her family about it. On the whole, village women didn't think much of domestic employment. But Mrs. Burt was old and her husband drank and her children were married and had gone off to live in the town so they didn't care, and her brothers said that so long as it brought her in steady money and she didn't go killing herself up there, she might as well oblige at 'The Lodge'. Besides, she could keep an eye on what was going on there. The village didn't much like having strangers in their midst, for whatever Mrs. Rockaby might think, she and her family were strangers.

Mr. Rockaby annoyed everyone by digging up things. He had always taken an interest in archaeology, and just by chance when helping his daughter with the heavy work in the garden (she insisted on double trenching) he had found a coin which turned out to be Roman. This had fired him, and ever since he had been digging and poking around all over the place. At first the villagers had thought he was after moles, and watched him with curiosity. He explained, and various people brought him old spoons and broken bits of pottery unearthed from a dump. But none of these was worth keeping, said Mr. Rockaby. After a bit he turned his attention to the church. The Vicar was only interested in the organisation of the living, not with anything to do with the dead, so he allowed Mr. Rockaby to do as he liked in the church so long as he didn't make too much mess and didn't trip people up with the paving stones when he raised them. But the village people were highly resentful that anyone should tamper with their church even though they didn't often use it. There were complaints. At length the Vicar's wife had the bright idea that Mr. Rockaby should lecture on archaeology to the W.I. in the village hall where they had a meeting once a week. Mr. Rockaby asked his wife to help with the slides, but she had one of her fits of laughter when she heard.

"Donald, you really are an old professor," she said. "Soon you'll be posting your umbrella. No, I'm not going to do the slides, it's your do. I'm not involved."

But Lavinia offered to help, so Mrs. Rockaby said if Mrs. Burt would come in, she would provide tea afterwards. Mrs. Rockaby was very fond of asking people in to tea. She did this suddenly, on the spur of the moment, and then regretted it afterwards. She had invited George like this one day. "Oh hullo!" she had said, opening the gate. And almost bumping into her—he was thinking very deeply—he had taken off his hat and said "Good evening" very solemnly.

"I say," Mrs. Rockaby said, "what about you and your wife dropping in one afternoon for tea?"

"That's very kind of you, very kind indeed," George said.

Mrs. Rockaby had thought very fast, and then said, "Well, what about Saturday? Saturday next. Not to-morrow. Saturday week."

And George had said yes. And she wished she hadn't been such an ass immediately. The truth was, Mrs. Rockaby was lonely. Both her husband and her daughter were out all day and although she made fun of people she liked company. She had always made fun of people, even her husband. It wasn't exactly his age, it was the way he treated her. Once he had loved her dearly, had wanted to put her in a golden cage as it were, had cherished and encouraged her, until far from the gentle creature he had imagined, a very different person had emerged. He had thought to train her in the ways of the world, bring her up carefully ("mould her character," he told her mother, who had smiled mysteriously), but suddenly, fully fledged, she had escaped him altogether. He had put it down to the birth of their children, coming so soon as they had. He hoped that later on, more would steady her. But she had not wanted any more. He continued to reverence in her something that she herself now had no use for. And this was why she mocked him. He was aware of it, but not humiliated as perhaps she wished; though it is difficult to see why a woman should want a humiliated husband. It never crossed her mind that she might leave him. In her way, she was as devoted as he was, and if ever he got exasperated, went to great lengths to calm him. Thus when he lost most of his money she never taunted him, but putting a brave face on it, agreed to give up the life to which she was accustomed, and without making a single scene, went to live in the country. Neither of them liked scenes. They elaborated their lives a good deal to avoid them, and yet they kept on happening. In this way, Bertram was a trial. Mrs. Rockaby adored him. Bertram did sculpting in Paris, despised his parents and refused to help them with money. Mr. Rockaby had very nearly forbidden him the house, but, to avoid a scene, ignored him when he was about. He didn't often come home except when he was broke or needed rest.

None of the Rockaby family was used to bothering about money, but now that they had so little, worry about it ate into their lives in every way. Only Lavinia, who was practical, faced the issue and tried to earn. Besides growing decent vegetables and so making the family that much independent, she also had a job at Hereward Hall. Three times a week Lavinia took reading. This did not mean she had to teach the girls to read, they could do that, but she had to read them the proper sort of books that were nice and all right, and that probably they wouldn't have time to read in later life. Mrs. Hardinger, the headmistress, had so far chosen *Silas Marner*, and three novels by Sir Walter Scott.

The school was very high class. Mrs. Hardinger, like Mrs. Rockaby (they were friends), also believed in keeping young, but not physically so much as young in spirit. It added up to the same thing really. She wore her hair in bubble curls (blue rinsed) and believed in equality, camaraderie, self-expression, and keeping up appearances. It was a hard life, but she managed it. Lavinia got very little pay, not rating as a teacher, but she was useful and gave the staff a rest. Mrs. Rockaby tried hard to appreciate her daughter. But as she said in a letter to a friend, "I have never felt that there is a generation between us, it isn't that, it's the extraordinary difference in our characters that makes it almost impossible for Lavinia and I to understand each other. For instance, Lavinia has worked like a slave in the garden which, because we were only here in the old days for the summer, was just a jungle of weeds. And my dear, she has grown the most wonderful vegetables. But, I said to her, what about a few flowers? All this veg. is terribly necessary and practical, but one also needs beautiful things as well. And too, the part of the garden near the house where she hasn't bothered is a fearful mess. My dear, she was furious!"

However, it is unusual for parents to understand their children, and most parents, having tried and failed, give it up like Mrs. Rockaby. But Mrs. Rockaby liked to think she understood people. She always identified herself with heroines in novels, no matter what their fate, so that, theoretically anyway, she knew something of life. Sometimes she read late. But she had to read by lamp-light as they were not on electricity and there was no gas in the village. If Lavinia remembered to trim the light and saw to it before going to bed, the light generally lasted. But to-night as Mrs. Rockaby read, there was something wrong with the lamp and she couldn't see properly. This was very hard on her wrinkles, but being absorbed in her book she frowned without knowing it.

Arriving home from an interesting evening spent in the organ loft where he had been checking up on its installation among other things, Mr. Rockaby paused when he saw a light was still on downstairs. It irritated him when people stayed up late chattering. But when he opened the sitting-room door he found his wife reading alone. Mrs. Rockaby belonged to a library that sent her two books a week, and looking at these sometimes, and reading a page or two while waiting for meals, Mr. Rockaby wondered what on earth she made of the stuff. Novels, books on psychology, travel books, autobiographies—she read them all. To Mr. Rockaby, who contented himself with Gibbon when at a loose end, this omnivorous reading was strange. For him reading was a diversion; it was always best to do things, to work out one's own ideas. But he had never voiced these sentiments, believing as he did that in the end if he behaved in the right way, others were bound to follow his example. If it was not in them to perceive what was good, it couldn't be helped. Just the same, one didn't have to defer to their standards. He was very strict with himself. So although it was late and she was reading a novel and he would have much preferred to have been alone, Mr. Rockaby just said, smiling, "Hullo, my dear. Isn't it rather late?"

Mrs. Rockaby, who had looked up and then gone back to her book when her husband had paused on opening the door, put a finger on the place where she was reading, and said, "Hullo, dear. Yes I know. But I want to finish this. Lavinia has gone to bed." Then she went back to her book.

"It's nearly twelve," Mr. Rockaby said.

Without looking up she said, "Yes, yes, I know. You go on up to bed."

With a sigh Mr. Rockaby began collecting his things, two note-books, a large box which contained photos of ancient pots, his fountain-pen, and some ink just in case. All these lay on his private bureau which stood in an alcove near the window behind a red curtain which was on an adjustable rod to keep out the draught. There were plenty of other rooms where he could have worked, it wasn't such a very small house, but Mr. Rockaby had said last winter that somehow they simply must economise, and as Bertram had left and Lavinia was most often out, it was ridiculous to heat the whole house for two people, and therefore they would have to do with one fire. The result was, everyone herded together in the one room and nobody had any peace. This was now a habit, so that even though it was summer only one room was used downstairs. Whenever he suffered too much, or as now, felt put out and grieved, Mr. Rockaby always collected his things with a deep sigh, and went off trying not to feel angry. But this retreat, although silent, had far more effect than the most angry protest. It was with the greatest difficulty that the person or persons in the room whose presence had caused Mr. Rockaby's upset could refrain from making a scene of their own. Indeed, the family had agreed that the only way to treat Mr. Rockaby when in this mood was to take absolutely no notice and conscientiously to go on doing what one was doing. This in itself was a strain.

But it was better than jumping up and accusing oneself of being in the way, to be sorrowfully contradicted, to be argued with, to have it thrashed out in a reasonable way, and at length to be left standing thwarted while Mr. Rockaby crept out with his things, softly closing the door behind him.

Mrs. Rockaby, whose nature, though not affectionate, was allergic to unfriendliness in others, had never learned not to suffer when her husband made one of his exits. She kept her eyes on her book now, but read nothing and waited almost without being able to breathe, listening for the sound of a book falling or a pen dropping, which was what generally happened on such an occasion. But this time Mr. Rockaby managed it without dropping anything. Only when she heard the door open did she dare to look up. It was just then that her husband turned round to look at her. Their eyes met.

"Sorry, my dear. Am I really such a nuisance?" Mrs. Rockaby said.

"No, no, no. You carry on," Mr. Rockaby said.

"But *can't* you work with me here? I'm only reading."

"It's these notes I'm trying to prepare. I must feel, well, completely without distraction."

"I won't distract you. I told you, I'm reading."

"I know, dear. You are reading a novel."

Mrs. Rockaby put a match between the pages to keep her place, and closed the book. "I know perfectly well you don't approve of me reading novels," she said. "It's obvious. But wouldn't it be better to say so and have done with it instead of making this fuss?"

Her husband looked wretched. "No. It isn't that at all," he said.

"Well then, what is it?"

"I have no right to interfere. You should be allowed to do exactly as you please."

"But if you disapprove?"

"That has only to do with me."

"But, Donald, it hasn't. I don't like people to disapprove of me—not in that way."

The clock on the mantelpiece struck twelve. Neither of them interrupted it, but when it had finished striking they both said how late it was. Then Mrs. Rockaby, with the book under her arm, said it really was time for her to go off to bed, and walking over to her husband tapped him with her fingers.

"Don't go on working too long," she said.

Her husband patted her hand and turned his face away. Not looking at her he said, "Don't take any notice of what I say. I have no right to judge others. I am not a good man. I know I have failed. But you know, Evelyn, sometimes you are very difficult."

"Am I?" Mrs. Rockaby said. "I wish I could understand you, Donald. If only you could try a little more with Bertram for instance, show him something of yourself—write him friendly letters, ask him to spend his holidays with us—don't you think that would make everything easier?"

"I was speaking of things as between you and me," Mr. Rockaby said. "I wish you wouldn't always confuse yourself with the children."

"But, Donald, what have I except the children? And of course, novels," Mrs. Rockaby said. She laughed.

Mr. Rockaby turned round and said sharply, "That Bertram of yours is no good."

Mrs. Rockaby stepped back away from the door.

"You have no right to say that," she said.

"I am afraid you are a little naïve, Evelyn," her husband said. "I have watched that boy very carefully during the past years, and believe me, he's nothing but a conceited double-faced rascal. That's what he is."

"I won't have you talk like that about my son," Mrs. Rockaby said.

"Our son," said Mr. Rockaby. "Beware of being possessive."

"But only just now it was 'Your Bertram', that's what you said."

"Well, that is exactly what you have made him. You have lavished all your affection on him. And it's very wrong. What do you suppose poor Lavinia must feel?"

"Oh, she's a girl. She'll find a husband. I do wish she would," Mrs. Rockaby said.

Mr. Rockaby dropped his pen. He stooped down to pick it up before answering. Then he said, "Evelyn, you have not been a very good mother to the children. It is painful for me to say this, but that is how it is. I hope I may be forgiven."

"I'm sorry you feel like that," Mrs. Rockaby said, "but as a matter of fact I've always thought you have never been a father to them at all. Now you had better get on with your notes or whatever it is. It's frightfully late and if we go on like this we shall be quarrelling. Good night."

"Good night, my dear," her husband said, making room for her to pass.

After she had gone, he took his things back to his bureau and then sat there a long while in thought.

Finally he shook his head, sighed, and unhooked some bills. On each side of his desk there were two large hooks like coat-hanger tops anchored to blocks of wood. On the left those bills which were outstanding and urgent were supposed to be stuck on one hook, while on the other his family had been told to put new bills which could wait. The right-hand side hooks were reserved for receipts and memoranda which had to do with money. These arrangements had been set up by Mr. Rockaby himself, but no one kept to the rules and the result was all bills were jammed down on one hook. The receipts were lost. Lavinia had offered to keep accounts for the family, but her father thought this an unpleasant job for a girl and not quite right. Every so often he dealt with the matter himself. It was a form of punishment he indulged in after being cross or nasty to his wife. First, to remind himself and in order to be able to tell them at breakfast exactly how little money there was, he looked at his cheque book. And having made sure of this, he next unhooked the bills and began sorting them out. He shook his head constantly. There were so many unnecessary things being bought. There always were. Long before he had got down to the business of signing cheques the lamp failed. It made a popping noise suddenly and began smoking in earnest. Hurriedly Mr. Rockaby got up and turned it out. He had never been able to master it and feared an explosion. He stood then, in darkness.

"Now what am I going to do?" he said.

But moonlight soon came to his rescue, and in a minute he could see again. He went to the window and looked out into the garden. It didn't look so untidy by moonlight and the unweeded paths, cut straight and edged with low box hedges, seemed less desolate. There were shadowy places where in daylight dead shrubs and struggling flowers cluttered up the beds; these now, mysterious and quiet, formed sanctuaries where stray cats slept. The hard clear light of the moon was only strong enough to make black shadows; there was no colour and no sound at that time of night. Nothing moved, nothing prowled.

"It's an odd world," Mr. Rockaby said. "I don't suppose I shall ever be able to understand it." He stood there a long time.

Eventually Mrs. Rockaby knocked with a hairbrush on her floor upstairs, calling out, "Donald! For God's sake— aren't you ever coming to bed?"

He called back, "Yes, yes. I'm working," stood about a few minutes more, and then, finding his way across the room very carefully so as not to bump into anything, he reached the hall, found a candle and went up to his own room, calling out as he passed his wife's door, "Good night, my dear."

They always called out a final Good night to each other like this.

CHAPTER FOUR

MRS. Henlow, housekeeper to Mr. Swan, had never thought much of her new master. It made her realise, now that the Doctor had gone and she had to do for the son, how good the old days had been. At first she had thought things would go on much the same, and had said to Mr. Swan, "You know what your father used to give, Sir, for my husband's rheumatism—those pills, the pink ones. I put them away in the bathroom cupboard myself. Now if you would kindly give me the bottle, Sir, I wouldn't always be troubling you." It had come as a nasty shock when Mr. Swan said, "Mrs. Henlow, certainly not. I am not a doctor." As Mrs. Henlow said to her husband that evening, she knew that all right, who didn't? If ever a man was missed, that man was the Doctor. Next day she told Mr. Swan again about her husband's rheumatics, his terrible sufferings, how he turned about in the night. She was good at describing pain. But although she went on and on about her husband, day after day, she had to give up in the end, because after suggesting that her husband paid a visit to the doctor in the town, Mr. Swan said, "You might try fruit salts," which showed how little Mr. Swan cared for her problems. Everyone in the village took salts—what good were they? So Mrs. Henlow didn't get on with Mr. Swan. She didn't like his cat, either.

"There's nothing worse than a dirty cat," Mrs. Henlow had always said. She had never been able to find anything that the cat did in Mr. Swan's house, which made it worse. So whenever Mr. Swan went out, she put the cat out.

One day Mr. Swan came in from the garden just after eating his breakfast, with a small bunch of roses.

"They don't last long this time of the year," she said, not thinking much of the bunch. Mr. Swan didn't answer, but after turning the tap on so that the sink got half full of water, he put the roses in.

"Like that they last better," he said. "I shall want them later. Please don't disturb me. I shall be working in the study." He went off.

"Now how am I supposed to wash up the breakfast things?" Mrs. Henlow said. She made up her mind then to give in her notice. At ten she made some tea, knocked on the study door and took it in.

"I thought I said not to disturb me?" Mr. Swan said.

"I'm ever so sorry, Sir," Mrs. Henlow said, putting on a blank face, "but I have to give notice."

"If you must go, you must," Mr. Swan said, taking the tea, "but it's most unfortunate."

"I'm ever so sorry, Sir," Mrs. Henlow said, "I do hope you'll manage. I don't know whether it's true, but I did hear— well, there's gossip you know, Sir."

"What on earth do you mean, my good woman?" Mr. Swan said.

"People talk," Mrs. Henlow said. "I daresay there's not a word of truth in it. But down in the village they say you are going to get married."

"That will do," Mr. Swan said. He didn't know how to treat domestics, and gave blunt orders and terminated interviews abruptly. Mrs. Henlow was hurt, and went, and didn't change her mind about leaving as she had been quite prepared to do gradually. Later on, Mr. Swan came out to the scullery for his roses. He found Mrs. Henlow there, very pink, cleaning shoes. He said nothing to her, but picked up the roses, shook them and did them up with green twine. He then went out. Mrs. Henlow heard the gate click.

"There's gratitude for you!" she said. She went off to put the cat out.

Picking the roses, it had been Mr. Swan's intention to take them to the Rockabys'. Mrs. Rockaby loved flowers, Lavinia had said. Not that Mr. Swan liked Mrs. Rockaby. He hated the way she always called attention to herself, the way she had, when you said something polite about the food, of spending the whole of the rest of the meal explaining exactly how she had cooked it and all about the oil stove. But the Rockabys had been very nice to him. People thought Mr. Swan cold and stand-offish in the village, but really he was puzzling all the time over changes they took for granted and he couldn't understand. His own kind had tried to welcome him back to the fold with tea-parties and so on, but he felt that they viewed him askance. This was not so with the Rockabys. Mr. Swan had decided on getting up that morning that it was about time he paid a formal visit to Lavinia's parents to ask for their daughter's hand in marriage. Therefore he had picked the roses with Mrs. Rockaby in mind. But two rather disturbing things had happened since then: first, the post had brought him a letter from Rupert Tyce apologising for Mrs. Tyce's unsigned letter (and he still couldn't understand how Mrs. Tyce, an educated woman, could have brought herself to do such a thing) and second, Mrs. Henlow's gossiping. Giving notice was bad enough, but he didn't like that sort of person knowing about his affairs.

And now, as he walks along, a third unpleasant thing happens; a magpie flies out from his garden in front of him. Mr. Swan is superstitious. But he has picked his best roses, and because his father has left the garden in such a mess, he hasn't many flowers. So he puts the roses down in a damp shady place near his gate, meaning to retrieve them afterwards. He has changed his mind, he will not go to the Rockabys', he will go to the Monsoons' and clear up the matter of the ditch. He goes through the fields down by the river, not by the road, because this way it is quicker. And this is the way he used to go when visiting the Monsoons' with his father.

At length Mr. Swan reaches the little bridge which crosses the river from the fields over to the Monsoons' property, and he pauses to look at the view. From here the garden with the yew trees and long green lawns can be seen in part; on the opposite bank over the bridge, the lawns slope down to the river edge. The river itself flows past, clear and untroubled by weeds. Rushes grow by the banks, and in their shade on the yellow stones on the river bed, fishes lie still, or becoming rocked in the currents, gently balance themselves, or sliding among the stones, disturb the sandy depths. These are Mr. Monsoon's trout, but just now no one is fishing here. Stepping on to the bridge, Mr. Swan intrudes on this placid life. His shadow causes alarm and the fish disappear. An old sheep-dog belonging to Mrs. Monsoon wakes up and growls from his place on the shady side of the bridge. But Mr. Swan walks past, and the dog returns to his sleep. Treading on the lawn (which has just been cut) Mr. Swan's feet make no sound. About eleven o'clock on this summer morning, the sun shines and it is very quiet. There are no farm animals here to make a noise, and except for the larks in the fields behind, the birds are silent. Nobody is about. William is having his mid-morning cup of tea inside the house. Mr. Swan doesn't know the Monsoons well enough to shout "Coo-ey," and besides he isn't the sort of man to do that. So he makes his way over the lawns, in and out round the hedges, past what used to be the herb garden, on down the path bordered by tiger lilies, walking slowly and looking round each corner rather uneasily, but not of course calling out. Thus he walks on, until at last, in the heart of the garden among the roses, he comes upon Amy fast asleep. She lies stretched out, comfortably, on a white bench; a pillow supports her head, which lolls to one side a bit, and her hands lie folded over a book on her lap. The sun is bright, and Mr. Swan wonders how she can sleep, or why, on a lovely morning like this. He stops to find out if she really is asleep. His shadow falls on her face, and he wakes her up.

"Oh!" Amy said.

"I'm so sorry," Mr. Swan said. "I do beg your pardon. I hope I didn't startle you."

"But however did I fall asleep?" Amy said.

Mr. Swan cleared his throat. He would have liked to have moved off. But Amy said, "Oh dear, I've just been dreaming I was lost in a forest and wandered about for what seemed like hundreds of years. Silly, isn't it?"

"Can't see the wood for the trees—ha ha!" Mr. Swan said.

Amy slipped her feet off the bench to the ground. "Won't you sit down?" she said.

Mr. Swan looked at his watch. "Well," he said, "I rather wanted to have a talk with your father-in-law about that ditch."

"Oh," Amy said. "Yes, the ditch. But, well—it's such a lovely morning isn't it? I suppose the ditch is important. What are you going to do with it?"

"It's a matter of bad drainage," Mr. Swan said, "you see . . . But really, you don't want to be bothered with this." He smiled.

"Well, I hope you won't think I'm always asleep in the mornings," Amy said. "And dreaming too. Isn't it ridiculous!"

"Funny things dreams," Mr. Swan said. He sat down, just on the edge of the bench. "Yes, you know, I sometimes dream I'm still in the Far East. I lived in the jungle, you know. Yes."

"Tigers!" Amy said, "but I suppose when one is used to them, even tigers aren't surprising. Like everything else. Or were there no tigers? I'm afraid I don't know very much about jungles and things."

"Yes, when one says 'jungle' everyone thinks of tigers," Mr. Swan said, "but there weren't any tigers. Of course I *have* seen them. . . ."

"'Tiger, tiger, burning bright,'" Amy said. She looked thoughtful. Mr. Swan, who was watching her face, noticed how she frowned, and supposing she had forgotten the next line, quoted it slowly in a coaxing tone of voice.

"'In the forests of the night,'" he said. And was surprised at the cross look Amy gave him.

"But that's right—that's how it goes—I'm pretty sure it is," he said.

"Oh yes, yes, I know," Amy said. "It reminds me of my dream, that's all."

"Do you know," Mr. Swan said, "I've just remembered something myself. Wasn't it about ten years ago you first came here?"

"Yes, I think so," Amy said.

"A long time ago."

"Yes, it is."

"And now you have two children. Dear me."

"Oh, but don't look so sad!"

"Don't you ever wish you were young again? I mean, of course, you are not old—no, no—a young girl again I mean."

"No," Amy said.

"I very much wish I could have my time over again," Mr. Swan said. "I've wasted so many years. Doing absolutely useless things. Fretting and trying to alter unalterable things. And making arrangements that nobody wanted arranged. But perhaps women are not so foolish."

"I've never *done* anything," Amy said.

Mr. Swan smiled and said "Tut-tut" quietly. They both thought for a moment. Then Mr. Swan said, "There's something peaceful about this garden. So quiet here, and so old. You are fortunate to belong to it."

"Do you think so?" said Amy. "It's because you've travelled about and seen the world, I expect. We are very shut off. Nothing happens here, nothing at all."

"No," Mr. Swan said. "I didn't mean that."

"Well, that's how I feel it."

"If only one could let it be, life is really very romantic," Mr. Swan said. "I mean, if, instead of always trying to arrange things one could just lean back and observe the way things happen from time to time, I don't say one would *learn* anything—life isn't a lesson—but one might catch something of life's irrational charm. It's hard to explain this, but the fact is, I was once awfully struck by you, Mrs. George. Please don't be insulted. I was only a fool of a boy at the time. Seeing you here reminded me of it. That is what I meant about life being romantic."

"But how nice of you to tell me that!" Amy said. "Ten years is a long time. Fancy you remembering."

"But I have only just remembered. Had I not come here this morning, I might never have been reminded of it."

"It's the garden, not me," Amy said.

"No. Something to do with the way we live. Time, you see, only goes one way. 'Time is God' as they say in the East. But sometimes the significance of an event can only be understood looked at backwards over the past. And without us, who live in the present, but who also know that we lived in the past, events would be meaningless. And, don't you think, Mrs. George, it is important to be detached sometimes, allowing events to take on significance, rather than letting them drown in the past? Forgive me. Perhaps these things don't interest women."

"You are a poet, Mr. Swan," Amy said. "You ought to write poetry."

"I'm afraid I am not very gifted. And I am not often inspired. So you see what you have done for me!"

"Oh not really. It's all in your head. I'm a nobody really. Just a wife and a mother," Amy said.

"*Just* a wife and a mother? But, Mrs. George, whatever else could you want to be?"

"Oh, myself," Amy said.

"What a mistake," Mr. Swan said. "You should try to take life more seriously. Find out what is important—I'll lend you some books if you like. As a mother you must have tremendous responsibilities. . . ."

"Oh please! You'll get angry—don't," Amy said. "Forget all about that. I would never have spoken if you hadn't startled me for a moment. I thought you meant something else. I misunderstood. No. Forget what I said."

"I'm sorry," Mr. Swan said. "I'm afraid I've been talking through my hat."

"Well, let's both take back what we said!"

"But I've been wasting your time, I'm so sorry!" Mr. Swan looked down and caught sight of his watch. He frowned. "Well," he said, "all this remembering doesn't do, you know. Time goes on, and we must get on too. One should look forwards, not backwards."

"Sideways," Amy said. "Sideways, don't you think? Otherwise it's so dull."

"You are laughing at me," Mr. Swan said. "Or are you being profound? One never knows with a woman. . . ."

"Yes. Well," Amy said, "you want to see father. Honestly, Mr. Swan, I shouldn't if I were you. Not about that ditch."

Mr. Swan jerked his shoulders straight and sat up. "Oh?" he said.

"No," Amy said. "You see the thing is, father isn't always in a very good temper in the mornings. Let my husband see about it for you. He'll be back early this afternoon. Or could I do anything?"

"Good gracious, no!" Mr. Swan said. "But one does want to get these things straightened out, you understand."

Amy sighed. "I quite see what you mean," she said, "only, it's a bit difficult."

"Not when one really gets down to it. All these things need is a little forethought, a plan of action. It's so simple when one gets down to it. All one needs is a plan."

"Yes," Amy said. "The ditch smells sometimes, doesn't it? I suppose that's a bad thing."

"It's unpleasant, insanitary and quite unnecessary," Mr. Swan said. "And to me, it is very surprising that Mr. Monsoon should have let this state of affairs go on so long. For that of course I also blame my father."

"Well, I suppose we just don't notice it," Amy said.

"But, my dear Mrs. George . . . !" Mr. Swan said—he was going to say "The thing stinks to heaven"—but heard someone coming along down the path, and turned round. It was Mrs. Monsoon with her gardening basket, come to pick some more roses.

"Good morning," she said. "What a lovely day, isn't it?"

Mr. Swan got up at once.

"Good morning. Yes. It's lovely," he said. "I was wondering whether, if, that is, it's convenient, I could have a word with Mr. Monsoon this morning?"

"With my husband?" Mrs. Monsoon said.

"Yes, concerning the ditch."

"The ditch?"

"Yes, you see, it smells," Amy said.

"Oh dear," Mrs. Monsoon said. "Well now, what do you want to do about it? Dig I suppose. Rather a hot day for digging. Still, you are used to hot climates. Yes, if you want to dig . . ." She began looking at the roses.

"I don't think you quite understand me," Mr. Swan said. He felt awkward.

Mrs. Monsoon began cutting roses. "I don't think my husband would be very much help at his age," she said over her shoulder. "My son George could help you dig. But then, he won't be back till this afternoon. And Stephen's away. I think it's rather a dirty job, isn't it, for Vivienne or Amy. You see, we are all rather busy, Mr. Swan, in our different ways. I am sorry though, that the ditch should cause you so much worry. Perhaps the wind will change, then you won't be able to smell it. Does it smell? I can't say I have ever noticed it."

Mr. Swan put his hands in his pockets and leaned back on his heels, holding himself very stiff at this angle and addressing Mrs. Monsoon as though she were turned round the right way and he didn't have to speak to her back; "I'm very sorry," he said, "but I must really insist on seeing Mr. Monsoon about this."

"Lovely roses, aren't they," Mrs. Monsoon said, "but prickly." She tried to remove her sleeve from a thorn, but got pulled farther than ever into the bush. "Yes," she said, after a bit. "Yes. By all means. He's probably shooting pigeons somewhere about in the garden. With a gun, you know. Yes, if you want to you must certainly talk the matter over with my husband."

Amy got up from the bench, forgetting her book. It fell, and Mr. Swan stepped forward and picked it up immediately. It had a French title, and he was unable in the short time between picking it up and handing it over to understand what the title meant. But even while Amy was saying "Thank you so much," he re-remembered his French. *Les Fleurs du mal*. Evil flowers.

"You shouldn't read that sort of thing, you know," he said in a low voice. "I'll bring you over some interesting books. What you need is philosophy. Women should have either religion or philosophy. Or so I am told."

"Amy will show you the way," Mrs. Monsoon said, turning round.

So after saying good-bye politely to Mrs. Monsoon, who smiled vaguely and then went back to her roses, Mr. Swan went off with Amy.

"A lovely old garden," Mr. Swan said as they walked along.

"Yes," Amy said.

Mr. Swan looked as though he had something sad on his mind, and Amy sighed. They didn't speak any more till near the house. Then Mr. Swan drew in a long breath and said, "A very fragrant smell that; reminds me of the East."

"It's the jasmine. It grows all over the house," Amy told him.

Mr. Monsoon wasn't shooting just then, but standing about on the lawn shaking his head over the dandelions. This part of the lawn hadn't been mown, and he had asked Amy that morning to help him with weeding. But she hadn't done this. He had got on with the job by himself and had just stood up to ease his back, when over the top of the hedge he saw Amy coming along with Mr. Swan. "Good morning, Swan," Mr. Monsoon said. "A long time since we've had you as a visitor. What brings you here?"

"Good morning. I would very much like to have a word with you, if you don't mind, Mr. Monsoon, about that ditch," Mr. Swan said.

"Can't hear," Mr. Monsoon said. "It's too hot to stand about chattering. Better go in. Amy, show Mr. Swan indoors."

Amy did her best to make things easier for Mr. Swan. She showed him into the parlour, saw that he had a comfortable chair, and brought sherry and biscuits in. But Mr. Monsoon, directly the ditch was mentioned, became trying. He said he couldn't hear, and edged himself very near Mr. Swan, not looking at him, but presenting him with what he said was his good ear. He said "Yes, yes, yes" several times in the wrong place, and then, looking hurt, said—"Can't quite make out, Swan, what you are talking about. Speak a bit louder."

Mr. Swan wasn't going to be done and roared out again about the bad state of the ditch.

"Which ditch?" Mr. Monsoon said. "Sorry, I can't hear."

"Very well then, I'll write it down," Mr. Swan said.

"What's he say? Can't catch it," Mr. Monsoon said, turning to Amy. But he had lost the battle because already Mr. Swan had got out a pencil and paper and was drawing a plan.

"If you want me, I'll be in the garden," said Amy.

"All right—no need to yell!" Mr. Monsoon said. Amy went out.

She found her mother-in-law still picking roses.

"Can I help?" Amy said.

"No, dear. You read," said Mrs. Monsoon. Amy sat down on the bench.

"I'm afraid father is making it difficult for Mr. Swan," she said.

"Not a very nice man. So domineering. And rather rude, don't you think?" said Mrs. Monsoon.

"But rather charming. He lives in a sort of dream. And he's honest," said Amy. Mrs. Monsoon snipped off one more rose, and then turned round.

"Blue eyes, you mean," she said. "I suppose so. But he glares with them. That's what makes him look honest. Blue eyes, cold heart—isn't it?"

"No. Cold hands, warm heart."

"Well, he has those then. He's not at all like his father."

"Yes, Doctor Swan was a nice man, wasn't he. Funny to think he brought my children into the world, and there they are, and he's gone."

"That's life, isn't it. Well, there we are. I think I've picked off all the dead heads. And now these ought to be put into vases."

"I'll do that," Amy said. She got up.

"My dear, you are very restless," Mrs. Monsoon said.

"The trouble is, I'm bored," Amy said. "I haven't anything to do these days. No children—nothing."

Mrs. Monsoon paused, holding the scissors in one hand, the basket with the roses in the other.

"Yes. Well, of course in my day boredom hadn't been invented," she said. "But then *we* didn't read novels in the mornings. It was unheard of."

"Well! Give me a job then, Mother, for Heaven's sake! And it's not a novel, it's poetry."

"Worse," Mrs. Monsoon said. "Poor Amy. I always find there is plenty to do if one wants to do it. Not another spring clean just now. But there's always a cupboard. Or you might start on the tallboy downstairs. Vivienne is always busy about the house."

"I should like to have a really necessary job," Amy said. "Something that I could do that made me feel wanted."

Mrs. Monsoon thought a moment, not looking at Amy. Then she said, "You never got on very far with that embroidery you started, did you? And what about George's book—he needs help I'm sure. He never reads it out now as he used to. It seems to me, dear, you are rather inclined to pick things up and then drop them half finished. If ever we got like that as girls my mother used to make us take pills. Iron Jelloids they used to be called. They were very good. You might try. And plenty of exercise, Amy—long walks. This morning for instance you could go down to the village with Vivienne and help with the shopping. That would make quite a change."

Large tears formed in Amy's eyes. "Didn't you ever feel, Mother, that the fun had gone out of life—that the whole thing was utterly pointless?" she said.

"I never suffered from self-pity," Mrs. Monsoon said in a shocked voice. "You had better go in, Amy, and ask cook for a cup of tea before things get worse."

"I suppose you never cried either," Amy said. "We are not at all alike, are we, Mother? But tea, I'm afraid, won't stop me from feeling sad. It's all right, I'll cry, and then I'll do the shopping."

Mrs. Monsoon said nothing but walked off with a stern look on her face.

Mr. Swan came back through the garden, not very pleased with himself. Things hadn't turned out as they should. Frowning, he passed by the rose garden. Amy looked up from her book. He saw her, and made a little bow and said, "Good morning. Or rather, good afternoon," and went on. He walked fairly fast, not liking the thought of the morning gone by and nothing achieved. Arriving at the bridge (which didn't look at all safe, he thought) he trod firmly across, making the boards shake. He noticed that the old dog was still asleep in the shade. And just then, from far away, someone began to call "Bob, Bob, Bob!" He stopped. "That's for you, I suppose," he said. He had a good look at the dog. "Shouldn't keep sheep-dogs as pets," he said. The voice still called out "Bob, Bob, Bob!" so Mr. Swan didn't exactly kick him, but gave him a poke with the toe of his shoe, saying, "Get up! Can't you hear your mistress calling, you lazy old dog?" But Bob, being deaf, could not. He was also bad-tempered, and in a sudden rage at being woken up, made a dart at Mr. Swan's leg, the one nearest. He missed the leg, but tore a hole in the trouser.

"Damn! Damn!" Mr. Swan said as he felt the stuff giving way. He hit out. But Bob loosened his hold and ran off back over the bridge. So, hoping very much no one had watched this very undignified incident, Mr. Swan, after looking round in a casual way (the place seemed deserted), pretended to take in the marvellous view for a moment before going off home through the fields.

CHAPTER FIVE

RUPERT Tyce had also set out on a walk that morning, but after breakfast in bed. He didn't like getting up early. He felt though, it was only right to be out of doors on such a lovely morning: after all, he was a countryman, being born and bred in the country meant something, and perhaps one shouldn't be lolling about like this with breakfast in bed. Having gobbled his breakfast, and excusing himself with the promise of taking the hell of a long walk, he at length set out in moderate spirits, not sure of enjoying himself. But the sun and the freshness of the air brought out the gay side of his nature, and before long he whistled and sang. "Early one morning, just as the sun was ri-hi-sing," he sang. He had a nice voice, untrained of course, so when he came to the high bits—"Ho-ow could you . . . ?" and so on, he whistled that part.

Arriving in the village, he quietened down. Walking fairly fast still, and swinging his arms, he looked round smiling and recognising things. Very few people were about as it was market day in the town and all the women who could leave their homes had gone in very early by bus, while the men were out working in the fields, or indoors at their jobs. But market day in the town held no attractions for Mrs. Rockaby, it just meant she had no help in the house because Mrs. Burt took that day off. Thinking of all the extra work, Mrs. Rockaby made up her face very carefully and stared out down the street. Thus, she saw Rupert pass. Her husband had had a letter from Rupert that morning. She had read it. It was just a formal apology for the unsigned letter his mother had sent, nothing more. "Let the dead bury their dead," Mrs. Tyce had written. In a way it made sense, though one couldn't exactly say what she meant. Mr. Rockaby had made rather a fuss. But now, having had an apology, he just said, "Well-well-well-well. Better ask the lad round."

"He isn't a lad. He's middle-aged," Lavinia had said. It was one of her days at the school. She was late and cross.

"So silly to harp on *age*," Mrs. Rockaby said. "He can't be older than Mr. Swan." An unwise remark. Mrs. Rockaby hoped now that she hadn't done any harm. She watched Rupert down the street. He hadn't looked up.

Mr. Rockaby was having one of those boring ego conflicts with the Vicar; boring, that is, to the listener—the combatants were flushed and spoke loudly, both at once. They stood close together by the entrance to the graveyard, arguing about the date of the font. Mr. Rockaby liked to get dates right and had been poking around that morning, pretty sure in his own mind that the thing was an eighteenth-century copy of some older font, when the Vicar breezed in leaving the door open, saying, "Heavens, my dear man, why shut yourself up on such a lovely morning—you ought to be out!" It reminded Mr. Rockaby of his wife, who always said that, whether it was a nice day or not, when she wanted to be alone in the house. "Do you mind if we have the door shut, there's a draught," Mr. Rockaby said. "But you ought to be out!" the Vicar insisted. Mr. Rockaby said something about the alleged antiquity of the font, and the Vicar said, anyway it was an ugly old chunk. And that had started the argument. The Vicar had won about going out. Still arguing, with the Vicar's hand on his arm, Mr. Rockaby had been led through the graveyard, and they had only stopped by the gate because the Vicar had made the outrageous remark that the font, for all he cared, might have been cast. Which had so shocked Mr. Rockaby that he had thrown off the guiding arm and refused to move on. "But, my dear Sir, fonts aren't *cast*," he said. "Rockaby old man, you have no sense of humour," the Vicar said. Alfred Grole, who was digging a grave (one of the old women in the alms-houses had died), leaned on his spade. It all sounded silly to him, but the Vicar and Mr. Rockaby were getting down to it hammer and tongs, no doubt about that. Mr. Grole liked a fight—the sort when sleeves were rolled up—but nowadays the gentry (so-called) were never rude enough to each other to stop being polite. Mr. Grole sighed, and thought about Mr. Tyce. It gave him a pleasant shock therefore when suddenly the Vicar broke off the argument and called out in a bell-like voice, "Why—my goodness! If it isn't Mr. Tyce!" It was only Rupert, of course, but it made Mr. Grole feel (as later on he said to his wife) that "You have to be careful with what you think in a graveyard. There's more in it than meets the eye."

"Oh, good morning," Rupert said. He would have passed on, but the Vicar held out a welcoming hand, saying, "You know my old friend, don't you—Rockaby the digging enthusiast?" And so Rupert was drawn in. The hidden joke about "digging enthusiast" was explained, they all laughed, and Rupert said, "How interesting."

"Now don't egg him on," the Vicar said, "or we'll be here all morning. And how do you find the old lady, Mr. Tyce?"

"My mother seems to be very well, thank you," Rupert said.

"Distressing this business. Very distressing," the Vicar said. "I suppose you'll be down here for some time?"

"Oh I must get back next week," Rupert said. "It's very difficult for me, you know. . . ."

"You must let us help," the Vicar said. "Now, is there anything we can do? You can be open in front of Rockaby here. He's an old friend."

"By the way, thank you for your letter," Mr. Rockaby said. "It was very kind of you, very kind."

"Not at all," Rupert said. He was furious and couldn't think how to be really rude and stared at the ground. Mr. Rockaby took this to be embarrassment, and said, "Mr. Tyce, my wife and I would so much like you to come to our house. My wife has asked a couple of friends to tea Saturday—would you care to come too?"

"What gay lives my parishioners live! Ah well," the Vicar said.

"I'm afraid I have no time," Rupert said. "This isn't a holiday for me, you know . . ."

"No-no-no-no," Mr. Rockaby said. "My dear man—just drop in if you can. We should be delighted to see you."

"And if I could offer some help . . ." the Vicar began. But Rupert said "Thanks" and walked off.

"Queer chap," the Vicar said when he had gone. "One of the rootless sort I'm afraid. Drifts about. Sad."

Rupert walked on, but without zest. Either he had to go through the fields to reach his home, which meant a long way round, or he could turn back and go through the village again, risking a second encounter. For a while he did neither one thing nor another but sat on a stile and smoked. He said "Damn mother," and thought about London, and sulked. Then he got up, crushed out his cigarette, and began walking back the way he had come, looking haughty and late on an errand, the sort of expression that kept people at bay in London and even made the more timid make way on the pavement except at the rush hour when more or less everyone wore just that expression. But alas, as soon as he saw Mrs. George and Mrs. Stephen coming along, he knew that it wasn't going to work in the country. In town it is easy enough not to notice acquaintances, or, if for the sake of politeness greetings have to be made, a man can raise his hat, look pleasant and then move on with the crowd. It is not quite the same in the country, and to make it more awkward, he hadn't even a hat on to take off. So he bowed. The two wives had been shopping and looked very matronly, each with a full basket under her arm.

"How do you do?" they said.

Rupert said, "How do you do. Lovely day, isn't it."

"Isn't it a lovely day!" said Amy.

"Lucky, because it isn't always like this in June, is it?" Vivienne said.

All three now stood about.

"Well," Rupert said. But then he noticed the shopping baskets. He also noticed that Amy had large eyes and looked sad. This made him unbend yet further. He said, with a very proper show of good manners, "I say, you look rather loaded," and speaking to Amy, "Can I help? It won't be out of my way really if I go back over the fields."

They refused, saying, no, the baskets were not terribly heavy.

"It's a long time since we met," Rupert said.

"Yes, you're a stranger, aren't you, these days," Vivienne said. "Well, we must be getting along."

But Rupert didn't like being called a stranger. "Oh, this is still my home town, you know," he said. "One doesn't forget. . . ."

"And how is your mother?" said Amy.

"Oh, not madder than usual," Rupert said. He laughed. "Forgive me," he went on, "but you can't imagine the ghastliness I've had to put up with about those idiotic letters. Don't say your father-in-law is going to have me up, Mrs. George—I wrote him an absolutely grovelling letter."

"Oh poor Mr. Tyce—what a shame!" Amy said. "No, father has taken it all as a joke."

"Good for him," Rupert said. "It is a bit of a joke really, don't you think? Perhaps I might drop in one day and Mr. Monsoon and I could have a good laugh. He might even tell me what my mother actually said. She tells me who she has sent them to, but not what she said in the letters."

"Why don't you come in and see us," Amy said, "any time in the afternoon?"

Rupert looked thoughtful.

"We simply must get home now," Vivienne said. "Lunch is at one, Amy!"

"Look here," Rupert said, "what about to-day? Are you doing anything? As it happens, I'm free."

"Oh but how nice," said Amy. "Could you come after tea?" She smiled, which made her look really pretty.

"Right!" he said. "Right. That's fine! Till after tea then. Sorry to have kept you." He bowed again, and Amy said "Bye-bye!"

"Goodbye, Mr. Tyce—come on, Amy—really we must hurry," Vivienne said. They walked away.

Climbing the hill, hurried along by Vivienne, Amy said, "Nice of him, don't you think?" And Vivienne, breathless and a little in front, said, "He's not a bit like his mother."

"How do you mean?" Amy said.

"Well, she may be dotty, but she is aristocratic."

"Oh?"

"In fact, if you ask me, he's one of those poisonous intellectuals!"

"But, Vivienne . . ."

"Yes. The sort that end up in some ministry and spend their whole time writing modern poetry while people like poor Stephen get driven mad filling up forms, or if he doesn't, they come down in Government cars to find out why not. Stephen says it's a shameful waste of public money. Come on, Amy."

"But how lovely of them to write poetry," Amy said.

"Are you sure, Vivienne, that such people do exist really? Or is that just Stephen?"

"He's a snob," Vivienne said. "Do come on, Amy. Didn't you notice when he first saw us? He only spoke because he had to. He was dying to get rid of us. *He* didn't want to be seen talking to the Monsoons."

"I should think not!" Amy said. "Us with our old coats on and no hats! A pair of frights."

"No. Country frumps, that's what he thinks we are. He was being ever so gallant. Anyway, bother Mr. Tyce. We're late."

They spoke no more, but walked along very fast until they reached home. Then, whilst hanging her coat up very carefully because of the mended rack, Amy said, "I shouldn't mention Mr. Tyce coming in this evening to father, Vivienne. Not before lunch at least."

"Why ever not?" Vivienne said.

"Well, you know about men and food," Amy said. "We don't want father upset. You should always let them eat first. They take things much more calmly afterwards."

"You do as you like if you think you know best," Vivienne said.

Although Mr. Monsoon would have discouraged any tendency towards wit among the members of his family, he often remarked on young people's total lack of fun. Remembering the buckets of water placed on top of doors, the banana skins, the squibs, the home-made bombs and all the other things that went off bang, he lamented the disappearance of practical jokes, saying, "You people have no sense of humour." And too, he respected eccentricity. When therefore his rage and surprise at Mrs. Tyce's note had blown over, he settled down to treat the whole thing as a joke. All the same, he was secretly rather pleased to have had Rupert's letter of apology, and now he looked forward to entertaining Rupert as his guest. "We'd better offer him some sherry," he told his wife.

Mrs. Monsoon took the whole thing much more seriously.

"I don't know why we should have to show our hospitality towards the Tyce family," she said. "After all, we have been insulted. In the old days Mrs. Tyce made it quite clear her sons had no need to be friendly with our sons. And if you remember, we were never invited to the big parties at her house. Not that it mattered. She had her friends, we ours. And Hereward Hall, although interesting historically, was very draughty."

"I see no reason to cold-shoulder them just because they've come down in the world," Mr. Monsoon said.

"It isn't that," his wife said. "It's because you are delighted to have been noticed at all by Mrs. Tyce, Charlie."

"Saying such things you merely reveal your own motives. I am prepared to accept unreservedly Mr. Tyce's apologies. It would be unchristian to do otherwise. One has one's ideals," Mr. Monsoon said.

Mrs. Monsoon put out a bottle of cooking sherry and went off to rest.

"You look very smart," George said when Amy appeared for tea in a new dress.

"Fancy you noticing," Amy said.

"But I always do. It's you who never notice what I do. For instance, I had my hair cut this morning."

"I know."

"Well, you might have said something."

"It's been cut too short. That's why I said nothing."

"Oh you two!" Vivienne said. She also had done something about her appearance, and Mr. Monsoon, not knowing quite how to put it, said, "Hullo, Vivienne—you look very odd. Something queer about your hair."

Vivienne blushed. "Well, you see, Father," she said, "I know Stephen's not here, but he's often spoken about me going grey. So I altered the parting. Perhaps it doesn't quite suit me. I wondered, but I thought I'd leave it to get used to it."

"Quite. Quite," Mr. Monsoon said. "Now come on, do let's have tea." He had on a new jacket and his best tie.

"I can't think why everyone has dressed themselves up this evening," Mrs. Monsoon said, pouring out.

There was a long silence. Then Mr. Monsoon said, "Pity about those gates. We shall have to get them mended. They won't shut."

"Yes, it looks better people having to open a gate," Mrs. Monsoon said. "Still, I don't see why we should have to spend money just for the sake of visitors opening gates."

"That reminds me. About that ditch," George said.

"Swan can go to hell!" Mr. Monsoon said.

Suddenly a door banged very loudly indeed. Vivienne jumped. Mrs. Monsoon sat up straighter than ever and the other three put on blank faces and lowered their eyes.

"I think that was the front door," Mrs. Monsoon said. "Pass me the bread and butter, please."

Footsteps sounded across the hall.

"Oh!" Vivienne said. "It's Stephen!"

"Hullo everyone!" Stephen said, coming in. He still had his hat on and carried a whole lot of cauliflowers. "Look!" he said, holding out these. "What do you think! I brought them along home just to show you what the old farm can grow. Fine, aren't they?"

"You'd better take them along to the kitchen and come and have tea," Mr. Monsoon said.

Vivienne jumped up from the table, and clasping her hands, ran over almost on tiptoe. "Wonderful!" she said. "However do you do it, Stephen?"

"All in the day's work," Stephen said. "Two acres of them. Not bad for a start, is it?"

"I didn't know you were coming home to-day, dear," Mrs. Monsoon said. "Go and get yourself a cup and saucer and . . ."

"It's too bad," Mr. Monsoon said. "This place is not an hotel. You ought to have let us know. Please take those things away. We are expecting a visitor."

"Oh?" Stephen said. But Vivienne shepherded him out.

"All this dashing about," Mr. Monsoon said. They went back to their tea.

Returning five minutes later, tidy and smelling of soap, Stephen beamed at his family, and drawing a chair in to the table waited till Vivienne had laid his place for him, and then between mouthfuls of bread and butter began to relate the story of his travels (he had been away a week), the excellent deals he had made and all about how his vegetables were got to Covent Garden, No one except Vivienne seemed in the least pleased, but she did her best with Ah's and No's and Oh's. Stephen had a loud voice, and as always when among his family it made the rest of them seem half asleep. He himself was a very wide-awake person. Mr. Monsoon grunted and sighed, gradually retiring into his thoughts, leaving the bread and butter untouched on his plate. George looked at his watch, and Amy, with her hands on the table, fiddled with her wedding ring. Mrs. Monsoon in the intervals of the flow of talk said, "Charlie? George? Amy?" lifting her eyebrows, meaning, "More tea?" And Vivienne leaned forward in her place opposite Stephen, absorbed, not eating anything. "Well, there we are," Stephen said at last. "What about a bit of cake now? Pass the cake, Mother, please." No one so far had touched it. It was a good cake, the fruit sort with almonds on top.

"Well, now," Mrs. Monsoon said, "don't you think as it hasn't been cut we might leave it? Have some more bread and butter, dear. Or one of those buns. Nobody's eating anything to-day."

"Well, I am," Stephen said. "I'm darned hungry. Don't forget, I'm a working man—out and about all day long. The trouble with all of you is, you sit around. Sedentary work. Look at old George—he's getting fat. Adipose tissue, that's what it is. I burn it all up in energy."

"What you mean is, you couldn't sit still if you tried," George said. "In any case, energy doesn't burn anything. You're mixing up cause and effect."

"Don't try and be funny. Come on, Mother, let's have some cake."

"If mother wants to keep it . . ." George said, but it was too late, because with a sigh Mrs. Monsoon had already passed it. Stephen cut himself a large slice and then carved out two more, handing these round with the cake. "Come on now," he said. "You can all have a whack now it's started." Nobody did. He frowned. "Come on, Vivy," he said to his wife. "There's no need to be shy. You'll get scraggy if you don't eat."

Vivienne wavered. "Well," she said, looking round, "if nobody minds—well, perhaps, just a bit. After all, it is cut, isn't it."

"If you wanted cake," Mr. Monsoon said, with his eyes shut, leaning back, "why on earth didn't you say so in the first place?"

"Oh, Father, please, won't you have a bit?" Vivienne said. But he never even answered.

"More tea?" Mrs. Monsoon said. Stephen nodded and handed his cup. He sat between his father and Amy, and Amy, who was next to her mother-in-law on the other side, handed the cup of tea back. She was careless and slopped it.

"Oh, Amy!" Vivienne said.

Stephen turned towards his sister-in-law. "What's up with you?" he said. "You're very silent. And all dressed up to the nines. And do I smell scent?" He sniffed. "Most peculiar," he said. "What do you call that? L'Amour, I suppose. Trust you to find something French."

"I'm sorry if you don't like it," Amy said. "Yes, of course it is French. It's a present from my mother. All good scent comes from France."

"Amy, you exaggerate," George said.

"The English make very good lavender water," Mrs. Monsoon said, "and personally, I prefer it if one must use scent."

"But lavender water and scent are totally different things, Mother," George said. "You see . . ."

"Don't, George," Amy said. "What does it matter?"

"Of course it doesn't matter," George said. "I was only going to tell mother . . ."

"Really, I am not in the least curious," Mrs. Monsoon said. "I just meant, I don't like strong smells but I do like lavender water."

"It's all a lot of nonsense," Stephen said, "women covering themselves with these things. Begging your pardon, Amy, I like you best when you don't smell."

"I think this sort of talk is perfectly disgusting," Mr. Monsoon said. He still had his eyes closed, but managed to look severe. "Please leave Amy alone," he said. "She's worth the whole lot of you put together. I like scent."

"Really!" Mrs. Monsoon said. "Well, as we're worth so little, and if you have finished, Stephen, we'll get on with our work. Perhaps Amy will be good enough to clear away."

"Sorry," Stephen said. "I've put my foot in it. But I want some more cake. Pity to waste it now it's cut. Don't go."

"We are expecting a visitor," his father said, "so please hurry."

"Yes, now I come to think of it, you all look terribly solemn and dolled up," Stephen said, eating cake. "Who's coming? The Pope?"

His mother repressed a smile. "One might well think so," she said. "All this fuss. And it's only Mr. Tyce."

"Good lord! But he's dead."

"Rupert Tyce."

"That bloke! Do you mean to say he still hangs around?"

Mr. Monsoon cleared his throat and opened his eyes. "There has been a little trouble between us and the Tyce family," he said. "Mr. Tyce is coming to make amends. But being such a stranger in this house, and taking so little interest in your own village, I don't think the occasion calls for your presence."

"You needn't worry, Father," Stephen said. "I don't want to meet Rupert if that's what you're driving at. The clever sort are not my type. No, thank you. And he used to cheat at hockey. Thought I didn't see. A rum lot the Tyces. No good the whole bunch of them. Shouldn't have anything to do with the family if I were you. Besides, the old lady's staring mad. Didn't you know?"

"For God's sake, eat and get out!" Mr. Monsoon said. He banged the table with a knife.

Afterwards, while Vivienne helped him unload the shooting brake (which smelt of vegetables as did his luggage), Stephen said, "Funny how I always manage to rub father up the wrong way. Still, it's old age I suppose. Pretty well in his dotage."

"Well," Vivienne said, "it was Amy really, wasn't it? Fancy putting on scent!"

"All the same, you could take a leaf out of her book. She's still damned good-looking," Stephen said. "Here, old girl, take this, will you? Mind, keep it straight! It's not all that heavy."

"Remove that van!" Mr. Monsoon shouted all of a sudden out of the bathroom window. (All the bathrooms and lavatories and less important rooms faced front because this was the north aspect of the house. There were a lot of drainpipes too which the creepers had not entirely covered up. But the front door was very splendid with an arch and studded nails in the wood part and seven steps leading up to it.)

"All right, all right," Stephen said; and then in an undertone to his wife, "I do wish father wouldn't call it a van. It's a shooting brake. A cut above the other firms, you know, to have a brake."

"I know," Vivienne said. She couldn't say more because the box Stephen had given her to carry was really very heavy. He opened the front door for her, and then went back, leaving the rest of the luggage on the steps, to put the brake away.

George and Amy met Vivienne in the hall. George took the box from her, saying it was far too heavy for a woman. She followed him upstairs to see that he kept it straight as Stephen had said, and Amy went out to see if there was anything more. She had just picked up a couple of suitcases, trying their weight, when Rupert came round the corner up the drive. She didn't see him till he said, "Good heavens! Let me." She laughed because he looked so worried.

"Oh, it's perfectly all right," she said. "My brother-in-law has just come home, and I thought I'd help."

"Hardly a woman's job," Rupert said.

"Well," Amy said, "let's take one each."

So they did. Mr. Monsoon, having put a few drops of brilliantine on his white head, was horrified when he met them coming upstairs.

"Mr. Tyce!" he said. "Amy! Really. . . . Allow me."

"Certainly not," Rupert said. "I like carrying luggage. Used to it. I travel about so much myself." They all went upstairs.

Mrs. Monsoon appeared on the landing and said, "Good evening, Mr. Tyce." Then George and Vivienne came down the top flight. Rupert put the suitcase down and was introduced and shook hands all round. It was a very long time since he had met the Monsoon family *en masse*, in fact he had never been a casual visitor to the house; the Tyces and the Monsoons had not been friends even though they lived near together. As Mrs. Monsoon had said, the Tyces had their own friends (who of course had not belonged to the village). However, all this was concealed, and to a casual observer it would seem that here was a happy reunion, not a formal occasion at all, except for the business of shaking hands. This over, they all began talking at once. Rupert said how nice it was to see everyone, and everyone else said how nice it was to see him. And then there were explanations about the luggage and Stephen and jokes about women doing the heavy work, and Mrs. Monsoon said what wonderful weather. It seemed they were permanently stuck on the landing with no room to move and Rupert still on the stairs so they couldn't go down. But at last Mr. Monsoon said, "Now perhaps, Mr. Tyce, you would care to join us in a glass of sherry?"

"Well," Rupert said, "if it isn't too early. . . ."

He stepped aside, making room for Amy. But Amy made way for her mother-in-law, who said, "No, dear, you go first." And then thinking of Vivienne, who stood behind, made way for her. But of course Vivienne was shy.

"No, no, Mother, you first," she said.

Trying to sound polite, Mr. Monsoon said, "Do get on down!"

So his wife gave Amy a little shove, and Amy went first. Mrs. Monsoon wasn't going to be second. In fact, seeing Amy go down like that, she decided not to go down at all just then.

"Amy will show you the way," she said. "If you will please excuse me, I have one or two things . . ."

"Oh, I do hope I haven't disturbed you," Rupert said.

Mr. Monsoon looked very angry, but said nothing.

The drawing-room smelt of roses and wood fires although the silver vases on top of the grand piano were empty and fire-screens stood in front of the fireplaces. It was a large room, and in winter, even with two fires, never warm. Now it was full of sun. Everything was polished and cleaned till it shone. But after Vivienne came in in the mornings with the carpet sweeper and dusters and so on, unless Amy wandered in with a book, looking for somewhere quiet to read, nobody ever came in except at week-ends sometimes, when George played the piano and Amy sang. This room was really reserved for social occasions, and the family, for ordinary everyday purposes, used what Mr. Monsoon called "the parlour"—"the sitting-room" it was called by the others.

The parlour was a small untidy room with books and knitting and sheets of writing-paper left all over the tables. Somebody was always looking for the envelopes, and the half-open drawers of the tallboy were choked up with bits of abandoned embroidery, candles, sealing wax and unravelled balls of string. Of course, Mr. Monsoon had his own study. This was where he did accounts and read books on fishing, and it was always kept extremely tidy by Amy, whom Mr. Monsoon trusted. She never put things away in unfamiliar places as the other women did, and she didn't get flustered when he roared out he had lost something, but said, "It's all right, Father," and found it. The pictures of family ancestors were too large to be hung anywhere except in the dining-room, which they dominated, and in the hall, where Mr. Monsoon's father glared down at visitors; while some forgotten woman in a mob cap hung half-way up the stairs where she couldn't be seen. It was dark on the stairs because Mr. Monsoon, in a fit of extravagance, had had coloured glass put in the staircase window. This window now depicted the family crest in yellow, blue and crimson. The crest was also on some of the serving spoons, though the rest were plain, being part of Mrs. Monsoon's dowry.

Annoyed that his wife hadn't bothered to put the usual sweet peas and gypsophila in the silver vases, Mr. Monsoon made a fuss about where people should sit, pulling up chairs himself and ordering his family now here, now there. When this was done and everyone sat in a state of nerves, except Rupert, who had sunk back into the depths of the biggest chair, he called over his shoulder to Vivienne, "Fetch the sherry." And turning to Rupert, "Well, it is certainly a pleasure to have you here. Afterwards perhaps we might have a few words together. But first, sherry." Then, speaking to George, "A bit warm. Let's have some air."

George opened the window. Two pigeons flew out from the jasmine above.

"Clumsy birds," Mr. Monsoon said, "supposed to be deaf. And there's a heron here. Feeding on my trout too. A difficult business stalking a heron—ever tried it?"

"No, I can't say I have," Rupert said.

"Got a gun?"

"Not these days."

"Pity."

"Mr. Swan used to be a good shot, wasn't he? I seem to remember my brothers saying Mr. Swan was the best shot in the County."

Mr. Monsoon cleared his throat.

"Here's the sherry," said Amy.

Vivienne came in with a tray, and began looking about for a suitable table to put it on.

"Here," Mr. Monsoon said, pointing to one near himself and Rupert. George drew it into the middle of the circle, and Vivienne put the tray down. Rupert and Mr. Monsoon looked at the label on the bottle at the same moment. Rupert lowered his eyes, but Mr. Monsoon, as though mesmerised, continued to look.

"And this time I haven't forgotten the corkscrew, Father," Vivienne said. She stood, waiting, at his elbow.

With the colour rising in his face Mr. Monsoon did his best to control his feelings, and in a quiet voice, very quiet for him, said, "My dear Vivienne, you may have remembered the corkscrew, but you have brought entirely the wrong bottle. One doesn't *drink* this stuff."

Instead of taking the bottle away, or at least keeping quiet, Vivienne stood on her dignity. "That's what mother put out," she said. "It was there with the glasses. You said sherry. It is sherry. But I'll bring in the gin if you like. There isn't much left."

Mr. Monsoon said something about women, pushed his chair back, picked up the bottle of cooking sherry, and went out.

Rupert caught Amy's eye. They almost laughed. George hadn't been paying attention, and said, looking puzzled, "What on earth's all this fuss?"

Vivienne, who was over-excited in any case by the unexpected return of her husband, said in a trembling voice, "I think father's awfully unkind." She searched about in her pocket and brought out a very small mauve handkerchief.

Amy jumped up. "Oh now, don't take it to heart!" she said. "Come on, Vivienne dear, you're tired," and turning to Rupert, "Please excuse us." The two went out.

"Dear, dear," George said. He missed not being able to smoke his pipe. Mrs. Monsoon didn't like people to smoke in the drawing-room. Rupert didn't know this and got out his cigarettes. He looked round the room, observing the little knick-knacks, silver boxes, ivory paper knives, miniature looking-glasses in elaborate silver frames, all of which lay about on highly polished gate-legged tables. Just beside him on one of these tables there was, among other things, a little prayer book bound in ivory with a silver cross on top, and "C.M." in silver initials on the bottom left-hand corner.

"I used to have one just like that," he said, "and inside, it talks about The Holy Ghost. I'm right, aren't I?"

"I really don't know," George said.

"Cigarette?"

"No, thank you."

Rupert lit one himself, blew out the smoke, and looked up. On the ceiling, two plaster cherubs looked down. This was confusing. Without them, the room would have been a museum, but with them it was somehow in keeping with life, a room that was lived in. "Good idea, the cherubs," he said.

"Oh, those," George said.

After a while, needing an ashtray, Rupert had another look at the objects on the table by his side; but found nothing suitable for that purpose. He leaned forward intending to use the fireplace. "Oh, so sorry. Wait," George said. "I'll get you something." He began hunting about among the other knick-knacks.

"Oh, please don't worry!" Rupert said. He almost got up. As he moved, a book, which had been stuffed in between the cushion and the side of the chair, fell out. He picked it up.

"Well, it looks as though you'll have to use the fire-place after all," George said. "So sorry."

"Hullo, what's this?" Rupert said, holding up the book.

"My wife's," George said. "She's always leaving her books about."

"Baudelaire," Rupert said. He smiled. "Who's reading Baudelaire? Là, tout n'est qu'ordre et beauté, luxe, calme et volupté'—ever tried to translate it?"

"No, no, no. It's my wife's. I don't speak French," George said.

"No?"

But Mr. Monsoon came back with another bottle just then.

"Here we are, try this!" he said. He poured some out.

They drank. There didn't seem much to talk about. Rupert proved unwilling to discuss his travels when given an opening, and when he asked his host about Stephen, whom he remembered from days gone by, playing hockey as it happened, Mr. Monsoon changed the subject. George tactlessly brought in Mr. Swan and the ditch, but his father said that could interest no one. Rupert asked after the boys. But they were at school. Mr. Monsoon hoped that Mrs. Tyce was well; and then, really, there was nothing left but the weather. So they talked about that. Then Mr. Monsoon said, "Well, George . . ."

And George said, "Well, if you will excuse me . . ."

"Oh please—if it has to do with mother's letter—" Rupert said, "Please don't go off because of that! I owe you all an apology—please."

George remained on the edge of his chair. So Rupert went on. "It's a bad show about this," he said. "I find myself in a difficult position, if you understand."

("Oh quite. Quite," Mr. Monsoon said.)

"My mother has always been a most responsible person. I am afraid she is getting old. Very old. I do apologise. I wouldn't say she is out of her mind or anything, but I see now, something will have to be done. Just what, I don't know. But obviously, people can't be annoyed like this. The trouble is, one doesn't know what mother said. She won't tell me. She let me know who she has written to all right, but she won't tell me what she said. I do hope you haven't been too much annoyed."

"Oh, my dear fellow, think no more about it!" Mr. Monsoon said. "Have some more sherry. It was a joke. Telling me to look out with my gun. And she was perfectly right. I shot our cook—didn't you know?"

"Really?"

"Father exaggerates," George said. "Our cook was not hurt, thank goodness."

"It's those damned pigeons," Mr. Monsoon said. The gentle sound of the pigeons cooing came in from the garden, a continual murmuring sound that was always there but did not strike the ear; like people talking together of grief, voicing their troubles unemphatically, without malice and so without despair, forgetting they are in company.

"What a sad noise they make, don't they?" Rupert said, "but peaceful really. Not damned souls, Mr. Monsoon, but ones in Purgatory."

"You like them, do you?" said Mr. Monsoon. "Well, I wish you'd take them away."

They listened a few minutes more, and then Rupert said, "But about that letter—I do hope, Mr. Monsoon, you will accept my sincere apologies."

"Why yes, yes of course. And now, some more sherry," Mr. Monsoon said. He had been holding the bottle since the last time he asked, and now poured some out.

"Well, it's good of you," Rupert said. "I hope everyone will take it in the same spirit."

"I shouldn't worry if I were you," Mr. Monsoon said. "After all, who else is there for your mother to write to? That chap Swan, I suppose. A fine man his father, my best friend. But I can't get along with the son. A nonentity. And Rockaby— what does he matter?"

"I can't say I really know them," said Rupert. "I don't think I've ever met Mrs. Rockaby. Aren't they those London people who used to come down in the summer? I met Mr. Rockaby this morning. He asked me to tea on Saturday. I didn't quite know what to say—I'm not used to social life in the country these days. Perhaps one ought to go?"

"Certainly not," Mr. Monsoon said. "There's no need to at all. They are only new-comers. Town folk. A shame really. The village needed that house. Can't think why they should want to come here. Totally out of place, you know."

Rupert sighed. "Yes," he said, "I wrote them a letter apologising about mother of course. But even so—if Mr. Rockaby still feels indignant—"

"Yes. Dear me. Just like them to thrust themselves on you, though. By the way, there's a letter of thanks from me, for your letter, in the post. And let me say now, it was most kind on your part, Mr. Tyce. Now don't let us say any more about it. But about Mrs. Rockaby. She's quite amusing, I believe. The daughter works at the . . . ahem . . . er, school, don't you know."

"Poor old Hereward Hall," Rupert said, "what *are* they doing to it! Turning the drawing-room into a gymnasium—I don't know how mother heard. Old Smyly is a bit of a gossip, and mother is lonely. You see how it is. . . ."

"Very sad," Mr. Monsoon said, "very sad indeed. In fact, it is very good of you to come back to the village at all."

"About my mother," Rupert said, "it really is rather serious. One doesn't want to be involved in a libel action or anything."

"My dear fellow, every decent person here knows how hard it is on your mother," Mr. Monsoon said. "After all, she has been Someone here, and to anyone with any sense of decency she still is."

"Still," Rupert said—but just then Mrs. Monsoon came in. The men got up.

Rupert was excellent at small talk, but Mr. Monsoon was very annoyed with his wife about there not being any flowers and about the sherry, and punished her by not offering her anything to drink and, in so far as he could, ignoring her presence. George, bored stiff, had long ago come to the end of all he had to say. The conversation therefore was sustained almost entirely by Rupert. Even he was unable to keep Mrs. Monsoon off her favourite topic, namely the weather.

"Soon, with all these hot days we must expect thunder I think. Don't you?" Mrs. Monsoon said.

Rupert had just been talking about gardens in a general way, so her remark made sense if one stopped to think. But Mr. Monsoon said, "Some people could do with a few thunderbolts dropped on their heads." Which was startling. Then Amy and Vivienne came in, and by the time seats had been rearranged and they had been given sherry, the threads of the conversations, such as they were, had become obsolete. Rupert tried again.

"Have you any plans for the summer—going away or anything?" he said. Amy sat next to him and he caught a whiff of her scent, which made him feel better. He still held her book.

"We don't go away," Mrs. Monsoon said.

"One day," George said, "we really must take the children to the sea."

"Yes, dear," Amy said.

Vivienne sighed and twiddled her glass. "Are you thinking of going off into the blue again, Mr. Tyce?" she said.

"Yes, vaguely I suppose," Rupert said.

"You ought to write a book about your travels, really you ought, Mr. Tyce," Vivienne said. "Such interesting places you've been to! Pekin, Lhasa—why don't you?"

"Because so many people have written about them already."

"Oh no, not really."

"But yes. Otherwise why should you think them such wonderful places?"

"You mean, they aren't," Mr. Monsoon said. "I thought not."

"Oh now, you're not going to destroy my illusions about them!" Vivienne said. "You mustn't do that."

"Exactly," Rupert said.

No one knew quite what he meant, and there was a pause. Then Mrs. Monsoon said, "The East has a very trying climate, I believe." And Mr. Monsoon said, "One has only to look at Swan. Bright yellow when he came back."

"Now he's the sort of chap who ought to write his experiences," Rupert said, "he has really lived in the East. I've only travelled."

"But that's what I like—*travel* books," Vivienne said. "I read such an interesting book only the other day. Now what was it called? Let me see. . . . It was one of the books Miss Rockaby said her mother . . ."

"Let's have some more sherry," Mr. Monsoon said. "Talking about the Rockabys," George said, "you mentioned before that you'd been invited—Saturday you said, wasn't it? Well, that's the same day my wife and I have been invited."

"Oh really?" Rupert said. ("No, thanks, I won't have any more—no, really.") "Well then, I look forward to meeting you all at the party."

"Not us," Mr. Monsoon said, "it is for the young."

"Dear, dear, that puts me with the old, because I haven't been invited, you know," Vivienne said.

"Oh, nonsense," Amy said, "I'm sure Mrs. Rockaby meant you too, didn't she, George?"

"Well, she said . . ." George began—but Vivienne interrupted him. "Oh no, no," she said with a laugh, "I wasn't invited and it doesn't matter a bit because even if I had been I shouldn't be going now Stephen's come home. So you see, it really, really doesn't matter."

"Before I go back to London we really must meet again," Rupert said, getting up, "but now, you know, I must be off."

After a few more soothing words about country life and the weather, Mrs. Monsoon changed the tone of her voice and said, "Well, Mr. Tyce, I'm sorry you have to go. But it has been a pleasure having you here." Mr. Monsoon began to get up. Rupert said, "No, no—please! I can let myself out. Don't disturb yourself. Really." Mrs. Monsoon said, "George— perhaps?" But Amy said, "I will, don't worry." And so after the usual cordialities and good-byes it was Amy who saw Rupert to the front door.

"I put your book back in the chair," Rupert said.

"I saw," Amy said.

"If it's not rude, are you French?"

"I was brought up in France, but I'm not French. Why?"

"Oh of course—I remember now. Please forgive me. But it was a bit startling finding someone buried away in the country reading Baudelaire and using the latest scent!"

"Do you like Baudelaire?"

"Yes, I must say I do. Very much."

"I read a lot now my children have gone to school and there's time."

"So you were brought up in France. Do your people still live there?"

"Yes. In Paris. My father is a novelist."

"Really? That's interesting. Look here, you and I must meet some time—if you'd care to. It's ages since I was in Paris! And I don't suppose you find many people here to talk with. About art and that sort of thing, I mean. What about coming round one morning to meet my mother? She'd love to see you. Would you?"

Amy frowned. "Well, I could, you know," she said.

Rupert looked pleased. "How about coming round Saturday morning then?" he said.

"Oh, but that's the day of the party."

"Party? Oh, that tea. You are going then?"

"Why, yes, we've been asked. All the same, I've got nothing to do in the morning."

"Good. Any time after ten. And your husband—would he care to come too?"

"I don't think . . . I don't know. . . ."

"Oh well, some other time. But you come. Goodbye then!"

They smiled at each other.

Just then Vivienne came through the hall. She was surprised that the visitor hadn't gone—she thought she had given him ample time—and was dying to talk to her husband upstairs. She said "Oh!", lost her nerve, and hurried back the way she had come. Amy looked round.

"Well, don't forget about Saturday," Rupert said. They both said "Good-bye" again, and Rupert went off. Amy lingered about in the hall. Stephen suddenly called down the stairs, "Is he gone?" and she jumped. "Yes," she called back.

"Thank God for that," Stephen said. He came down like an elephant and began shouting, "Vivienne! Vivy old girl—where are you? Come and give us a hand." Seeing Amy standing about doing nothing, he said, still coming downstairs, "You'll do! Be a sport will you—one of the locks has got jammed—a hairpin or something. . . ."

"No, thanks," Amy said.

He was hurt. She had never behaved like that before. Telling Vivienne about it afterwards Stephen said, "What's happened to Amy?—she's suddenly awfully stuck up. What's bitten her?"

"Oh, it's always Amy, Amy, Amy," Vivienne said. "But as she's father's favourite one can't say a word against her. So you'd better not start."

"All I asked was, what was the matter with her. Generally she's so easy to get on with. The obliging sort."

"She was certainly getting on very well with Mr. Tyce just now in the hall," Vivienne said.

"What an age that bloke took to take himself off!"

"So you noticed it?"

"My dear girl, he kept me waiting at least ten minutes. I wasn't going to come down and be polite after the way father spoke. To hell with him I said to myself, I don't want to meet him!"

"Did you hear what they said?"

"No, how could I up there? Anyway, one doesn't listen, old girl, what do you mean?"

"Nothing. Except that when I came into the hall thinking he must have gone, he was still there. They were talking."

"Well, I don't know why they shouldn't."

"They looked rather awkward as I came in. That's all."

"Hm. I suppose you women would call him good-looking. Not my idea of good looks at all."

"Oh, Stephen, what do you mean?"

"Don't be an ass, Vivienne. And leave Amy alone. And do let's get on with the unpacking."

In the drawing-room, Mr. Monsoon was holding forth over a final glass of sherry. Mrs. Monsoon had her lips pursed, and George had on his not-listening look. Amy came in and George tapped the chair at his side, and she sat down.

"You are not going to tell me that there is nothing in heredity," Mr. Monsoon was saying, "don't we all carry our past with us? And if one happens to be a member of a great family that has always known and lived up to responsibility, it seems fairly obvious that one would grow up to be a very different person from the ordinary run. And there are the weaknesses in bad strains. Take dogs, for instance, and I don't believe human beings are so very different. . . ."

When Mr. Monsoon chose to go off like this on a subject it was useless trying to stop him and they all knew it. After a while George got out a pencil and an envelope which was covered with notes concerning appointments and such like that had to do with his work at the office. Mrs. Monsoon, who had never yet been offered a drink, looked nipped and hurt, and Amy leant back, lost in thought.

"And now if you please," Mr. Monsoon was saying, "and now if you please, they would have us believe that we are nothing more than machines. It's a question of nerves and responses like some horrible slot machine. Instead of being part of a plan, we aren't even playthings. Nobody's laughing, Nobody's interested, Nobody's there at all. I ask you, without religion, without fate—and mark you, with no free will at all because what you do must happen like the platform ticket that comes out after you've put in a penny—I ask you, where in this ghastly mechanic's nightmare is there room for man's dignity? And if there is no dignity, that is the end. That finishes it." With eyes on some distant vista, his face very red and the veins sticking out on his brows like forked lightning, he groped about for his drink; and finding it, drank it down at a gulp.

After this, nothing more was said. The group dispersed: George to get on with some work before dinner, Amy to write to her children, and Mrs. Monsoon on some errand or other to the kitchen. At dinner Mrs. Monsoon's place was not laid. She had left word with cook that she didn't want any dinner. At once, after seating himself, Mr. Monsoon said to George, "Where's your mother?" Mrs. Smith, who was handing round soup, repeated the message her mistress had given her.

"Rubbish!" Mr. Monsoon said.

Mrs. Smith got on with her job. So when Stephen, who was last, was served, he said, "Well, somebody'd better go up then to see what's the matter."

"I'll go," Vivienne said. "Poor mother, I expect she's tired."

"Take up some soup," Mr. Monsoon said.

After a minute or two Vivienne reappeared. "Mother won't even let me in," she said, her eyes getting big.

"Don't goggle," Mr. Monsoon said.

Amy wiped her mouth with her table-napkin, and got up. "Perhaps if I went," she said.

Mrs. Monsoon's door was locked. Amy tried. "Please, please, Mother, let me in," she said. There was no reply. "Oh please!" Amy said. There was still no answer. "Mother, if you don't open the door I shall make Mr. Smith get a ladder. . . ." The door was unlocked. There stood Mrs. Monsoon with a shawl over her head, in a voluminous wrap, very angry indeed. Behind her, Bob sat on her bed. He looked silly and panted.

"I've had enough of you, Amy. Please go away," Mrs. Monsoon said. "How dare you! I don't want to see anyone, do you understand? And I don't want anything to eat. Take it away at once." Amy had brought up some soup on a tray. She hesitated a moment and then said, "Let me just put it down in your room. You needn't have it if you don't want to." And, with considerable courage, brushed past her mother-in-law. But, following close behind, Mrs. Monsoon picked up the bowl of soup as soon as Amy put the tray down, and with a queenly gesture of contempt threw the soup out of the window.

"There!" she said.

Amy was rather alarmed. "But what's the matter, Mother?" she said. "Don't you think you ought to be lying down?"

"Of course! What do you suppose I was doing before you compelled me to get up?" Mrs. Monsoon said. She stroked Bob, and he slobbered.

"Oh, Mother, I'm sorry," Amy said.

"It's not your fault."

Mrs. Monsoon sighed and leant on a corner of her bed. "I know animals are not capable of love as we know it," she said, "but they seem to enjoy the company of human beings, some of them, so I brought Bob in. No one in this house cares for my company, I am only too well aware of that."

Amy tried to put in a word, but Mrs. Monsoon held up her hand and went on. "It has always been so, I don't mind," she said. "But it is you, my dear child, not me, one should feel sorry for. I'm afraid you have married into a very dull, stupid, unkind family. Yes, and even George is morose these days. Do you think I haven't noticed it? No wonder you hang about crying all day! What your parents would think, I don't know. Perhaps really it is my duty to tell them of it. You look terribly tired and drawn, Amy. You should go to bed." Having turned the tables so successfully, Mrs. Monsoon felt quite well. She glanced at the tray. But there wasn't anything else. "Now leave me," she said. And so Amy did.

After dinner, Mr. Monsoon went off in search of Mr. Smith, feeling that he needed the company of someone of his own age and sex. Besides, he knew how silly and obstinate Mr. Smith was about biology (which he called "Nature"), and still fuming inside with ideas conjured up by the Machine

Age, he wanted to crush Mr. Smith's sentimentality with the full weight of that slot machine. He found him watching the sun go down, by the bees. There was a bench there, a little way off from the hives, so he sat down beside him. He rather hoped Mr. Smith would be first to speak. But Mr. Smith said nothing. Mr. Monsoon sighed.

So, looking up, they watched the birds, who passed by to their destinations, silent and swift. A few late bees came homing in and the inevitable pigeons cooed, hidden in the fruit tree branches. From here, on the borders of the apple orchard which stretched unfenced into the neighbouring fields, there was nothing much to see except a few flowers Mr. Smith had planted near the hives, and of course the sun going down, and the glow of the sky and the symmetrical pattern of shadows made by the trees. It was growing cold, and the two old men must have felt it. But they did not speak and continued to look at the sky. A star appeared. More birds passed by. And somewhere in the distance far away a cuckoo who had changed his voice called out "Cuck-uck-uck-uck-cuckoo." To be answered even farther away. "It's all very strange," Mr. Monsoon said at last. "Really, I don't know, I don't know at all."

"It's cold," Mr. Smith said. He got up slowly.

"Ooch," Mr. Monsoon said. He was stiff. Mr. Smith helped him up.

"Now don't you go fretting yourself," he said.

"Fretting myself? Who said I was fretting myself?"

"I'm not going to get into any argument."

"No," Mr. Monsoon said.

Actually, he felt relieved, telling himself it would be a pity to spoil such a very peaceful evening; and besides, what was the good?

CHAPTER SIX

"EVELYN my dear, you are overdoing it," Mr. Rockaby said. "Why kill yourself for these people? Really, there is no need."

"You mean you want supper, I suppose," Mrs. Rockaby said. "Well, you can open a tin. I can't do everything."

"Let me boil father an egg," Lavinia said.

But Mrs. Rockaby said no, she wanted the stove to herself. As usual, she was performing wonders. Petits fours, éclairs, and dozens of langues de chat covered the kitchen table, and a cake made with eight eggs cooked in the oven. There was a delicious smell.

"Couldn't I have one or two of these?" Mr. Rockaby said, eyeing the things on the table.

"No! No! No!" Mrs. Rockaby cried, beside herself. "Can't you understand? These are for the party, not just to *eat*."

"But, dear, I'm hungry."

"Well then you'd better have bread and cheese or open a tin as I said."

"And what about you? *You* must eat."

"Donald, can't you see I have quite enough to do without orders from you? For God's sake leave me alone and stop complaining about being hungry. It's impossible the way you treat me, really it is. I'm supposed to be chef, cook, housemaid, char and everything else in this house. And on top of everything, hostess. And do I ever get a day off, a day out? Never. And I'm expected to look well-dressed and gay at the party—I ask you! Anything more?"

"But it's all so unnecessary," Mr. Rockaby said. He went out.

"Sardines," Mrs. Rockaby said, "in the bottom cupboard. And use marge or dripping. I'll need the butter for biscuits. And he can't have cocoa to-night, it's such a business making it. Later on, perhaps, tea. But there's only boiled milk. Now come on, Lavinia, do help."

Lavinia, who was washing up the debris: greasy pudding bowls, wooden spoons, knives, forks, an egg whisk and so on, took no notice of her mother, but bending over the sink said over her shoulder, "Why haven't you asked Mr. Swan for Saturday, Mother?"

"Because, dear, I have more sense," Mrs. Rockaby said.

"Oh?"

"Yes. You don't want to make it look as though you were running after him. Now's the time to give him the cold shoulder for a bit."

"I see; what you mean is, you're terribly keen I should marry him."

"Oh how crude!" Mrs. Rockaby said. She fluttered her hands.

"Sorry," Lavinia said, "but, Mother, have you thought how you'll manage without me?"

"I am not such a materialist," Mrs. Rockaby said, "I was only thinking of your good."

"And you think marriage is a good thing?"

"Yes, definitely. And, my dear, think how incredibly lucky you are to find in a God-forsaken place like this a man like Mr. Swan! It's providential. Quite extraordinary. You never said anything, so I didn't, but now you've mentioned it—well, Lavinia, I'll say straight out—I'm terribly pleased! Look, I tell you what, take in a handful of petits fours and eat them with father. After all, this is an occasion!"

"How did you know he had asked me?"

"So he *has*! Oh, darling, why didn't you tell me? But it doesn't need half an eye to see how madly in love he is."

"Really?" Lavinia said. "And me?"

Mrs. Rockaby turned round, but Lavinia had her back to her. "Well," she said, "still waters run deep. It's always been difficult to tell, dear, what you are thinking. Just a minute—the cake."

But the cake was not quite done yet.

"The great thing is, not to hurry things," she said.

Lavinia finished the washing, emptied the bowl and looked about for a cloth to dry with. Owing to the work done that evening, they were all wet.

"Well?" Mrs. Rockaby said.

Lavinia chose the least wet one and said, "Me or the cake? I was wondering." This bewildered Mrs. Rockaby, who said, "Oh dear, now I don't know what I'm doing! We mustn't get excited, or what will it be like on your wedding day?"

"Wedding day?" Mr. Rockaby said, coming in. "Whose wedding day? In any case, I don't care whose it is. I must have food."

"So like a man," Mrs. Rockaby said, laughing.

But Lavinia said, turning round from the sink, "Shut up, Mother!" Which made both her parents nervous as they feared a scene.

"Now, now, now," Mr. Rockaby said in his calmest voice. "We've all been working, we're all tired, we're all a little on edge."

"Working! I like that!" Mrs. Rockaby said.

"I know you think I do nothing, my dear, but I assure you, that is not the case," Mr. Rockaby said.

"Oh yes," Mrs. Rockaby said, "you do the real work, don't you? You men make the world go round, while we, us miserable women, just do the odd jobs, the unnecessary things like cooking and cleaning!"

This was a terrible old favourite of Mrs. Rockaby's. In fact she had used it on and off even before the sad days when the family had come down in the world. And now of course Mr. Rockaby couldn't say, "Well, anyway, it's I who earn the money." But Lavinia, who didn't often butt in on her parents' arguments, said, "Well, it's pretty obvious, isn't it, I'd better marry Harold Swan at once, and then, instead of me, perhaps you'll be able to afford a full-time char."

This was indeed the last word, and all Mr. Rockaby could think of to say was, "My dear, such things are not done."

"I don't care, I'm fed up," Lavinia said. She hung the drying-cloth on the line and walked off past her father.

"Lavinia!" Mrs. Rockaby said.

"The cake's burning," Lavinia said. She closed the door behind her and was gone.

Mrs. Rockaby got the cake out, placed it on a wire grid and then became hysterical. There was no brandy, so Mr. Rockaby gave her gin.

Meanwhile Lavinia went up to her room and wrote a letter to Mr. Swan.

"Dearest Harold (she wrote)—I'm awfully sorry, but I've just let the cat out of the bag. I had to. I'm terribly sorry. I know you said I was to say nothing until you asked father. But I told you it wouldn't work, and that mother would nose it out. You don't know mother. So please, for my sake, could you come round when you get this and ask father and get things on a proper basis? It's really too difficult otherwise. If you come round one day during the morning it would be best because I shall be out of the way—or if not, I shall make myself scarce—and father is generally home in the mornings. So very sorry about all this. And please forgive your Lavinia."

She read this over carefully, put it in an envelope, stamped it, and then ran out just as she was to catch the last post.

Mrs. Rockaby wasn't the sort of woman to be knocked out by one gin. After a good cry, she told her husband all about Lavinia and Mr. Swan. He was surprised. But she said she had known about it all along.

"Well, I think he might have asked me. Are you sure about this, Evelyn?"

"Quite sure," said Mrs. Rockaby. "He's terribly shy, Donald, that's what it is. Oh *what* a pity! Why ever didn't I ask him Saturday for the party! Then he'd have asked us, of course he would. I tell you what, I'll ring him up now!"

"Evelyn, you are making a mistake—you'll make us look foolish," Mr. Rockaby said.

But nothing could stop Mrs. Rockaby in this mood.

Mr. Swan was very surprised to be rung up and asked to tea the day after next like that. But Mrs. Rockaby said it was quite informal, just a gathering of friends, and she would so much like to see him because really he too was a friend of the family. And Lavinia would be so disappointed if he didn't come. So he said, yes, all right. And Mrs. Rockaby said that was lovely, between half-past three and four then, just a little informal party, so sorry not to have asked him before, but she never liked to make a fuss with proper invitations and things; that made it all so formal and stiff. This was just a friendly little party. Eventually, she rang off.

"There now, that's done," she said.

"I'm sorry, but I don't approve, Evelyn," Mr. Rockaby said. She brushed him aside.

"Now Dora," she said. "I must get Dora to come. After all, in a crisis one does want one's friends."

"I wash my hands of this," Mr. Rockaby said.

Dora was Mrs. Hardinger. Being head-mistress, she naturally had other engagements. But she never liked to hurt people's feelings, and even though Mrs. Rockaby could never be, *vis à vis* the school, a 'parent,' she didn't like to disappoint. So, making one of those snap decisions as head-mistresses have to, she said suddenly, after saying no twice, that really, Evelyn was such a darling, she couldn't refuse. Tea at four-thirty. Right.

"So lucky I started early with cakes and things for the party," Mrs. Rockaby said. But Mr. Rockaby said, "It's quite ridiculous. You'll be tired out. For goodness' sake go to bed now and get a good night's rest!"

"Donald, I'm *not* tired," Mrs. Rockaby said.

She stayed up till one that night, just fussing about.

Mr. Swan got Lavinia's letter at breakfast next morning together with some circulars. He opened the circulars first. On coming to Lavinia's letter he frowned very slightly. Then he opened it and sighed. At length, putting the letter down, he said to himself, "Well, once having put one's hand to the plough I suppose . . ." Ting his cat jumped on his lap and he stroked him absent-mindedly.

Later on Mr. Swan took a walk round his garden. He had brought his scissors out with him, meaning to cut some roses; but there weren't any out, only buds. He picked these. They made a very small bunch. He looked round for something more to put with them, but could find nothing else suitable. Later still, he set out intending once more to call on Lavinia's parents.

Mrs. Rockaby, taking a moment off, sat at her bedroom window looking out and smoking a cigarette. She said "Oh Lord!" when she saw Mr. Swan approaching. There was still a lot to be done that morning. Mrs. Rockaby always took at least two full days to prepare for a party; Mrs. Burt had to be watched now the best china was out—it needed to be cleaned and polished up most carefully—and as always, there were ever so many other little arrangements that had to be thought out if one wanted to give a really nice tea-party. "I want to have nothing to do to-morrow," she had said to her husband at breakfast, hurrying him up. He had complained of the fuss, saying, "Evelyn, really—why on earth can't you leave all this till to-morrow?—the party isn't to-day!"

Lavinia had done the dusting and made the beds and gone off to work at the school, and Mr. Rockaby said he must deal with some bills, would she please not disturb him, and Mrs. Burt would arrive very shortly to wash up the breakfast things: so Mrs. Rockaby had said to herself, "Just time for a cigarette!"—and had rushed up to her bedroom. She had her overall on and watched Mr. Swan coming down the street with some anxiety, waiting about, not sure if he really would come in at the gate. He did. She pulled off the overall quickly, fluffed her hair up and powdered her nose. Then, holding her breath, she stood still, listening for the bell to ring. But Mr. Rockaby too had seen Mr. Swan, and before Mr. Swan could ring, had opened the front door and asked him in. Because of the porch over the door, Mrs. Rockaby couldn't see any of this. She waited and waited. And still the bell did not ring.

"Well!" she said at last. "Either that wretched bell has broken again or I'm deaf." She then gave herself a brief inspection in the glass, said, "I do wish people would 'phone before calling!"—brushed her dress, and ran off downstairs. Long before she reached the hall she could hear Mr. Swan and her husband speaking, so she didn't go into the room at once but stood about within earshot, half-way down, just above the sitting-room door.

Mr. Swan sat on the edge of one armchair, Mr. Rockaby on another. They sat a bit sideways, not quite facing each other. The bunch of rosebuds lay on the sofa disintegrating, because Mr. Swan hadn't put enough knots in the string and the string had come undone. He had put the roses down at once on coming in, glad to be rid of them, but sad because he hadn't managed to give them to anyone. And now man to man Mr. Rockaby and Mr. Swan were seeing the thing through. They had got over the awkward part of mentioning the word marriage and Mr. Rockaby had already said, "Of course my daughter knows she can do as she likes—it's for her to choose." And Mr. Swan had said, "Oh quite. Absolutely. Quite."

Mr. Rockaby now said, "We don't want to lose her. It will be a great loss."

"I quite understand," Mr. Swan said. "But I promise you, she will be well looked after."

"I'm afraid we have not been able to do all that we ought for Lavinia," Mr. Rockaby said. He sighed. "If I'd had my way," he said—but Mr. Swan cut him short and said, "Quite, quite."

"There will be no dowry," Mr. Rockaby said.

Mrs. Rockaby came in with quite a flourish.

"Oh *hullo*, Mr. Swan!" she cried.

Both men got up from their chairs. She said, "Oh, please!" and sat down beside the roses. There was a silence, so she said, "What heavenly flowers! Roses. Yes, don't you adore roses? I do. So English and nice. From your own garden I expect. Lavinia is a very keen gardener too, you know." There was another silence, and then Mr. Swan said, "Mrs. Rockaby, I have come to ask for your daughter's hand in marriage."

"Oh but how sweet! How terribly old-fashioned of you!" Mrs. Rockaby cried. She got out her handkerchief.

"There will be no dowry," Mr. Rockaby said.

Mrs. Rockaby waved her handkerchief about. "Donald, must you?" she said.

"Well, my dear," said her husband, "one must get these things clear. It is only right Mr. Swan should know."

"It sounds so terribly, terribly—well, I don't know," Mrs. Rockaby said.

"I know what you mean," Mr. Swan said, trying to make things easy. "It makes it sound like Bride Price and all that, though that would be the husband's dowry—quite the usual thing in Far Eastern societies where I come from!" He laughed.

"Really?" Mr. Rockaby said.

"You are not thinking of going back to the Far East?" Mrs. Rockaby said.

"No, no," said Mr. Swan. "My jungle days are over. So you won't have to worry about Lavinia among the tigers." He laughed again.

"So there really were tigers then?" Mrs. Rockaby said.

"Well, no."

"But you lived among savages?"

"So-called. We are all much the same really, only our skins are a different colour. That is my belief."

Mrs. Rockaby laughed briefly.

"Seriously though," she said, "*au fond*, one is civilised, isn't one? And there are ways of doing things properly. When would you like us to put a notice of the engagement in *The Times*?"

"My dear—" Mr. Rockaby began, but she waved him aside.

"I'm right, I know, it's the bride's mother who does that. And we do the wedding breakfast and the decorations. But I think (I'm not sure though) that you pay for the church. I suppose it had better be a local wedding. Such a pity because all our friends are in town."

"Yes, well, I thought Lavinia . . ." Mr. Swan said. "The dear child. Of course she shall choose," Mrs. Rockaby said. "And now, to celebrate, what about a glass of something?"

"No, no, not for me if you don't mind," Mr. Swan said, "not so early in the morning. I mean . . ."

"Oh, have some sherry, you *can't* refuse!" Mrs. Rockaby said.

"But just a minute, just a minute, my dear," Mr. Rockaby said. "*Is* there any sherry?"

Alas, there was not.

"Donald, you really should remind me," Mrs. Rockaby said. "Wine is your job."

"Oh goodness, don't you go worrying because of me," Mr. Swan said. "You must want to be rid of me anyway. I hope you'll forgive me calling like this on the morning before your party."

"It's just friends dropping in for tea," Mrs. Rockaby said. "Nothing really. But it was so nice of you to say yes when I asked. We're so pleased you can come."

"Very nice of you to ask me," Mr. Swan said.

"I tell you what," said Mrs. Rockaby. "How would it be if we made an announcement of the engagement to-morrow?

Then it would be an engagement party! And I've made rather a splendid cake."

"Oh no, my dear," Mr. Rockaby said. "I don't think . . . it isn't really that sort of party, is it? You said yourself . . ."

"But it *is* just that sort of party," Mrs. Rockaby said. "After all, one wants one's friends to know, doesn't one, before they read about it in *The Times*."

Mr. Swan cleared his throat. "I would very much rather keep it private," he said, "otherwise there's talk. And please do not put it in *The Times*. Let us say nothing about it."

"Now why?" Mrs. Rockaby said. "One's friends ought to know. And all the arrangements are made, they are coming to-morrow in any case. And I've made such a beautiful cake!"

"No," Mr. Rockaby said. And Mr. Swan said, "No, if you don't mind, Mrs. Rockaby." She tossed her head and said "Oh!"

Soon after this Mr. Swan got away. He felt very exhausted and went straight off to the pub. The pub had stone floors, thick walls and narrow windows, so it was cool. There were a few men, drinking and standing about, but no women. Mr. Henlow was there describing his rheumatism. He saluted Mr. Swan, and Mr. Swan went over to him. They spoke then about the weather, the unusual dryness of the season, with the old man remembering years gone by when cracks appeared in the earth. And then when the storm came, lightning set fire to the corn. "But you need lightning," he said, "at the proper time of the year. It helps ripen the corn."

"I'm sorry about your rheumatism," Mr. Swan said, after a pause.

"Wouldn't know myself without it. That's the truth," Mr. Henlow said.

So Mr. Swan ordered himself and the old man another pint of bitter. He said, drinking his beer, "Sorry to lose your wife. I don't know why she gave notice."

"Oh her!" Mr. Henlow said. "You'll see, she'll turn up again next week just the same."

"Really?" Mr. Swan said.

"You don't have to worry," said Mr. Henlow. He returned to the subject of the weather: how hail-storms followed unusual droughts, and after that, great winds which laid the corn flat. Mr. Henlow remembered some dreadful things. He went on to tell of the floods when the bridge broke down and only the tops of trees showed in the bottom meadows. Mr. Swan ordered some more beer. He felt rested and peaceful again. He looked at the clock, made his mind up to leave at one sharp, and relaxed.

"It made the womenfolk wild it did," Mr. Henlow was saying, "with chairs bobbing and floating about, nowhere to sit and the stove gone out. It was good-bye to the hens all right, and the pigs got drowned. Cut their own throats you know when they try to swim, and that's what they did, cut their own throats the foolish creatures, they did that. But the ducks was in their glory! Floating about, nibbling the tops off the hedges . . ."

Just then, Mrs. Henlow came in. She had finished at Mr. Swan's, laid the cold meat ready, and left a little note under his plate, saying, "To oblidge will come Monday as usual. A. Henlow." She now came to remove her husband, who on Friday morning always went to the pub. She looked about.

"Here, Albert," she said. "Time you stopped gassing." Then she saw Mr. Swan. "I hope you haven't been listening to him, Sir," she said, "he's a rare one for talking."

Mr. Henlow sighed, finished his beer and got up.

"Next time you come along, I'll tell you about the fire," he said.

"Albert!" said Mrs. Henlow.

"Well, so long all," Mr. Henlow said. He followed his wife out.

Mr. Swan, alone at his end of the bar, felt sad again. He ordered another pint and drank it slowly. Mr. Gerald Grole, who owned the pub, got out a rag and began cleaning the bar.

"It's a hard life," Mr. Swan said.

Mr. Grole was deaf, so he smiled.

"And how are you getting on up there?" he said.

"It's a pity my father was not more interested in the garden. It's in a poor state," Mr. Swan said.

"Ah. He was a good man your father," Mr. Grole said. "A real doctor. One of the best."

"Still, he did leave things in rather a mess," Mr. Swan said.

"You find it lonesome up there I daresay?" Mr. Grole said.

"No, no. Being alone has never troubled me."

"That's right, you need someone to help."

"I beg your pardon?"

"He's very deaf," one of the men at the far end of the bar called out.

"Oh I see. I see," Mr. Swan said.

"It comes to us all," Mr. Grole said, "and it's right that it should. Man wasn't meant to live alone as they say."

"Quite," Mr. Swan said. "Now I must be off."

Mr. Grole looked surprised to see him go, but went on polishing.

On his way home, nearly at the end of the village street, Mr. Swan met Lavinia. She too was on her way home, having finished her duties at the school that morning, Mr. Swan waited till she had come pretty near him before making any show of recognition. When something had to be done he said, "In future, please leave important decisions to me. I got your letter."

"Oh Harold! So you've told mother and father!" Lavinia said. "I'm terribly pleased."

"Well, I'm not," Mr. Swan said. "See you later." He went on.

Lavinia looked back at him. "Surely, surely," she said to herself, "he hasn't been drinking!"

It is Saturday. Mrs. Hardinger is taking a stroll in the woods with her husband. Although the sun is already filtered here she carries a parasol because her skin burns so easily. All her summer dresses have long sleeves and she always wears stockings no matter how hot it is. These woods, inside the wall, are all that remain of a great forest that long ago covered the countryside, and the immense trees which still exist have been guarded for several centuries by the owners of Hereward Hall. Now there are no more gamekeepers and the only two gardeners have work elsewhere on the estate so that the rides, so beautifully kept before, are invaded with brambles, and a vast undergrowth of brambles and twisted saplings shoots up between the trees. But there is still order among the confusion, and there are green grassy places where one can wander, where light is, where the eye can take pleasure of distance on distance; where there is solitude, but no fearful wildness. And it was in such a charmed environment as this that Mrs. Hardinger and her husband came, drawn out by the summer weather. Among those ancient trees the human pair took on a certain dignity; they strolled, taking their leisure, lost to the usual world, Mrs. Hardinger in her creamy summer dress and gay pink parasol, and a little behind her, Mr. Hardinger. They spoke as they walked of something dear to them both: the project of a gymnasium for the school.

Now although Mrs. Hardinger was head-mistress Mr. Hardinger was in no sense head-master. For one thing, Hereward Hall was a girls' school, not the sort employing male instructors. And, too, Mr. Hardinger had none of those credentials proper to a head-master, while his wife could follow her signature up with the capital letters of her degrees. However, Mr. Hardinger was excellent with parents; he showed them round, making them feel they were visitors being entertained on a gentleman's estate: they liked this. Also, he was good at carpentry, amateur plumbing, and could do all those little, tiresome jobs—fuse mending, elimination of cats, minor boiler repairs—for which goodness knows how many other unnecessary servants or hired workers would have to be employed. The Gym had been his idea. It was to be made out of what had been the drawing-room, a room which when emptied of its furniture looked unfortunately cold and square. Mrs. Hardinger had been at her wits' end to know what to do with it and had (most unusually) agreed at once when her husband said, "I know—a Gym!" Owing to the enormous expenditure required to equip classrooms, dormitories and proper kitchens, and all the other things like mending the wall which surrounded the school, they had not at first been able to get on with the Gym. (Mrs. Hardinger had vainly tried to insist on its being called 'the Gymnasium'; it appeared as such under the heading 'In course of construction' on the prospectus, but otherwise was spoken of universally as 'the Gym.')

"Well, my dear," Mr. Hardinger said now, whirling his cane, "it won't be long. We have the bar, the ropes, the proper flooring. Yes, it won't be long now."

"Oh, I'm not worrying. You've got things coming along splendidly," Mrs. Hardinger said. "It's just the horse, isn't it?"

"Oh, I daresay I shall be able to manage that," Mr. Hardinger said.

"Yes. But it's got to be stuffed."

"Yes."

"Yes. It's got to be stuffed, hasn't it?"

"Perhaps, in a way, it might be better to buy it? Second-hand of course."

"Oh! Just when we've got square! And I did so hope this year the school would show a profit."

"Patience, patience, my dear," Mr. Hardinger said, catching up. "After all, we are not a vulgar business affair."

"No," Mrs. Hardinger said, "but we've sunk all we have. One must be practical."

"But what's just one horse? Pity to spoil the ship, my dear . . ."

"Yes, yes," Mrs. Hardinger said.

Farther on in the wood there was a ruined temple. This temple, now a really ruined place with lumps of masonry sprouting weeds and covered with ivy, had been built in conformity with the spirit of a past age, when to own a ruin had been almost essential if one was aristocratic and wealthy enough to be able to follow the fashions. Not owning a ruin, Squire Tyce had built one. The carefully half-constructed arch still stood, but the weather and the weeds had torn down the rest, and the delicate fluted columns had fallen into the waiting brambles and were now lost in that all-engulfing embrace. Even so, something of the Idyll remained. There was still a clearing where trees did not grow, and on sunny days such as this, lizards and little insects came out to play on what was left uncovered by weeds or leaves or earth on the tumbledown bits of masonry. And here, although it no longer belonged to him and he was trespassing, Rupert had brought Amy.

Mrs. Tyce had been difficult that morning. She said the Monsoons were terribly worthy and dull and she didn't want to meet Mrs. George a bit.

"But she's quite different, Mother," Rupert said. "She's a square peg in a round hole. Really."

"There's no such thing," his mother said. "Take her out for a walk."

And so Rupert had. The ruined temple was one of his favourite spots; he remembered it from his youth, when in order to escape—from his nurse, from his tutor, or from his brothers, who, unlike himself, adored sports and lived for hunting—he would find his way to this solitary place and spend hours watching the lizards, or just lying on his back in the sun, thinking. He didn't tell Amy about this all at once, of course, they discussed modern literature first, but he led the way; and thus it was through the wood and towards the temple that they walked. The Dower House stood inside the wall near by the main gates to Hereward Hall. Crossing the drive which passed the Dower House gates, Rupert and Amy walked over the grass edge, jumped the ditch, and went straight on in between the trees. They were enclosed immediately in a calm world where silence prevailed; calm in spite of sudden death among the animals, and still in spite of the moving birds who winged in and out high in the trees: calm and still because the trees lived long and slowly. And there was a continual sighing caused by the winds of the upper air which the branches, heavy with leaves, could not resist. Here and there the trunks had names carved on them, names of people long ago dead, and the bark was closing up on them, distorting the hearts and arrows and the deeply incised initials so that they had become just part of the tree; scars of very little significance. Here Rupert brought Amy. They spoke in low voices, troubled by human affairs, not observing the trees about them, stepping carefully over the brambles, being polite about who went first: absorbed in themselves. At length they came to the clearing. Rupert explained about the temple, how his ancestor had built it, and they sat down on the rubble, scattering the lizards. They had finished with literature and the talk had become more personal. They spoke about life, and were sad. Everyone has a life history which he or she, given the right person, is willing to tell. And when a man like Rupert, who thinks of himself as a bird of passage, feels the need of calling attention to himself, and perhaps getting a little entangled with a woman he finds attractive, nearly always his tale is just a bit sad. Amy listened sucking a stem of grass, keeping quiet, but sometimes nodding her head. She had never had any illusions, but of course, being a woman, felt much more warmly about love for instance than Mr. Swan did.

At length Rupert paused. He had come to the end of all he wished to tell, and feeling he might have given away too much of himself too early on in their acquaintance, and not wanting Amy to feel left out because he did not like to be thought an egoist, he said, hugging his knees, "Your turn now. Tell me about yourself." But Amy had nothing to say it seemed. She made some observations about women in general and families, and then fell silent. This rather annoyed him. He stifled a yawn half-heartedly. It was so hot. And a number of butterflies they had disturbed before returned to sun themselves on the weeds, unfrightened.

"Look!" Amy said.

"Yellow brimstones. Quite common," Rupert said. "Look here, I can't go on calling you Mrs. George."

A slight wind blew in their faces, and all at once, from far off, they heard voices. Rupert got up.

"Who the hell!" he said. He was most indignant.

But Amy said, "The Hardingers!" and looked rather afraid.

"Who? Oh . . ." Rupert said. He took Amy's arm, and they fled.

The sun poured down and the lizards came back to play. Some sort of animal life went on in the undergrowth, and every now and then dragonflies skimmed past on their way to forgotten ponds near by.

"I never feel quite at home here," Mrs. Hardinger said to her husband, coming out from the wood. She pointed at the ruins. "One doesn't feel one belongs somehow," she said.

"It's all these beastly insects," Mr. Hardinger said, hitting out with his stick. "I say—who's that?"

"Where?"

"Somebody in the wood over there—I swear I saw somebody there! In a yellow dress. . . ."

"Good heavens!" Mrs. Hardinger said.

"But not one of the girls," Mr. Hardinger said with authority.

The woods were out of bounds, and although it was Saturday, which was marked on the Staff time-table as 'Holiday,' nevertheless the girls were all in class being read to by Miss

Rockaby. Because of roll-call, playing truant was hardly possible.

"But who was it?" Mrs. Hardinger said.

"One of the maids, I expect," Mr. Hardinger said.

It was not the first time they had had differences with the domestics concerning moral behaviour. The domestic staff was composed of foreigners, which, as Mrs. Hardinger said, was part of the trouble.

"Don't let it spoil our walk," Mr. Hardinger said.

But Mrs. Hardinger said, "This place is haunted."

So they turned back.

CHAPTER SEVEN

"HULLO, going to the bun fight?" the Vicar's wife said, passing Amy and George. She had just been down to the shop and had seen Mr. Swan go by, rather dressed up. "Where's he off to?" she had asked Mrs. Burt (not Mrs. Rockaby's but the grocer's daughter), and Mrs. Burt said, "Oh, it's that Mrs. Rockaby. Having some sort of a party. Been asking for paper doilies, but we've run out of stock." The Vicar's wife was rather annoyed she hadn't been asked.

"We're just going to have tea with Mrs. Rockaby," Amy said. "I don't think really it's a *party*."

Just then Mrs. Hardinger passed in her car. It was slowing down, and they all three watched it draw up farther along the street by the Rockabys' gate.

"Well, well," the Vicar's wife said, "and how are the boys?"

"Quite all right, thank you," Amy said.

George said something indistinctly, and the Vicar's wife smiled and nodded and said, "There now, I mustn't keep you. Enjoy yourselves at the party!" and went off.

"Oh Lord! What on earth have you let me in for?" George said, frowning. "The Rockaby woman said 'just drop in any time after three Saturday,' she didn't say it was a party."

"She asked you and you said yes. It wasn't me," Amy said.

Arriving at 'The Lodge' they found the front door open. Not a sound came from inside the house.

"Well," George said, "do we ring, or what?"

"I should think so," Amy said.

George pulled the bell handle, and the bell rang just once inside the porch. They waited. Nothing happened.

"Ring again. Pull harder," Amy said.

George gripped the handle and pulled hard. The chain, amateurly put together by Mrs. Rockaby, broke in the mended place. George found himself holding the handle and part of the chain, while the bell rang violently.

"Hell!" George said.

"For God's sake put it down!" said Amy.

Still nobody came.

"Do you know, I think they're all out in the garden," Amy said.

"It's all very well, but we can't just go round like that. We don't *know* them," George said. He put the chain and the handle down in a little heap inside the doorway.

"Of course we can!" Amy said.

"Well, you go. I'll wait. Because if somebody comes to the door and finds no one, it'll look queer."

"No! I'm not going alone. That'll look as though you hadn't come."

"Well, Amy, it's no good us standing here."

"All right then. Let's go in."

But a strange house when it is quite silent is always frightening, and after peering inside the dark hallway, they just stood still.

Amy was right, everyone was outside in the garden at the back. Mr. Rockaby had had a dreadful time that morning, weeding and sweeping and tidying things up. As soon as Lavinia had come, she had been made to help too. "But it *must* be made to look tidy!" Mrs. Rockaby said, waving her arms about. "All those people coming—what do you think I'm going to do with them before tea? And the room is so small I can't both have tea laid ready and people standing about!" And just afterwards, in the middle of giving old Mrs. Burt instruction as to how to make proper sandwiches, it had suddenly struck her that, of course, they must have paper doilies. She rushed out. But there weren't any. Back in the kitchen again she said, "Much too thick!" to her Mrs. Burt. "I'd better do it. Lay the table. For eight."

"It's time now for me to go home," Mrs. Burt said. "It's gone one."

"Well, you can't," Mrs. Rockaby said.

"I'm ever so sorry, Mum, but I said just two hours," Mrs. Burt said. "It's gone one—I've been here two hours."

"Oh go then! I'll manage," Mrs. Rockaby said. "Go then!" And so Mrs. Burt had gone.

Later, over a tin of bully beef in the kitchen (the dining-room table was laid for tea, and besides, the room had been cleaned), Mrs. Rockaby started fretting about the doilies and whether the table-cloth was going to look all right. Mr. Rockaby just sighed. But Lavinia said, "I'm not ever going to let you give another party. Asking Harold and Mrs. Hardinger like this is too much. I shall get married at a Registry office."

Mrs. Rockaby said darkly, "We'll see. Have you got that garden tidy?" They had of course; Mrs. Rockaby went to look afterwards. "Yes, it's all right I suppose," she said, "a pity, though, there are no flowers. Show them round a bit, Donald, but don't go pointing out things; there are still quite a lot of weeds. And don't forget, this is an absolutely *informal* party—I asked them just to drop in for tea."

But the art of being informal at a tea-party is more difficult in some ways than holding a slap-up formal dinner-party. The guests don't arrive at a set time, for instance, but being asked any time after three for tea at four-thirty, some walk in at half-past three (as Mr. Swan did) and have to be persuaded they are not early, and have to be taken out into the garden to be marched round (informally—passing the time of day that is, but without drinks which help so much before a dinner-party), and of course in Mr. Swan's case making him feel one of the family. All the time Mrs. Rockaby had to be ready to answer the bell too. So she hopped about, agitating everybody. After Rupert had come at about four and been let loose in the garden, and Mrs. Hardinger had been met at the door and gathered in safely, Mrs. Rockaby felt a bit more happy. She left the front door open, telling herself there were only those Monsoons to come now; they could let themselves in. They were late anyway.

It was a bit of a strain in the garden, talking and being amusing informally, because there were so few flowers to admire and nowhere to sit.

"Take them to see the vegetables, say they're your work!" Mrs. Rockaby hissed in her daughter's ear. So they went there. The vegetables grew at the end of the garden by the wall which shut off the fields. Unfortunately the wall did not surround the whole of the garden; the two boundaries on each side were just marked by hedges. Neighbours didn't exactly watch what was going on in the Rockaby garden, but one could see them. And of course one could see their washing.

In fact it was a neighbour, an old woman called Mrs. Lang, who came to the Monsoons' rescue as they stood about by the front door. She had been hanging out dishcloths at the back just before, and now looking through the curtains in her sitting-room to see whether any more cars had come, she saw Amy and George. She opened her window at once on realising their predicament, and called out, "They're all at the back, dear, in the garden. I should go round."

"Thank you," Amy said.

"I'm not coming here again, that's flat!" George said as they made their way.

"It's because we're late," Amy said.

"And whose fault is that?" George said.

"Oh do stop it!" Amy said.

"Oh dear—the Monsoons," Mrs. Rockaby said, looking up from the cabbages (she stood next to her husband). "I'd quite forgotten. Donald dear, go and meet them. Then we'll have tea."

"Thank God," Mr. Rockaby said to himself.

He saw the curtains part in the next-door house, and feeling watched made haste to get over the greetings. "Do come and look at the garden," he said to George, after the usual how-do-you-do's. "Come along, we're all in the garden!"

His two guests registered no enthusiasm, so he said, "I expect you're like me—no gardeners. But my daughter is. Won't you come down perhaps and join the rest?"

"I'm very sorry," George said, "but I broke your bell."

"Oh!" Mr. Rockaby said, "don't mention it. My dear fellow, it keeps on happening. Now, if you'd like to come down . . . oh, Evelyn, here's Mr. and Mrs. George."

Mrs. Rockaby, just coming in to see to the tea, paused and said, "So glad you've come. Look, you'll find the rest of them down at the end of the garden. Donald, do you think you could come in a moment and help me? You will excuse me you two, won't you? It's such a job single-handed. And I'm a bit late with the tea."

Mr. Rockaby looked distressed, and Amy said, "Can I help?"

"No, no, no," Mrs. Rockaby said. "Donald!"

"If you'll excuse me," Mr. Rockaby said. And inside, having closed the door, "My dear, wasn't that rather rude?"

"Oh, this isn't a formal party," Mrs. Rockaby said. "Everybody knows everybody."

"If this were mine," George said, walking slowly with Amy down the length of the garden, "I shouldn't want people to look at it. It's more like a blasted heath."

"Shush," Amy said. She had caught sight of Rupert. "But they might have asked whether I wanted to powder my nose," she said.

"Oh dear," George said. "Well, you'd better go in. I can't very well barge about asking where the lavatory is."

"I said powder my nose. And I meant it."

"Nonsense. Your nose is all right as it is."

"You know perfectly well I dressed in a hurry, George."

"You look splendid. Now for goodness' sake, Amy, forget all about that, and talk. You do the talking and I'll look at the beastly peas and cabbages."

Rupert appeared to be discussing something very seriously with Mr. Swan, while Lavinia stood a little apart, talking to Mrs. Hardinger. Mrs. Hardinger had already noticed Amy's smart dress. She herself had dressed carelessly as Mrs. Rockaby had said twice it was not a real party, just friends meeting for tea, so she was annoyed at having on an old dress. Besides this, in the general hurry, she had forgotten her parasol and was afraid of the sun, which was even now strong. But every time she had said, "Well, I'm glad to have seen the garden . . ." or "It's rather hot here, don't you think . . ." Mrs. Rockaby had mentioned something about the vegetables that needed comment. It was most frustrating.

"My dear," she said to Lavinia now, "don't you think we might go in? One gets so tired standing."

"Oh, here are the Monsoons!" Lavinia said, "just let me introduce them."

George had already been drawn into the talk with Mr. Swan and Rupert, so Lavinia introduced Amy. "We have met, haven't we, of course," Mrs. Hardinger said.

Meanwhile Rupert said to George, "Swan here tells me you have trouble with ditches. Now I was just saying . . ." Amy couldn't hear any more. "I'm afraid I'm dreadfully untidy," she said to Lavinia, "perhaps before tea . . ."

"*Un*tidy!" Mrs. Hardinger said, "My dear Mrs. George, just look at me!"

Without thinking, Amy did, with a sort of stare because she was trying to hear what Rupert said. It was terribly rude, Mrs. Hardinger thought. And certainly, it didn't make it better when Amy said half-heartedly, "Oh, but you're all right."

"I'll just see whether I can't help mother with the tea," Lavinia said. And before Mrs. Hardinger could make any move, Amy said, "Lovely weather. Just look at those enormous cabbages."

"I daresay, I daresay," George was saying, "but what no one seems to realise is, I can't *afford* it."

Rupert happened to look up and caught Amy watching him. She smiled, but he nodded his head, briefly, so she turned her back on him. Mrs. Hardinger was observing the scene in a general way, having walked off a little apart. Amy went up to her now and said confidentially, "Oh, Mrs. Hardinger, do you know, I've got something to confess!"

Mrs. Hardinger looked startled and said, "Oh."

"Yes," Amy said. "I hope you'll forgive me, or us rather, because this morning Mr. Tyce and I went for a walk in your wood."

As Mrs. Hardinger told her husband afterwards, it was such a shock you could have knocked her down with a feather. In fact, she closed her eyes (which was what she always did when confronted with girls who were sent to the Office for misbehaviour). Opening her eyes again she allowed herself that long, soul-piercing look which often reduced the most hardened culprits to tears. Even Amy didn't feel too happy about it.

"Really?" Mrs. Hardinger said.

"Yes," Amy said. "I think Mr. Tyce rather forgot, you know. But I thought I'd say I was sorry."

"Putting up notices is rather vulgar, I think, don't you?" Mrs. Hardinger said. "But you know, the wood *is* private property."

"Tea's ready! Tea's ready!" Mrs. Rockaby called from the house.

"Amy—tea!" George said.

"Come on, they're gossiping," said Rupert.

"Oh, Mr. Tyce, just a moment," Amy said.

"Come on, we'll go in," George said to Mr. Swan, "now, as I was saying, about that ditch . . ." They went up the path towards the house.

"I was just confessing about our crime," Amy said, "how we went in the wood."

Mrs. Hardinger smiled in a lofty way. "I expect you are still very fond of the place," she said, "still, next time, just ask me."

"I am extremely sorry," Rupert said, "it won't happen again."

"You really must come and see what the school is like one day," Mrs. Hardinger said. "But didn't I hear Evelyn say tea? . . ." She began to walk off.

"Amy—and after that you are going to be Amy whatever you say—what on earth made you do that?" Rupert said very quietly. She didn't answer, so he said, "I shall have to talk to you severely about this afterwards. Let's meet in the pub."

"Come on—tea," Amy said.

Mrs. Rockaby stood with her back to the window, watching her guests come in. She was terribly disappointed when Mrs. Hardinger, who came first, the men having waited, didn't even say "Oh!" when she saw the spread; she just said, "Er, where shall I sit?"

"Show her, Donald," Mrs. Rockaby said.

"What a wonderful cake!" Amy said. But somehow it came too late—it wasn't the same thing.

"You don't mean to say you made it?" Amy said.

"Yes, of course," Mrs. Rockaby said. "Do all sit down. Come along. Anywhere!"

"No, not there," Mr. Rockaby said to Mr. Swan, "here."

He put Mr. Swan next to Lavinia as had been arranged. This meant uprooting George, who had already sat down.

"Careful, George!" Amy said. He was taking the table-cloth with him. There wasn't much room.

"Frightfully sorry," George said. Amy rearranged things.

"Donald, for goodness' sake!" Mrs. Rockaby said.

"But, my dear, you said . . ."

"What on earth does it matter *where* people sit? It's all quite informal," Mrs. Rockaby said.

Mrs. Rockaby sat down herself. The big teapot, the silver one which they didn't generally use, was too full of tea. She spilt tea all over the table-cloth.

"Oh dear!" Mr. Swan said. "Let me help. Shall I get something to mop it up?"

"No, no, no," Mrs. Rockaby said.

Mr. Rockaby produced a handkerchief, surreptitiously. It wasn't very clean.

"Look, George has one," Amy said.

"My dear, don't make such a fuss! We've got more than one table-cloth," Mrs. Rockaby said.

No one spoke, so she said sharply, "Lavinia, hand round the sandwiches."

"Well, how's the Law these days?" Mr. Rockaby asked George, who sat next to him. He didn't know George at all well, but remembered now he was a solicitor by profession.

"Oh, all right," George said.

"I suppose you have slack times like everyone else," Mr. Rockaby said, "or are there always crimes going on? One wouldn't think so in the country."

"Oh, I don't know," George said, "not much. Just the usual, you know."

"What? Contested wills? That sort of thing? And I suppose people getting had up for trespassing, and so on."

George said, "Yes, yes." And there was a long silence.

"But trespassing by itself is no crime. Or so I believe?" Mr. Swan said. "Strange how we don't know our own laws."

"It's all rather involved," George said, "you see . . ."

"My husband, you know, is much more interested in butterflies," Amy said.

Mrs. Rockaby helped pass the scones round her end. "Oh, really?" she said, "that's interesting."

"But about this trespassing," Mr. Swan said. "Now, if I build a fence round my property . . ."

"A scone?"

"No, thanks. Now if I build a fence . . ."

"Have one of my langues de chat then?"

"Oh, yes. Thank you. Thank you so much. Now, Mr. Monsoon, if . . ."

"Honestly, George wouldn't know," Amy said. "Honestly not. Do you know what he does all day? Writes books on butterflies!"

"Really?" Mr. Rockaby said, "so you write, do you? I do too, you know. In a small way."

"Donald dear, pass the langues du chat round, will you?"

"Isn't it langues *de* chat?" Mrs. Hardinger said in a far-away voice. "I think so."

"Oh my dear, I am sure you are right," Mrs. Rockaby said. "Anyway, Donald dear, *do pass them on.*"

"I bought a little book on the Law just the other day," Mr. Swan said. "One of those cheap editions. Quite good too. All the things one wants to know. For instance, if a hen that doesn't belong to you lays an egg in your garden, who do you think the egg belongs to?"

"Oh, but you mean a peacock," Lavinia said. "Or don't you?"

"Yes, that's it. It's a joke, that's the one you mean, isn't it?" Amy said.

"A joke?" George said. "What did he say? I'm afraid I wasn't listening."

"Mr. Swan said . . ." Amy began. But Mr. Swan laughed and said, "No, no, no! I was being perfectly serious. No. I know the one you mean about the pea*hen*. Ha, ha. No." He went on to repeat what he had said about the hen. George helped himself to another scone, saying to himself, "Peahen, peahen. What's he mean?" This irritated Mrs. Hardinger (who sat beside him). She said, "Peacock, peacock. Don't you see? *Peahen*."

"Cocks don't lay eggs, dear," Amy said, leaning over the table.

"But the point is, if one owns the hen, one can't go and fetch the egg in one's neighbour's garden without permission. Otherwise one is *trespassing*!" Mr. Swan said.

"Would you believe it," Mrs. Rockaby said. "More tea anybody? More tea?"

"But if *they* can't fetch the egg, and *you* can't take it—what happens?" Lavinia said.

"Well, the egg goes bad, I suppose. Ha, ha," Mr. Swan said. "That's right, isn't it, Mr. Monsoon. Let the Law speak!"

"Yes, certainly. Certainly," George said.

"Well, I think that's rather ridiculous," Mr. Rockaby said.

"People who go to law *are* ridiculous," George said. He found everyone looking at him as though expecting more. He put down the scone he was eating.

"Lavinia, you might start cutting the cake," Mrs. Rockaby said in the pause.

"But litigation is sometimes a necessary evil," Mrs. Hardinger said.

George said, "Quite." And picked up his scone again.

It was really too soon to cut the cake, but Mrs. Rockaby, having spent so much time on it, longed for it to be really noticed. And being nervous she just said anything that came into her head. The cake was very magnificent, covered with snow-white icing and cunning little decorations in pink. It stood on a silver stand on the best plate in the middle of the table.

"You know," Rupert said, leaning forward, "that's a very wonderful cake. Is it somebody's birthday? Are you twenty-one to-day, Mrs. Rockaby?"

"Oh come now, Mr. Tyce," Mrs. Rockaby said, frightfully pleased at last, "even you are older than that!"

As far as a tea-party can, the party now went with a swing. Everyone ate, everyone talked, and when some hot water was wanted to fill up the teapot, Mr. Swan got up quite naturally as though he were one of the family, and said, "Let me." Of course he didn't know his way about, so Mrs. Rockaby said, smiling, "Lavinia, you show him, dear." And when they had gone out, "Such a nice man. So nice," she said vaguely. Mr. Rockaby frowned. But Mrs. Hardinger raised her eyebrows and began cutting up her slice of cake into little bits, thoughtfully. Thus Mrs. Rockaby knew her remark had not fallen on deaf ears.

"Dora, you don't have to hurry back directly afterwards, do you?" she said. "It's ages since we had a really good talk. Don't rush off."

"Well, I mustn't be *too* late, you know," Mrs. Hardinger said.

"How about coming to the pub?" Rupert said to Amy quietly.

"But tell me, how do you manage to house all these butter-flies—they must take up such a lot of space in boxes?" Mr. Rockaby said.

Mr. Swan and Lavinia came back with the kettle.

"We'll see," Amy said. And before George could really explain about his collection, Mrs. Rockaby had interrupted him to ask, "Anyone? More tea?"

He sat next to her, and said, "Yes, please."

"Ladies first," Mrs. Rockaby said, smiling. "You're as bad as my husband—head in the air—he always forgets where he is." She reached over and took Mrs. Hardinger's cup.

"Oh! So sorry," George said.

"You know, it's frightfully difficult teaching the girls manners," Mrs. Hardinger said. "You'd think, coming from good homes, wouldn't you, that they'd have good manners. But no."

Suddenly Rupert said, "Do you happen to know a song called 'L'Absence' by Berlioz?" He was talking to Amy, but hadn't lowered his voice; so everyone tried to think, quickly, how this and the subject of manners could be related. Mrs. Rockaby realised at once that the song he meant was in French and put on a dreamy smile and said, "Oh. Yes, yes. Oh yes." Amy said, "No."

Rupert waved his hand. "Never mind," he said.

"I adore Berlioz," Mrs. Rockaby said. "Strange how he has never been really appreciated by the English, don't you think?"

Rupert shrugged his shoulders and spread out his hands.

"One can see you know France well," Mrs. Rockaby said. And turning towards Mr. Swan and her daughter, "Perhaps—for the *lune de miel*?" she murmured.

"Me?" Mr. Swan said. "Oh, I see what you mean. Er, well . . ."

"For myself," Mrs. Hardinger said, speaking to George, "I prefer German Lieder, don't you?" She hadn't expected a reply, but was being polite, and had already turned to her other neighbour, Mr. Rockaby, to say something interesting about Hugo Wolf, when George said, "Yes. Personally I am very fond of Lieder. But my wife says they are sentimental. She sings, you know, and I accompany her on the piano."

Mrs. Hardinger had to say, "Er, sorry," to Mr. Rockaby, who hadn't quite caught what she said, and turn back to George and say, "*Oh*. How interesting though."

"Yes," George said. "A pity we've rather let it drop lately. We must take it up again. Hard on my wife, you know, the children both being off at school."

"One should always have outside interests," Mrs. Hardinger said.

"But honestly, Dora, for a woman, that isn't possible," Mrs. Rockaby said, clasping the teapot. "What with a house and children and a husband to look after, one simply hasn't got time."

"One should make up one's mind what one wants to do," Mr. Rockaby said.

"What better interests could a woman have than those centred around her home?" Mr. Swan said.

Mrs. Rockaby burst into fits of laughter. "Oh, oh," she said. "*So* like a man!"

"So you sing, do you, Mrs. George?" Mr. Rockaby said. "I've always thought you had something of the Arts about you."

"Oh, nothing very interesting," Amy said.

"Her father writes very interesting books," Rupert said.

George frowned. "Didn't know anybody read them though," he said.

"Have you?" Rupert said.

"What on earth are you talking about over there?"

Mrs. Rockaby called out. "You all look terribly serious. Look everyone, would you mind all going out now you've finished? Lavinia and I will clear up."

Pushed out into the garden, the guests wandered about. Mr. Swan smoked a cigarette by himself. George watched some cabbage whites thoughtfully and Amy strolled along the path with Rupert.

Mrs. Hardinger, who had come out last (she had offered to help with the washing up, but Mrs. Rockaby had said, "No, good gracious!"), went up to talk to Mr. Swan. They spoke of this and that. She thought he seemed a bit vague and rather short. George looked at his watch. "How much longer, I wonder?" he said to himself.

"I say," Rupert called out, "what about you and your wife coming round with me to the pub afterwards?"

"Oh no. Thanks very much. I must get back," George said.

"Oh, George, get back for what?" Amy said.

"You know perfectly well, I've got work."

"Couldn't you give it a rest, just for once?"

"No, Amy," George said. "You go along with Mr. Tyce if you want to. I must get on with my work. Sorry."

Shortly afterwards Lavinia came out.

"Really, don't you think your mother might let me help now?" Mrs. Hardinger said.

"Well . . ." Lavinia said.

"There now, I thought so," Mrs. Hardinger said. She went in, leaving Mr. Swan with Lavinia.

Mr. Swan had made a great effort at tea. He was tired now. "Lavinia," he said, "this has been rather a trying day for me. I don't want to spoil your mother's party, so if I went off now, just quietly, would you explain that I didn't come in to say good-bye because naturally the other guests don't want to go yet, and if I start saying good-bye it will make them feel awkward. So I'll just go away very quietly."

"Oh but, Harold, you can't," Lavinia said. "Whatever will mother think? And what about me?"

"I shall write your mother a letter of thanks, of course," Mr. Swan said, "and doubtless you will wish to talk to the others and help entertain your mother's guests. You must understand, Lavinia, I am not used to company. I hope you don't mind living quietly?"

"No, not a bit. But when do you think, Harold, we should get married?"

"I have had quite enough for one day," Mr. Swan said, "we can discuss that afterwards."

"I'm sorry about the letter, really I am," Lavinia said. "Honestly, I never knew, Harold, that mother was going to invite you to-day."

"I find the way your mother behaves a little extraordinary, I must say," Mr. Swan said, "but then, I don't pretend to understand women."

"You are not going to marry mother, you are going to marry me, Harold. So don't worry."

"We shall see," Mr. Swan said.

"Look, Harold, there's something about all this I don't understand," Lavinia said.

But Mr. Swan began walking away. "Not now, not now," he said, "we don't want to get into any discussion. Good-bye. I'll go round through the garden. Good-bye."

Lavinia sighed. "Not exactly love at first sight," she said to herself. "I must try and behave sensibly." Out of the corner of her eye she saw George coming along down the path, so she put on a smile and turning in his direction said, "Hullo. Hope you haven't been too bored." She liked George, but not Amy. Working with him in his study, she had certainly got to know George, but Amy had always made her feel uneasy. She had formed the impression too, that Amy didn't appreciate George, or her children, really. Lavinia loved children, but because Amy always said "Come along now, children, you don't want to waste Miss Rockaby's time," when she started to play with them, she had had to leave the children alone. After the book had come back from the publishers the last time, she hadn't been asked to help any more. So she knew nothing about George's desperate efforts with jokes.

"Hullo," George said. "I must be off, you know. Of course I'm not bored."

"Well, I am," Lavinia said. "How's the book?"

"So-so."

"Oh dear. Any help wanted from me?"

"No, thanks," George said.

She didn't like to say any more, thinking perhaps George was hard up, because of course he paid her the usual rates. She changed the subject. "How are the children?" she said.

"Oh, coming along, coming along," George said.

"And happy?"

"Oh yes. Thoroughly enjoying themselves. They needed school, you know."

"I'm so glad."

"Did you do this?" George said, nodding at the vegetables.

"Yes. Father helped with the double trenching."

"Hard work. One day I must get down to gardening. I've rather given it up these days. My book, you know . . ."

"If ever I can be of any help . . ."

"Thank you, Miss Rockaby. But just now—well, I haven't got to the stage when you can help."

"Well, just let me know."

"Thanks. I won't forget. Decent of you. Wonderful peas you've got there. You work hard, obviously."

"Yes, it's a hard life."

Lavinia sighed. George heard, and looked up.

"Don't you go killing yourself," he said. "Look here, there's far too many vegetables for us at home—we'll never eat them all. And you know my brother grows them. Why not have some of ours? I'll send William down. Gardening is much too hard work for a young woman."

"Oh thank you," Lavinia said. "But we are all right really." She sighed again, which made George wonder about the girl.

"I say, just look at George and Miss Rockaby!" Amy said to Rupert. "They've been talking at least ten minutes. And he never opens his mouth at home. Odd how much people have to say to strangers, isn't it?"

"And that goes for you and me, Amy," Rupert said.

They were standing together by some shrubs near the house.

"Let's will him to say good-bye," Amy said. "I can't think why he's hanging about. It's not like him to spend hours being polite."

But this effort of will proved unnecessary, for at that moment George took his leave with a friendly wave of the hand and called out, "Well, don't work too hard, Miss Rockaby!" and came down the path. Being deep in thought, he didn't look up as he passed, so Amy called out, "Bye-bye, George."

"Oh, bye-bye," he said, "see you later," and went into the house.

"We'll give him five minutes to take himself off, then we'll make a move ourselves," Rupert said. He looked at his watch.

"Better make it ten," Amy said. "Mrs. Rockaby's bound to make a to-do about saying good-bye, and George never knows how to go."

Indoors, in the sitting-room where they had eaten, Mr. Rockaby had been put on to sweeping up crumbs. Mrs. Hardinger had gone upstairs "to powder my nose" as she said, and was just coming down.

"Well, what on earth are you going to do with all these people now, Evelyn?" Mr. Rockaby said.

"Shush!" Mrs. Rockaby said. She had heard George. In the moment before he came in she snatched the brush and pan from her husband's hands and pushed them under the sofa.

"Hullo, Mr. Monsoon," she said.

"I'm leaving Amy behind with Mr. Tyce," George said, standing in the doorway, "but I simply must go myself. Such a lot of work, you know. I hope you don't mind. And thank you so much for the party."

For the sake of politeness Mrs. Rockaby held him talking. But when for the third time he said he really must go, Mr. Rockaby came to his rescue and took him off to the front door. Mrs. Hardinger stood at the foot of the stairs apparently looking at prints of old London with much appreciation. She had heard George's efforts at saying good-bye, and not wishing to involve him in any unnecessary complications hadn't gone in. Now, after smiling and saying "Good-bye" in such a way as not to delay his exit (she knew exactly the way to say "Good-bye" with finality having had to deal with so many parents), she went in to the sitting-room, hoping to have a chat with her friend Mrs. Rockaby.

"Such a nice man," Mrs. Rockaby said. They watched him depart down the street.

"What do you think of her?" Mrs. Hardinger said. But Mr. Rockaby came back, so the chat had to be put off. He found the brush and pan, and resumed picking up crumbs.

"My dear, *what* a wonderful tea!" Mrs. Hardinger said to Mrs. Rockaby, after a pause. "Oh dear, I simply must sit down! But tell me, honestly, isn't there just *something* I could do?"

"No. Honestly. Nothing," Mrs. Rockaby said. "Donald and I were just finishing. I sent Lavinia out. What's she doing, do you know?"

"Talking to Mr. Swan when I last saw her," Mrs. Hardinger said.

Mrs. Rockaby hummed a gay little tune to herself.

"Excuse me," Mr. Rockaby said, knocking against Mrs. Hardinger's chair with his brush.

"Mr. Tyce and Mrs. George seem very friendly," Mrs. Hardinger said. "Oh, so sorry, am I in the way?"

"No, no," Mr. Rockaby said. "I've just finished more or less. You carry on."

"Very much lord of the manor, isn't he," Mrs. Rockaby said, "but all the same, quite nice. I, for one, like a bit of flattery."

"I do wish he wouldn't trespass, though," Mrs. Hardinger said. "Do you know, this morning those two were in the school wood! And without any permission."

"*Really?*" Mrs. Rockaby said. "Donald dear, there's no need to go over it with a tooth comb, don't overdo it."

"But I dislike crumbs and this room was quite disgusting. As indeed it usually is," Mr. Rockaby said.

"One in the eye for me!" Mrs. Rockaby said. She laughed.

"If, instead of spending your time gossiping and fussing over parties, Evelyn, you took a bit more interest in the house. . . ."

"Donald—Donald!"

"Oh dear, you should make your guests useful, really you should!" Mrs. Hardinger said. "Both of you are dead tired." She got up. "Now, Mr. Rockaby, the brush and pan!" she said, and held out her hand.

"I assure you, it's quite clean now," Mr. Rockaby said. "I've been over it most carefully. Really, I wish you wouldn't!"

But Mrs. Hardinger wasn't going to be outdone. She shifted the chairs, said "Tut-tut!" and swept under some of the carpet.

"It's going to be frightfully hard when Lavinia's gone," Mrs. Rockaby said.

"Evelyn!" Mr. Rockaby said sternly. So Mrs. Hardinger pretended she hadn't heard. After a time Mr. Rockaby said, "Well, hadn't we better get the rest of them in from the garden?" But his wife suggested he might go out himself and keep them amused for just another ten minutes, then the room would really be ready. So Mr. Rockaby went.

"As you were saying, my dear, about Amy Monsoon," Mrs. Rockaby said. "She's always frightfully well dressed, isn't she? Not really in keeping with the country. But I daresay Mr. Tyce, being used to London life, finds the rest of us dowdy."

"There!" Mrs. Hardinger said. She put down the brush and pan and relaxed. "No, I must say," she said, "Mrs. George isn't my type. She's sly, don't you think? Like some of my parents, the mothers especially, who want to get out of paying for extras. Oh, what trouble I have!"

"They say the old man simply adores her."

"Oh, my dear, she knows which side her bread is buttered!"

"But there's absolutely no money, Dora—they're as poor as church mice."

"Rather silly. I wonder why they don't sell up and live in a smaller house."

"Such people don't, you know. Partly sentimentality, the old home and all that, and then lack of imagination. They don't know when their number is up."

"Ah well," Mrs. Hardinger said.

"Of course, you were very lucky, my dear, to get Hereward Hall when you did, weren't you?" Mrs. Rockaby said. "Since then, the market has gone rocketing up."

"Couldn't you sell this place, Evelyn, and perhaps live in a flat?" Mrs. Hardinger said. "It has often struck me that you are not very happy in the country."

"Look, there's something I simply must tell you," Mrs. Rockaby said. She began to tell Mrs. Hardinger, rather hurriedly, fearing any minute her husband might come back, the great news about Lavinia and Mr. Swan, Meanwhile, Mr. Rockaby had had a good look out through the kitchen window. He had seen Lavinia bending over the cabbages, and while he watched, she was joined by Mrs. George and Mr. Tyce. "Well, they seem quite happy," he said to himself, and, being tired, decided to take a few minutes off. He closed the kitchen door, got out some notes from his pocket and sat down by the stove. He had meant to keep an eye on things through the window, but soon forgot and became absorbed in the notes.

Out in the garden Amy and Rupert were saying good-bye to Lavinia.

"Don't bother, we'll find your mother," Amy said. Lavinia was worried about the cabbage whites laying eggs, so she said, "So nice of you to have come," and let them find their own way. It was dark inside the house after the shadeless garden, and feeling, rather than seeing, her way, Amy opened the wrong door. "Oh dear," she said. "Where on earth have we got to—it must be the other door. I'm the wrong way round. Coming in, of course, it's the right, not the left."

"Let's see," Rupert said. He peered over Amy's shoulder.

It was the sort of room most people would have made into a drawing-room even though it was a bit near the kitchen. The windows looked out on to the garden; there was a large fireplace with a basket grate, an ornamental mantelpiece with heaps of room on top of it for china dogs and photographs, and enough floor space for a sofa and a couple of arm-chairs and the usual bric-à-brac. But on leaving London Mrs. Rockaby had left behind the drawing-room side of her life; all that remained was a black baby grand which she had refused to sell because Lavinia played (and Mr. Rockaby agreed that girls should play the piano), a stack of pictures shoved into a corner—reproductions of Matisse and Picasso which no one had bothered to hang up after Mrs. Rockaby said it was no good, they didn't "go"—a Madame Recamier chaise-longue, two Empire style chairs and a gilded looking-glass with an eagle on top. All these were scattered about.

"How queer. It's a sort of dump," Rupert said.

Amy went in, and crossing the room, opened the piano lid and played a few notes very softly. The uncertain, quivering notes—for the piano hadn't been used for months and was out of tune—expressed exactly the dry sadness of all abandoned dusty rooms.

"Play," Rupert said. He shut the door. Amy pulled up one of the chairs and began playing Mozart, a minuet she knew by heart. But she felt nervous, and after a few bars, faltered and then stopped. "Do go on, Amy," Rupert said, "it sounds so sad and right. So full of memories."

"What of?" Amy said. But she started playing again, so Rupert never answered.

In the kitchen, opposite, Mr. Rockaby was not aware of the piano being played, but in the front room, during a pause in the conversation, Mrs. Hardinger suddenly lifted her finger up and said, "Evelyn! Isn't that someone playing the piano?" They listened.

"How sweet," Mrs. Rockaby said. "It's those two. Lavinia's quite good, you know. I knew I was right hanging on to that piano! The world doesn't alter a bit. I used to play for Donald."

"These lovers!" Mrs. Hardinger said. "Well, Evelyn dear . . ."

"Shush!" Mrs. Rockaby said, "just listen a minute—the past comes back. What a lot of the past there is. That means I'm old."

"You should get it tuned, my dear, it's fearfully out," Mrs. Hardinger said. "And now, truly, I must be off."

While Mrs. Rockaby hung on to her friend a bit longer, Amy and Rupert slipped stealthily into the passage, closing the door with care. By the time they had reached the front part of the hall, Mrs. Hardinger had torn herself loose and was ready to go. She opened the sitting-room door, and they all met in the hall. Mrs. Hardinger left first. No one knew where Mr. Rockaby was, so Amy and Rupert said good-bye to Mrs. Rockaby and thanked her, and after a few more polite words, they too went off.

Much later, when Lavinia had explained at least twice about Mr. Swan feeling tired and why he hadn't come to say good-bye, and still Mrs. Rockaby said she failed to understand, it was most peculiar, and Lavinia had gone off for a walk by herself in a huff, Mr. and Mrs. Rockaby had a drink together, finishing up the last of the gin.

"I suppose it's all right about that fellow Swan and Lavinia," Mr. Rockaby said.

"Oh, don't fuss, Donald," Mrs. Rockaby said. She was tired.

"Well, when *I* was a young man," Mr. Rockaby began—but Mrs. Rockaby interrupted. "Let them be," she said, "he is a bit rude. But what does it matter? Did you hear them in there playing the piano? He must have slipped out round the back just as Dora was going. Perhaps he felt embarrassed. Men do, don't they? So silly. But one's only young once."

"Yes. But the young make such dreadful mistakes sometimes," Mr. Rockaby said.

"You mean, I suppose, Donald—us."

"Us? I said no such thing! Really, Evelyn, sometimes you seem to wish to misunderstand me on purpose."

"Can you say honestly, Donald, that you think our life's been a success?"

"Well, I have always done my best. . . ."

"So have I! So have I. . . ."

"Of course," Mr. Rockaby said, "of course. That's what matters."

"But how on earth could one do anything else? It's so silly, Donald," Mrs. Rockaby said.

"Women never seem to understand that true happiness lies in doing one's duty."

"How nasty that sounds. And what a lot it leaves out."

"You may think so. But that is what comes from reading novels. However, don't let us quarrel."

"It must be fun having a really good quarrel sometimes," Mrs. Rockaby said. "I mean, the sort when you throw plates about and shout—a first-class row I mean."

"It's not like you to be vulgar, Evelyn," Mr. Rockaby said, "you are tired. Perhaps I shouldn't have given you gin."

"Oh nonsense—let's have some more!" Mrs. Rockaby said.

But there was none. Soon afterwards Mr. Rockaby went across to his bureau, and Mrs. Rockaby went to her bedroom to change. Her shoes hurt and she had on her smart dress, the only smart one left, which she kept just for parties. And, taking her shoes off, forgetting her rings, something caught, and she found she had laddered her last pair of nylons.

CHAPTER EIGHT

WHENEVER there was a particularly dry spell, water failed in the upstairs taps at the Grange. If, after a week or two, it still didn't rain, then, sooner or later, one day there would be a gurgling and a few drops of dirty-looking water, and no more, when cook turned on the sink tap. George always got sent up into the attics at the first signs of trouble, and generally Mr. Monsoon got someone in from the village who dug up the drive a bit, said the plumbing was queer, water couldn't run up-hill and filled up the hole again. What made the women so cross was seeing the river at the bottom of the garden, lower perhaps than normal, but certainly not dried up. All that water going to waste!

"I know," Mr. Monsoon said, when his wife pointed this out, "but water always finds its own level."

She didn't quite know what this meant, so was silenced. But Vivienne said, "I suppose that means, then, we'll have to start carrying buckets." It did mean that. As the lawns rose quite steeply up from the river towards the house, and water is fearfully heavy, everyone had to do his bit, even Amy. Mr. Monsoon watered his flowers in secret when things got bad like this, and Mrs. Monsoon forbade unnecessary cups of tea.

"I don't know what's going to happen to my trout," Mr. Monsoon complained.

"As you told me the other day," Mrs. Monsoon said, "it's bound to rain soon and then we'll have floods. Why worry?"

"Well, one good thing anyway, the drought has got rid of the heron," Mr. Monsoon said. It was true, the heron had not been seen for many days. On the other hand, the pigeons were now an absolute pest. They ate everything young and green in the garden, even the lettuces, which were so pecked as to be no good for the table. And William said he wasn't going to prick out any more seedlings or set any seeds, it was no darned good. But these days Mr. Monsoon seemed to have lost interest in the pigeons. He just said, "Yes, yes," when anyone mentioned them, and went off to his room.

"Your father is getting very old, I'm afraid," Mrs. Monsoon said to George.

"It's the heat," George said. "It's really frightful in the office; and when I get home I'm so done in I can't get on with my book."

"Oh dear," Mrs. Monsoon said, "where have you got to? Why don't you read it out as you used to in the evenings?"

But since putting in those jokes, George hadn't thought fit to read what he had written during the day to his family in the evenings. His family, it seemed to him, were not the General Public. Nor, in spite of her having suggested the jokes, was Amy. Because one day, after spending hours making a pun fit in about Painted Ladies, Amy had called him for dinner, and he had said, "Time for dinner already? Time flies. . . ." And then, half remembering, "Time flies, you cannot something something—what's that, Amy?" And Amy said, "It's not at all a *funny* joke."

"Well then, what *is* funny?" George said, and had rather lost his temper. Afterwards he felt ashamed, but at the time it had been a relief to be able to blame Amy. First, he blamed her for the jokes, because, he said, having suggested taking such a step to sell the book, surely it was up to her to find the jokes; naturally he would work them in. But had she done this? No.

"I know you think I'm no damn good," he said. "And, of course, by your standards, I am not. I don't spend my time rushing about in cars with you for instance. I haven't time to pay attention to you all day long. One doesn't change, Amy. You always knew I was not that sort of a man. I often wonder why you married me. Why did you?" Attacked in this way,

Amy sulked. George knew she would, and not pausing for an answer, went straight on. "And another thing," he said, "you are not interested in the things I'm interested in." He spoke of the children then, how Amy never wrote unless he nagged her, what a fuss she'd made about that boarding school, how now they'd gone she didn't seem to mind. And did she realise the holidays would be here soon? And had she any plans for keeping the children amused? And what about new suits? Yes, she should be alive to all these problems; he was, and it was her job, not his.

"So it's no good mooning about with a long face, Amy," he said in conclusion. He was really angry. But George never stayed angry. And he knew that getting stuck at chapter fifteen was his fault, not Amy's, and that putting jokes in, though her idea, was a matter for his decision, definitely. And if Amy wanted a bit of fun with Mr. Tyce, why shouldn't she? Because if a man cannot trust his wife, that was the end.

"I'm so dull," George told himself. "It's a wonder she's stuck to me!" He didn't mean this seriously of course. He was out in the garden picking an enormous bunch of flowers, and feeling lonely and trying to make himself cheer up. When he had picked some delphiniums and columbines and two of his father's best lilies, he went on to the rose beds. No one was there, so he picked half a dozen of the best roses. And these, with the delphiniums, columbines and lilies, Amy found when she went to lie down after lunch, arranged in Mrs. Monsoon's best vase, bang in the middle of the dressing-table.

But Amy had changed. Looking back, Mrs. Monsoon put it all down to the Rockabys' party when George had come back alone. Amy hadn't even come home for dinner that evening.

"Where's Amy?" Mr. Monsoon had said, sitting down. Everyone looked at the empty place at the table. "Oh, she 'phoned," George said, "Mr. Tyce wanted to take her out to dinner."

"Take her out—where?" Mrs. Monsoon had said, but Mr. Monsoon hadn't taken the matter seriously and just said, "Ha! Gadding about! Let's have some beer. George, fetch the beer, please."

At ten, Amy still wasn't home. Mrs. Monsoon pointed this out.

"Well, I'm a bit of a dull dog really," George had said. "Amy doesn't get very much fun."

"Quite right," Mr. Monsoon said, "don't be such a Mrs. Grundy!"

Of course Mrs. Monsoon had gone upstairs then, and stayed awake. But she never heard Amy come in. And next morning Amy was not in her place at breakfast.

"Sleeping it off," George said, when she asked.

Nobody in the Monsoon family approved of breakfast in bed, so Amy had gone without.

After that, and looking back, Mrs. Monsoon wondered how no one except herself had noticed the difference, Amy changed rapidly. She was never about when anyone wanted her, and naturally, Vivienne—who had to do everything by herself if Amy wouldn't help—complained. Then Stephen wrote a letter.

"Dear Mum (the letter said)—I'm frightfully busy just now so I can't come home. But Vivy sounds awfully run down. She writes that she has to do everything now, and the beds hurt her back. Also, she's not helped with the housework at all, or the shopping, and the poor old girl is a bit fed up. She says she always feels tired. Now I don't know what on earth's come over Amy. She used to be a good sport but she seems to have folded up completely. Or rather, as I'm bound to say, knowing something about it, changed her spots. You know I'm not the sort to spread gossip, but it's all over the place since Mr. Tyce got hold of that second-hand car (if you can call it a car) that he goes hurtling about with Amy. You might point out to her, that whatever she thinks, other people take a pretty dim view of it. And it's not fair on the family. Please try to buck Vivy up. I'll be writing to her. Love, Stephen."

"I should like to have a word with you, Charlie," Mrs. Monsoon said to her husband, coming upon him suddenly one evening. He had thought he was safe at that time of day, safe from the bothers of daily life and lost to the rest of the world, his family, his house, wandering about in the garden he loved so much. On evenings such as these, after the heat of the day, sounds of children playing or cattle lowing carried across the valley and from far away bell-ringing practice in the next village could be heard intermittently. The stillness, when it came, was full of peace. And then remote sounds coming to life again and the children's shouts repeated after a silence of minutes foretold that some hours yet must pass before night's quiet, and it seemed that there never would be an end to the weariness of this too long summer day. Mr. Monsoon had forgotten where he was really. The heat had been steady, the skies had been cloudless, and now that the sun sank low in a haze of dust, it was pleasant to think of the night which must follow, of the night breezes and of the dark. He was watering some of the flowers which had collapsed, and jumped when his wife spoke. "Only just one canful— dirty water from the kitchen," he said, recovering himself.

"I don't know what we are supposed to do with the washing," Mrs. Monsoon said, "there's two weeks now, and the water is still low."

"These things happen. It's no use worrying," Mr. Monsoon said.

"All very well for you to say that. But when there is no more linen and you can't have clean sheets—what then, Charlie?"

"I shall complain, of course I shall. But it won't make the slightest difference. Patience, my dear. There will always be droughts. And there'll always be rain afterwards."

"Floods. I suppose we shall have those awful floods again."

"Yes, I daresay we shall have floods again. One must expect it in these valleys."

"I must say, I envy you your philosophical attitude. But then it's always the women who have to deal with these things. Three weeks' washing. And then going out in useless boots in a flooded garden."

"Two weeks' washing, didn't you say? And now is the time to get some Wellingtons if you want them."

"Charlie, one has other things to do than waste a whole day buying boots."

"I know, I know, my dear. And now, please could you leave me alone? I must finish this watering."

By this time the can was empty.

"Enough. That's enough, Charlie," Mrs. Monsoon said.

"You go in, my dear," he said, "you are tired. I like to walk about in the garden in the cool of the day."

"Cool? You must be ill, Charlie—it's frightfully hot still."

"Oh do leave me alone."

Mrs. Monsoon touched his arm. "I have something on my mind," she said, "I must speak to you, Charlie."

So Mr. Monsoon put down his watering-can, and they strolled in under the shade of a tree and then seated themselves on two old garden chairs which faced away from the house so that they looked at the orchard, and beyond that, the fields and hills.

"I don't know whether you have noticed Amy lately?" Mrs. Monsoon said.

"She's looking very pretty," Mr. Monsoon said.

This was true.

"Is she? Oh. Well, I rather wanted to have a word with you about Amy," his wife said.

"Amy. . . . Yes," Mr. Monsoon said, "but remember, we are old-fashioned. One of the worst things for an old man to be told is that he doesn't understand. But it comes to us all I'm afraid. And one day George's sons will tell him that he doesn't understand. The trouble is, our children remain children to us, they only grow up to others. Human beings never allow for change unless they are forced to; but really, our children have changed. That is the difficulty."

"I was talking about Amy," Mrs. Monsoon said.

"I know," said Mr. Monsoon, "and I am very fond of Amy—I love her—isn't that enough? But George worries me. He doesn't look after her. All this business about his book! It's getting worse and worse. These days he's always shutting himself up. Is he blind? Because for a long time now I've seen that those two are drifting apart. More children is my answer, but one can't very well put it like that."

"I don't think you quite understand," Mrs. Monsoon said. "It isn't George at all who is at fault—not as I see it. You know perfectly well what I mean really, Charlie. Amy and Mr. Tyce."

Mr. Monsoon sighed, and looked out over the fields. "It's no good pretending you're deaf," Mrs. Monsoon said, "or blind, you know, Charlie."

"It's so quiet and peaceful this evening," Mr. Monsoon said, "I do wish you wouldn't fuss. Amy's a good girl. She has given us two grandsons, hasn't she? And as for the rest, well, it will pass. It's only a storm in a teacup, my dear."

"Indeed it is not—it's very scandalous!" Mrs. Monsoon said. "The whole village is talking about it. You should see Stephen's letter! I haven't shown it to you before, but now that you seem to want to be such an ostrich . . ."

"No," Mr. Monsoon said, waving away the letter his wife brought out. "Amy is all right. If you interfere you will provoke a catastrophe, a meddling woman always does. I'm too old for that."

"Well, you can't say I haven't warned you, Charlie."

"Someone's always been warning me all my life."

"Yes. And just look at your life!"

"What's the matter with it?"

"Oh Charlie. . . . No money, nothing achieved. . . . You can't say you have really had a worthwhile sort of life."

"I have enjoyed it."

"But that isn't enough."

"Well, I leave two children and their children to get on with it."

Mrs. Monsoon got up. "You have a lot to answer for," she said, looking down at her husband not very sympathetically.

"God knows what you mean," Mr. Monsoon said, "unless you are talking about the way I have lost all my money. But I enjoyed even that. It's up to the children now to make some more if they want it. It's very easy. Then their children can spend it. As for the rest, well, we shall see. I am old, but not old enough to repent yet. If you like, you can do that. But leave me in peace."

"And Amy?"

"So long as Amy is happy she won't go far wrong. Don't interfere."

"But if she makes everyone else unhappy?"

"Then it's up to George, not me. I can't be responsible for everyone's life!"

"But it's your own family."

"Oh do go away!" Mr. Monsoon said.

She went. Slowly and with dignity she walked straight back to the house, across the lawn, up the steps, over the path and in by the Parlour door. Mr. Monsoon watched and then sank back into himself, half closing his eyes.

"Now for a bit of peace perhaps," he said. He almost fell asleep.

Mrs. Monsoon was not present at dinner, and when Amy suggested taking up soup, Mr. Monsoon said, "Leave her alone for God's sake!" Which certainly relieved Amy.

*

George's flowers had come too late. Amy had noticed them of course, but just thought "How pathetic." And after a short rest, dashed out to meet Rupert. It was more than a month now since Rupert had come down to stay with his mother, and truth to tell, Mrs. Tyce was getting a little tired of her son. Originally, when pressed to stay, he had said, "Well, Mother, if you promise me there will be no more letters and you'll be good when I'm gone, I'll stay till your birthday." This he had done. Mrs. Tyce achieved the age of eighty-two, spending the day with Rupert very happily (he gave her a book on Chinese painting, and Smyly gave her a new gong), and after dinner that night she said, "Don't forget to order a taxi. And if you are going early, please don't wake me."

"Oh, there's no hurry. I don't think I'll be going just yet," Rupert said.

"Oh," Mrs. Tyce said.

And so Rupert had stayed and stayed. It had been Amy who had persuaded Rupert to borrow money from his mother to buy the car. He had mentioned casually to Amy once that one day he hoped to go to Greece to potter about in the sun; only just now, he couldn't afford to buy a car. And later, reminding him of this, Amy said, "Why not borrow money from your mother and have the car now? After all, she's bound to leave you something, isn't she—why wait for her to die, because that's rather nasty, don't you think."

To have to ask his mother for money didn't bother Rupert, he was only afraid she hadn't got any to give, and £80 which he would have to raise somehow or other to put with the £100 he had saved in order to be able to buy the car was rather a lot. He enquired delicately into the state of his mother's banking account. Now actually the old lady's object-ive outlook on life was fading; more and more she tended to rely on herself alone, not what other people said about the world. Even books became unpleasant. She sat all day long in her sun hut (in the shade, it had to be continually turned round) lost in recollections of the past, which, as she mused, became ever more vivid than the present. Rupert contributed to this shadowy existence among shades; he was such a nuisance—always there at meals looking like his father. And too, because of him, she had had to give up writing letters. She put the *Parish Registry* away, relying still for a little while on Burke's *Landed Gentry*; but the fun of looking people up had gone, and soon she put that book away as well. Now there was nothing to do. So she just sat about all day long remembering Queen Victoria, a nice Queen to remember in one's old age. Gradually, though, the Queen absorbed her (or she absorbed the Queen, it's hard to say), and so, when Rupert asked her for the second time what was the state of her banking account, she said, "Ah yes. Largesse. It's time we made a gesture." Rupert, used to his mother's eccentricities, just raised his eyebrows.

"Yes," she said.

So he brought her cheque book. "How much?" she said to herself.

"Eighty pounds?" Rupert said. He hesitated. She began to write out the cheque. "Are you *sure* you can spare it, Mother?" he said.

"Ask them to give it you in sovereigns, please," Mrs. Tyce said. He was too absorbed in other things to bother very much about his mother. He thanked her, told her not to go short because of him, herself, and went off to meet Amy.

Sometimes they met at a distance from the village in the fields, sometimes in the wood in a particularly overgrown and weedy place. This last was a bit dangerous, and Amy ruined her stockings finding a way through the brambles; but it was not easy for these two to find a safe, secluded place to meet where no one would disturb them. The car was an absolute blessing. Rupert, who had had his eye on it in London, went up to get it immediately he got the money, and drove back in triumph. It was shabby and old and would leak when it rained, but it was a car.

"I'm going out for a drive with Mr. Tyce, if that's all right," Amy would say most afternoons.

"Right-o," George would say, "—back for tea?"

"No."

"Well, don't be too late."

And off Amy would go. Soon everyone in the village knew about Amy and Rupert. No one approved. But perhaps in his heart of hearts Mr. Grole was glad, because a scandal like this entailed long discussions among the menfolk, and so much beer was drunk in the pub. No word of this, except for what Stephen had said in his letter, reached the Monsoons. But Smyly, well trained in gathering gossip (she was friends with the postmistress), tried to warn Mrs. Tyce. A year ago, Mrs. Tyce would have been delighted to know, she wouldn't have minded a bit that her own son was involved—such things happened—and she would have been all the more tickled to think of those worthy Monsoons, dismayed beyond words, caught out by a Tyce. But not now. She waved Smyly away, and said in her new, grand voice, "We are not interested." So poor Smyly read all Rupert's letters (the two wrote when they couldn't meet, and Rupert was frightfully careless and left letters lying about) and kept what she read to herself, because, really, one couldn't tell that sort of thing to the postmistress.

Like the drought, this state of affairs dragged on and on. But in the end, it rained. Not, as Mr. Monsoon had prophesied, in floods, but gently. It poured down day after day. No one could go out. To make it worse, Stephen came home. He contented himself at first with being rude to Amy. But when she bore it with indifference, he spoke his mind to his father. There was a row. At meals, everyone kept silent. Only Amy dared to look up from her plate. After dinner, Mr. Monsoon said, "Amy, I want to speak to you. In my room." George, who knew of the row that morning from his mother, but not of its cause, said nothing. He was fed up with Amy. She had been in what he called "her perverse mood" so long now, he couldn't remember her nice. And this interfered with his work. But soon the children would be back from school. That would cure her, he thought. He went off to his room.

Mr. Monsoon only kept Amy two minutes.

"Well," he said when she came in, "what have you been up to?"

Amy looked very obstinate. "Nothing," she said.

"It's all very well, we can't have this," Mr. Monsoon said.

"What?" Amy said.

"It isn't dignified."

"Just what do you mean?"

"Don't look at me like that, Amy. You know you're my favourite. Don't make me sad."

"What has Stephen been saying about me, please?" Amy said.

"I'm not going to repeat what Stephen said."

"Well, can I go now, Father?"

"Oh Amy . . . Is that all you've got to say to me?"

"Yes," Amy said.

"You have changed. Be careful, my dear," Mr. Monsoon said, "and if you're not happy, come and tell me. Don't forget, I'm your friend." He gave Amy a long look, but the obstinate expression remained, hardening her face.

"You'd better go then," he said.

CHAPTER NINE

THIS sort of weather made Mr. Monsoon's legs ache, so he lay about a good deal in his bedroom. He had finished *Riders of the Purple Sage* and was now on to *Hamlet*. He read this aloud to himself. Mrs. Monsoon was also confined to her bed. She had very bad indigestion. Her husband's reading disturbed her peace. She complained through Vivienne.

"Tell her it's all nerves," Mr. Monsoon said when Vivienne told him about the complaints and the indigestion. Rather naturally, Mrs. Monsoon said when she got the message, "Tell him his legs are just nonsense!" But Vivienne didn't care to do this.

Everyone was being terribly nice to Vivienne. It had just become obvious that she was going to have a baby. Cook rushed about saying, "Now, Mrs. Stephen, don't you go carrying heavy things!" And Stephen, having explained to each member of the family individually why he stayed at home—Vivienne was in a bit of a flap, the first always made a woman feel nervous—said things at meal-times like "Come on, Vivy—eat up! Now you're eating for two, don't forget." Which was thought to be rather coarse, as the others said afterwards. And Vivienne rested and had milk instead of tea and was allowed to use Mrs. Monsoon's ancient sewing machine for turning the ends up round nappies. The other things, little night-dresses and infant garments, she sewed by hand.

"I always think making the baby's clothes oneself makes such a difference," she said to Amy, "even though one's stitches aren't so small as those made by the sewing machine."

"As I never learned how to sew properly and hate it," Amy said, "I wouldn't know. But still . . . Would you like some of the boys' old things?"

"No, thanks," Vivienne said, "we can afford to have all new things. Besides, it may be a girl. Who knows?" She smiled to herself.

"In the beginning it couldn't possibly make any difference," Amy said.

"But then," said Vivienne, "you are not the really terribly mothering sort, are you, Amy dear? How do you know what a baby thinks and feels?"

"Oh, wait till you've had ten!" Amy said.

Vivienne looked rather alarmed. "You don't mean to say that you . . . ?" she began, screwing round in her chair.

"Good lord, no," said Amy.

By this time the row had blown over, though nothing had changed. Owing to the appalling weather (and how that car leaked!) Amy was more often at home. And because Vivienne had said rows and Stephen's attitude to Amy upset her and made her feel sick, Stephen had bought Amy a box of chocolates and said, "Look here, old girl, sorry. But you know Vivy's state. It makes a man a bit jumpy when his wife's in the family way. Here's some Cadbury's chocs. If you think of it, leave one or two of the pink squishy sort for Vivy, will you? She seems to want that kind of thing just now—it's the baby."

"Another time, mind your own business, please," Amy said.

"Well, you tuck into those chocolates," Stephen said. He pushed them towards her.

"I know what you think. And I don't care. I don't care what anyone thinks," Amy said.

"So I said something like 'keep your hair on, old girl' or 'there, there,'" Stephen told his wife afterwards.

"What did Amy do with the chocolates?" Vivienne said.

"If she had any sense, she ate them," Stephen said.

"I do wish you'd buy me some," Vivienne said. "Is it likely, Stephen, that Amy would keep me the pink ones even if you did ask?"

"This baby business is getting a bit expensive," Stephen said.

Another time, when Vivienne was talking about babies to Amy (he had heard the word 'baby' on coming in) and Stephen said, "Hullo you two—having a mothers' meeting?" and Amy got up and went, Stephen said to Vivienne, "The trouble is, she's got her nose out of joint. That's what it is." But Vivienne just smiled and said nothing.

When Mrs. Monsoon's indigestion got better and she was off Benger's Food and on to pigeon pie and that sort of thing again, she took meals with her husband upstairs in his room sometimes. "You know, Charlie," she said on one of these occasions, "if you're not careful you'll become bedridden. That's what will happen to you."

"I shall die in my boots," Mr. Monsoon said. "And what about you?"

"I'm up, Charlie."

"No good getting up this weather. One can't get out. But when I do I'm going to start shooting those pigeons seriously. George says they are a pest."

"Poor George," Mrs. Monsoon said.

"The trouble, my dear, with George," her husband said, "is that he's such an ostrich."

"I once said that about you."

"Women are no judge."

"Well, so long as you think everything is all right . . ." Mrs. Monsoon said.

"Amy's a sensible woman. You leave her alone," Mr. Monsoon said. "And now, my dear, if you don't mind . . . Where's my book? . . . Ah, here it is. Get well and don't fuss. We can all look after ourselves."

"So like your father. No help," Mrs. Monsoon said to Stephen that afternoon, "and he won't even get up."

"Let him be," Stephen said. "After all, Mother, he's getting pretty ancient, you know."

"It's all very well for you to speak, Stephen," Mrs. Monsoon said, "but you don't have to take the responsibility. Something has got to happen about George and Amy. Eternally cross like this, they upset the whole house. And you said yourself that Amy was misbehaving herself and causing gossip."

"Oh forget it, Mother!" Stephen said. "Mr. Tyce will take himself off and the whole thing will blow over. The important thing is that Vivy shouldn't be upset. And I can't always be at home, you know. Keep calm. That's best."

"Perhaps," Mrs. Monsoon said. "Well, I hope you are right."

It continued to rain. One morning George came out of his room to look for another pencil, his old friend the indelible one being lost, and met Amy in the passage with her mackintosh on.

"Good lord!" he said. "You'll get soaked—you're not going out, Amy?"

"I'm not a child, George," Amy said. "There's no harm in getting wet."

"But it's daft!" George said. "Why should you go out? Don't tell me you're off on a walk, not this sort of weather."

"Oh, shut up and let me pass," Amy said. "I'm just going out."

"Look here, Amy, this sort of thing's got to stop," George said. "I've had enough of your filthy temper. And in another week the children will be back. You might think of that."

"Why bring in the children always?"

"Oh to hell with you, Amy! I haven't time to mess about dealing with you in a temper. Go out. And get wet." He brushed past her.

"Thanks," Amy said. Neither of them looked back.

But that morning, in the car, just after he had picked Amy up by the signpost some distance from the village, Rupert said, "We can't go on like this, Amy."

"Please don't you start," Amy said. "Everyone's shouting at me this morning."

Rupert liked driving fast, but the car wouldn't do more than forty and made a deafening noise doing that. Conversation was ruled out once he put his foot down on the accelerator, and so the two just sat, looking cross. When they stopped some time later on in the town, they had their first quarrel in the car park. Had Amy not said, "Well, you've made it quite obvious, Rupert, that you loathe me," when Rupert said, opening the door of the car, "Oh for goodness' sake let's get out!" they might have made it up. But this remark put Rupert straight back on to the main argument which had started the quarrel: love.

"Love, love, love, love!" he said, "that's all you women ever think about! It never strikes you that a man has work!"

"Shush! Don't talk so loud," Amy said.

"Oh what do I care—I'm fed up," Rupert said.

And so they continued like that. As Rupert said, it was Amy's fault. All the same, she was bound to stick up for herself.

And she was still sticking up for herself when she came back.

They parted where they had met, by the signpost.

"Good-bye" Amy said. Rupert drove off. In tears, almost, Amy began the long walk home. It was one o'clock, not the time of day when many people were about. She hurried on, knowing she would be late again for lunch. At that time Lavinia also came home when she had had a morning at the school (partly to help her mother, but also because staff meals were eaten apart, not with the girls, and Lavinia didn't really get on with the staff) and so, just beyond the Rockabys' house, the two women met.

"Oh hullo, Mrs. George," Lavinia said. Amy said "Hullo" but didn't stop.

"Oh, Mrs. George," Lavinia said, running back.

"Yes?" Amy said.

"About your husband's book," Lavinia said a little breathlessly (Amy made her feel shy). "If you think, if I could help—I mean—don't let the question of cash come into it—it isn't that. But if your husband needs help . . . well, I'd be only too glad. You see, I am interested in the book."

"I'm sure my husband would let you know if he wanted help," Amy said.

"Yes, I just thought . . ." Lavinia said.

"As he never does anything else except write, I shouldn't think he needed help."

"Well, when he's at a more finished stage perhaps. But I won't keep you, you're in a hurry, Mrs. George."

"Yes I am," Amy said.

They said good-bye and parted. "Oh poor Mr. George," Lavinia said to herself.

"Your lunch is outside keeping warm, Amy. We didn't wait," Mrs. Monsoon said when Amy came into the dining-room.

"Where have you been?" George said.

"Oh, just out," Amy said.

Stephen and Vivienne exchanged looks, but Mrs. Monsoon kept her eyes on her plate. Mr. Monsoon was still in bed.

"Well, you'd better change. You must be sopping wet," George said.

Amy went out to fetch her lunch. She paused at the door and said, "But I'm *not* wet."

"Such dreadful weather," Mrs. Monsoon said. She sipped a little hot water, closed her eyes and tried not to think about indigestion. But she had it again.

Next morning the post brought a short note for Amy from Rupert.

"Sorry, (it said) but I hate this sort of thing. I can't stand quarrels and you were beastly angry yesterday, Amy. Perhaps I was too. So I'm going to London to cool off. Don't be unhappy. I want to get an objective view of the whole thing, and this is impossible while we're together. You see, we must make up our minds what we are going to do. If you say you can't leave your children, that's that, isn't it? But there's no need to drag in this business of me not loving you, that's a lie, Amy. Think it over and write. I don't know how long I'll be away. Yours, Rupert."

He gave his London address underneath. Amy took this letter outside and read it in the rose garden in the pouring rain and caught a chill and spent the next two days in bed.

"I told you you'd catch cold," George said. But Amy was too unhappy and felt too ill to argue. So he went back to his book.

By the time the children came home the rain had gone and the sun shone once more. William mowed the lawn and the lovely smell of freshly cut grass filled the garden and seeped into the house. The flowers perked up, and Mr. Monsoon sat out on the verandah watching the children play. Mrs. Monsoon fussed over the housekeeping and ordered suitable food for the children (Irish stew, *not* pigeon pie). Vivienne sat about sewing and telling lies to the children when they asked why were the clothes so small, no one was as little as that, and Stephen had to go off on business most days. George went on with his book, but with the window open as it was warm and he was smoking a tremendous lot. And Amy was well again. So, on the surface, things looked all right and quite normal. However, watching her children and listening how they talked, Amy complained to George that they weren't hers any more.

"What on earth do you mean?" George said. He was taking time off to think, and didn't want to be disturbed. They sat by the river in the shade of some trees. Mr. Monsoon had just been fishing, but he had gone in.

"Well," Amy said, "they don't behave as they used to, for one thing."

"Of course not!" George said, "they've been to school. You don't want to have them tied to your apron strings, do you?"

"It isn't that," Amy said. "I can't even talk to them any more. When I asked, what did they do with themselves at school, they just nudged each other and giggled."

"They haven't settled down yet. Give them a chance."

"And I don't like the language they use. Not exactly swear words—that's bound to happen. But they seem to have a sort of secret language. I don't know . . ."

"You're fussing," George said, "just leave them alone. Can't you remember when you were young how maddening it was to have parents fussing?"

"If you call that fussing when your own children won't have anything to do with you—won't come when you call—are downright rude when you make suggestions—call you disgusting names . . ."

"Perhaps you brought them up badly after all, Amy."

"Everything's always my fault." George sighed and looked away.

"Next you'll be telling me that I never loved the children really," Amy said.

George knocked the ash out of his pipe and said in a toneless voice, "One wonders. Got anything more to grouse about?"

"It's no good talking to you, obviously," Amy said. "It's quite clear I'm not wanted."

She got up and then lingered a few moments, but George said nothing, so she went away.

Later that day Amy brought up the subject of the children's behaviour when speaking to her father-in-law, hoping to get some help from him. But he was tired and didn't want to get involved in any discussion and fell back on platitudes. "Boys will be boys," he said.

"But, Father, I don't like the way they behave," Amy said.

"One must live and let live," said Mr. Monsoon.

Amy went off to the stables all by herself and cried with the pigeons.

Mr. Monsoon still didn't feel well enough to go shooting those pigeons, but he bore them in mind. Every morning at breakfast he said, "Well, to-day I'll have to see about getting my gun out. . . ." But when William had been to see him about the garden and he'd had a chat with Mr. Smith, the best part of the morning had gone, as he said, and he lay about on a chaise-longue watching the children. Lately, he had handed all business affairs, all plans that had to do with the house or the garden and everything that had to do with money, over to George. All the same, he liked William to keep him informed about the state of the garden, and of course said "No" when William said Mr. George had said it would be a good thing to plant celery in a different bed this year. But one thing he never interfered with now was money.

"You spend what you like, how you like, on what you like," he told George, "I don't want to be worried."

"It isn't a question of *spending*, Father," George said. He had just learned that Mr. Monsoon had taken out a second mortgage on the house.

"Well, you can have the run of my study—find out about things—Amy knows where everything is," Mr. Monsoon said.

"You really ought to have told me before about this," George said.

"Now it's yours, my boy. You can do as you like with it."

"Stephen ought to be consulted."

"Consult him as much as you like. Only don't bother me," Mr. Monsoon said.

"Obviously the old boy is going to peg out," Stephen said to George when, after dinner that night, the two sons sat in their father's study, reviewing events. They had got out all the relevant papers and were shocked at the mess Mr. Monsoon had made of the family accounts. The trouble was, not being able to lay his hands on any ready money because George dealt with all business affairs and investments, the old man had been juggling about with the property. Although, years ago, the whole of the Grange property had been made over to Mrs. Monsoon, when her husband said—"Sign this"—she signed it. She would in fact sign anything, one only had to ask.

As Stephen had already remarked when told of the second mortgage, "Father's made a blasted mess of it. If we're not careful, we'll be out on our ears."

"Yes," George said now. "Yes. I don't quite know what to do about it. It really is very irresponsible on father's part to throw in his hand like this."

"Senile decay," Stephen said. "Well now, what are we going to do about it?"

They spent some long time in argument. It was not the first time they had found themselves in such a predicament; before, though, it had always been Stephen who took the line that they must sell up. Now, when George suggested this, Stephen held out against it. The result was as usual: the two sons would contribute more, keeping less for themselves, nothing was to be spent on luxuries, and the women, somehow, must be made to spend less. And sums should be set aside each month to pay off the mortgages. They said nothing of this to their wives, nor indeed to their mother, but dropped dark hints such as "You are lucky to have anything *at all* to eat" when she complained of the everlasting pigeon pie. For try as she would, Mrs. Monsoon could not keep pigeon pie out of the menu. Banned for lunch (being unsuitable for children), it turned up at supper for adults.

"No wonder I get indigestion," Mrs. Monsoon sighed. Amy was told that she simply must make the children's clothes herself. And when she said, "But, George, you can't sew—why should I suddenly be able to?" George said, "Well, you've bloody well got to."

There was talk of dismissing some (meaning one or other) of the servants. "It's quite ridiculous," George said, "to have five people—and I don't count Stephen—he's not at home really—looked after by two servants. And when the children are away at school, that's three looked after by two. And that's not counting William."

"But I'm going to have a nurse for baby when baby arrives, aren't I? Amy did!" Vivienne said. And when Stephen said, "No, old girl. You can't. That's flat," she had hysterics. It was all very unfortunate. "The thing is," Stephen said, "we ought to sack Mr. Smith. He does nothing but eat."

But to sack Mr. Smith meant sacking Mrs. Smith too, which was unthinkable; so, as George said, "That means William must go." Nobody wanted William to go. He had spent all his working life in the Monsoons' service, and no family likes to sack an old servant. "Well, we've got to economise somehow or other, you know," Stephen said. "The fact is, we damn well must. So William had better go. I'll do my bit when I'm home—and you're lucky to have a chap like me in the know. And you'll have to learn, George."

George said Stephen had better give William his notice, and Stephen said no, that was George's job. In the end, all that happened was that George got up early and worked in the garden. This made Amy complain. She never got any sleep she said, George came to bed late because he would work at night on his book, and now, when he got up at six, she never got any proper rest.

"There's no other time for my book with the children home and all the time I have to spend at the office," George said. "One doesn't need all that sleep!"

"Well, I do."

"Don't wait up for me then. There's no need to."

"Very well then, George," Amy said, "I shall sleep in the dressing-room. Then you can come to bed at four and get up at five if you wish."

"Just as you like," George said.

"It's hopeless," he told himself, alone with his book. He tried not to show it, but was in fact very disturbed and put off his work by Amy. He was more than annoyed.

Considering it his duty to take the children out at least once a week, George remarked at breakfast the next day (it was Saturday) that really the boys were old enough now to enjoy a bit of sport. He proposed borrowing William's terrier and trying the new ferret out. Amy, who loathed the ferret anyway but had bowed to family opinion when the children said every boy at school owned a ferret, and the family said, of course—all boys love ferrets, don't be silly, Amy—Amy said, "But, George, what on earth do you think you're going to do with it?"

"Rabbiting," George said.

"No. That's cruel," Amy said.

"I quite agree," Mrs. Monsoon said, most unexpectedly. But this lost Amy a more potent ally.

"You don't want to turn them into milksops do you, Amy?" Mr. Monsoon said. "Silly womanish prejudice! Rabbits are vermin, you've got to keep down rabbits."

"Yes, Father, but not like that," Amy said.

"Well, how would you set about it?" George said.

"Not that way," said Amy.

"No, you'd put salt on their tails I suppose!" George said. Everyone laughed.

"Oh poor little bunnies—it's rather a shame isn't it—but still . . ." Vivienne said. "What a pity Stephen's away. He always says he loves ferreting."

"You women don't understand sport," Mr. Monsoon said.

"No," George said, "you just keep out of this, Amy."

"That'll do now, please. This is breakfast," Mrs. Monsoon said.

Afterwards, when Amy refused to help dress the boys— they had to put on special boots as it had rained in the night and now it was muddy outside, George said, "Really, Amy, you treat me like dirt."

"You never take any notice of what I say. You never take any notice of me at all," Amy said. "It serves you right."

"Oh please, Amy, must we go on like this?" George said. The children were in the nursery next door, waiting, so they had to speak quietly.

"You never really cared for me," Amy said.

"Cared for you? What do you mean, Amy? You are always bringing that up these days. I suppose you mean I don't love you. Well, I must say, you behave as though you don't *want* to be loved. I'm sure you don't love me!"

"That's what your girl friend thinks," Amy said. "Oh, you know who I mean! Miss Rockaby. I met her the other day. She's hoping you can't get along without her. You'd better give her a summons and she'll come rushing up and finish off your book—free! That's what she said. Stupid girl. And she thinks, 'Oh that poor Mr. Monsoon—with that dreadful wife of his,' that's what she thinks, every time she sees me. It's written all over her face. Yes, ask her up, George."

"*Amy!*" George said.

"And it's no good trying to be fatherly, George. All that nonsense about me getting wet—as if you cared! You know very well you never loved me . . ."

"Amy," George said, "look here, we've been married more than ten years. We are husband and wife. You can't expect to be madly in love for ten years. Instead, we should be able to understand each other because we have grown up together."

"Have we?" Amy said. She burst into tears, and ran off, leaving George calling out—"Amy! Where are you going? Come here!" She never replied. So George went into the nursery, helped the children on with their boots, and took them out.

Meanwhile, downstairs, Mr. Monsoon was having an argument with Mrs. Monsoon. She said, never mind about Amy or the boys or milksops, the thing was, cruelty was never right. And he said she was making a ridiculous fuss—all this nonsense about blood sports!

"And next, Charlie, you'll be telling me the fox enjoys being hunted," Mrs. Monsoon said.

"That's your idea. Trust a woman to know what a fox thinks!" he said.

"It's wrong to teach children cruel sports," Mrs. Monsoon said. The whole thing went round and round. In the end Mr. Monsoon got so furious he said, "Just to show you who is master in this house, I'm going to have a little sport myself! To hell with you women!"

Mrs. Monsoon let out a deep sigh, waited till he had gone out, and then said, "Oh, those poor pigeons I suppose," and went off to tell cook, who was still, after all this time, nervous about guns going off.

Looking back, Vivienne said she knew something awful was going to happen that morning. But cook said that was because she was carrying; women in her condition were always nervous. What happened was this. Mr. Monsoon blazed about with his gun for a bit in the garden. He brought down two birds (the pigeons were pretty tame by this time, having been left alone). "That'll teach them!" he said. He meant the women, especially Mrs. Monsoon, not the birds. But he hadn't quite worked off his temper yet, so he went to the wood. Being old, he was very long-sighted and could see things far off. He caught sight of a pigeon sitting on a branch—a bare one, half broken off by the children, who used it for a swing. This was near by the drive on the edge of the larch wood, a coppice really, but Mr. Monsoon liked it called the wood. He approached the drive extremely warily from behind some rhododendrons, walking on the grass edge. Even so, the pigeon either heard him or saw him. It flew off. He took aim, slipped off the grass edge, and the gun went off. He missed the bird, but as Stephen said afterwards (though not in his father's hearing) "he winged Amy." It was only a graze, but she cried out and her arm bled and Mr. Monsoon was very afraid.

That evening he greased his gun, wrapped it up in its case, and put it away in the attic. "For ever," he said. Nor did he ever go back on his word. He never went shooting again. And so the pigeons were left in peace for a while.

"Nature takes care of her own," as Mr. Smith said. But when the whole thing had blown over, Mrs. Smith asked permission to have a couple of female cats that were going in the village. All the cats at the Grange, except one, were neutered; cook saw to that. And the old mother was dead. The one that hadn't been neutered was Mr. Smith's pet. His wife hated it, but now, all of a sudden, found nothing against it.

"But why females, Cook?" Mrs. Monsoon said, when asked.

"For our Tom," cook said. And so in the course of time (though this was much later on) the trouble lay not so much with the number of pigeons, but with the number of cats at the Grange.

Saturday was the day the grocer came with the orders. Cook always gave him a cup of tea when he came, thus the grocer was there when Mr. Monsoon brought Amy in. The news was all over the village in no time. Mrs. Burt, the grocer's daughter, heard first. She told all her customers before they had time to open their mouths to say good-morning. Lavinia came in to buy sweets, and Mrs. Burt said at once, "Have you heard?" and told her every detail of the accident. Lavinia chose the sweets in a hurry and rushed off to tell Mrs. Rockaby. But she ran into Mr. Swan at the door. He was coming to buy some tobacco. The two were not on very good terms.

"Good heavens!" Mr. Swan said, "you might look where you're going. I must say . . ." But Lavinia cut him short.

"Mr. Monsoon's shot Mrs. George," she said.

"Shot Mrs. George?" Mr. Swan said.

"Yes, Mrs. George," Lavinia said, "—you know who I mean—Amy. Not dead. In the arm."

Mr. Swan looked frightfully upset. "Can one do anything? When did this happen? Have they a doctor?" he asked all in one breath.

Lavinia drew him outside beyond Mrs. Burt's interruptions. "Oh, it's all right," she said, closing the door of the shop, "allowing for exaggerations, I should say it was only a graze. If that."

"All right?—how do you know it's all right?" Mr. Swan said. "I must go. They may need help."

He left Lavinia standing there, and went off at a run, up-hill. "Well!" Lavinia said.

Mrs. Rockaby, too, thought Mr. Swan was making rather a fuss. "Still, they are neighbours, you know," she said. Later, she rang up. "Just as I thought," she said, putting down the receiver, "nothing much. Nothing to make all that fuss about. Perhaps Harold will come and tell us when he's seen for himself."

But Mr. Swan did not go down to the Rockabys, he went home after seeing Amy. He had asked to see her, and been so insistent about it that cook, who had opened the door, said, "Well, I don't know, Sir," and let him in. The family—Mr. and Mrs. Monsoon and George—not Vivienne, who had gone bright green and fainted, or the boys, who had been sent out to play—were all standing about in the study, where George, summoned in from the lanes, had carried Amy. The study (Mr. Monsoon's) was just off the hall, and the door was open, so Mr. Swan walked in. Amy saw him first. She smiled and said, "Hullo, Mr. Swan," in a perfectly normal voice. "Thank God," Mr. Swan said.

Everyone turned round.

"If you've come about that ditch . . ." Mr. Monsoon said.

"Indeed I have not!" said Mr. Swan. "I have come to see Mrs. George."

"So you know," George said, "but *how* do you know?"

"Gossip," Mrs. Monsoon said, "it's probably all round the village."

"Tom-toms—like your natives. Or weren't there any tom-toms either?" Amy said.

"My dear Mrs. George, I can't tell you how glad I am you're all right," Mr. Swan said. "Well, I'd better be off now."

No one stopped him, they hadn't quite come to themselves yet. Only Amy was calm.

Later on, just before lunch, Mr. Swan sent Mrs. Henlow round with some roses for Amy.

"How kind," Amy said, "and they are red ones."

CHAPTER TEN

FOR the rest of that day Mr. Monsoon wandered about slightly stunned; he couldn't read and he wouldn't lie down and when it was time to eat he pecked at his food and groaned.

"It's all right, Charlie, you know. You have given us all a fright, but you haven't really hurt Amy," Mrs. Monsoon said at lunch.

George confirmed this. "Amy's all right," he said.

Naturally the children were interested, and began to ask questions. So Mrs. Monsoon changed the subject.

"I suppose really one shouldn't complain," she said, "it's seasonable weather, isn't it? But rather oppressive. I expect we shall have some thunderstorms soon."

Amy had been forced to lie down, and Vivienne too was confined to her bedroom, but George and his mother, like Mr. Monsoon, were inclined to wander, not doing anything much after lunch. Mrs. Monsoon wandered about between the bathroom and Amy's bedroom with a bottle of disinfectant and some cotton-wool in one hand, and some pills she had found in the other. These last she referred to as "M and B," and meeting George in the passage she told him they would be good for Amy. But George very firmly said, "No."

So Mrs. Monsoon went back to the bathroom and put everything down and began hunting for a hot-water bottle.

"But she's quite warm, Mother," George said, "it's a hot day. Honestly, I'm sure Amy doesn't need a hot-water bottle."

"For shock," said Mrs. Monsoon, "that's what the book says."

"If you ask me, father's shocked, not Amy," George said.

"Oh I know, I know. But he won't lie down."

"Well, you rest, Mother. Leave Amy to me."

"Just help me find that hot-water bottle, dear."

"Are you sure there is one?"

Mrs. Monsoon paused, and thought for a moment. "Yes, there was," she said, "but where on earth could it be?"

George made several suggestions, and they searched. But they couldn't find one. Mrs. Monsoon had been upset to find Amy in the dressing-room and not in her own bed. And the dressing-room bed had been made up some time, it hadn't just been made up, because it hadn't got new sheets on. She didn't say anything about this, but thought it was wrong. Looking for the hot-water bottle, she said to George casually, "I hope Amy's all right in that bed." And George said, "Yes." And after that she never mentioned it.

The children, left to themselves, played hide and seek in the garden. They shrieked, trampled the flowers down, made machine-gun noises and were happy as the day was long. Upstairs in her bedroom, Vivienne was looking after herself. She had just had a glass of milk for lunch, and now ate biscuits to keep up her strength. She tried to make her mind a blank and to forget the morning's excitement. Not being able to do this successfully she made a great effort to think about nice things such as hymns and daisies. But breaking under the strain, she sat up.

"Oh I do wish Stephen was here!" she said.

Stephen was away, due back in three or four days. But, it occurred to her, she might write to him.

"All this excitement's so bad for the baby," she told herself. Nevertheless, she got up to find her writing-things and spent the rest of the afternoon very happily telling Stephen all that had happened.

Amy too was writing. Every time Mrs. Monsoon came in, and she did frequently, Amy shoved the letter under the pillow. She was writing to Rupert. It was an important letter and she longed for peace. Since Rupert had left for London, she had never yet written to him. But she had kept his letter, and so had his address. She had always expected that he would write again, but he hadn't, and feeling proud and hurt, she had never written to him. Perhaps in any case she would have changed her mind, climbed down and sent a letter to Rupert after a time, and being shot by Mr. Monsoon merely hastened events; or perhaps she really was shocked as the First-Aid book said. Whatever it was, she was determined now to get in contact again with Rupert. In spite of the many interruptions, she found it a great relief to write. She put on a blank exhausted look when her mother-in-law came in, but smiled as she wrote.

George would have liked to have fussed a bit over his wife, but when at first he had tried this, she had snubbed him. After a time he got tired of wandering about the house and went out to do some gardening. He heard the children, but not wishing to see them, went off to the other end of the garden to see the irises. They were over, of course. He hadn't expected this. Like Lavinia, he was more concerned with vegetables than flowers when he gardened, and so far his activities had been confined to things like potatoes, onions and peas. In fact, what one ate. With his hands in his pockets, he stood in a daze looking down at the ditch. William found him like this. Now William knew all about Mr. Swan and the ditch. He rather agreed with Mr. Swan. But digging and laying down drains wasn't gardening, so whenever George had mentioned the ditch, William had changed the subject. But he had a kind heart.

"In a bad state the old ditch," he said to George now. "Yes, I'm afraid it is," George said, turning round. "I don't know quite what to do about it."

"We shall have to dig," William said.

"Oh, you couldn't manage it, William. Besides, it's not really your job, is it?"

"I daresay I could lend a hand. These are troubled times," William said.

George sighed. "Yes, very troubled," he said.

"You don't want to take it too hard, Mr. George. It was an accident that could have happened to anyone. How is Mrs. George, may I ask?"

"Oh, she's fine. Not really hurt, you know."

"And the master?"

"He's bearing up. A bit of a shock for an old man though. But he'll be all right."

"Then you don't have to worry. I'll just go along and fetch the spades."

So George and William spent the afternoon digging. They didn't get very far. It was hard work, and the ditch smelt horribly and there was no shade and it was hot. But it kept George's mind off his worries. Also it meant that William would never be sacked; not after that.

There was another caller that day at the Grange. Mrs. Rockaby came round after tea with some homemade buns. Handing these over to cook at the front door, Mrs. Rockaby said, "Tell the family we are so sorry. And I thought these might help."

Cook looked down at the buns. "You'll be wanting the basket back, I daresay," she said.

"Is Mrs. George allowed visitors?"

"Well, I'll ask. I couldn't say," cook said. She left Mrs. Rockaby waiting outside the front door. *"Buns!"* she said to herself on her way to find George. She was annoyed because she hadn't thought to make any herself. She rolled them out of the basket on to the kitchen table, where later on Mr. Smith found them and ate them with relish. There were six, and not being able to manage them all, he broke two up into bits, poured milk over them and gave them to the cats. It was always better, he found, to make a clean sweep of tit-bits, otherwise Mrs. Smith, finding some left, either accused him of greediness because he had eaten some, or else said, "Waste! Wicked waste" about the ones he had left, and was cross in either case.

Cook hadn't closed the front door; Mrs. Rockaby, bored with waiting, opened it more with her toe. She looked in. Mr. Monsoon's father glared at her from the wall opposite. Mrs. Rockaby pulled a face at him, saying, "You nasty old Victorian! I suppose, though, the frame is worth something." Having said this, she felt superior, and when at last George came she was able to greet him with just the right touch of condescension that was necessary for this type of visit.

"Oh *poor* you!" she said, "what a time you've had. Tell me, can I do anything?" George was very dirty she noticed (he had only just come in from the ditch).

"Very nice of you," George said, "but Amy's all right, you know. Just resting. They exaggerate so in the village. And thank you for ringing up this morning. Won't you come in?"

"Are you quite sure I'm not a nuisance?" Mrs. Rockaby said, walking in. George said "No, no" and led the way. Amy watched all this from the landing. Determined to get her letter to Rupert posted, she was waiting for an opportunity to slip out when no one was looking. She had told her mother-in-law that she didn't want any tea, what she did want was sleep, and just before Mrs. Rockaby arrived, she had come out of her room. As soon as George and Mrs. Rockaby went into the drawing-room, she ran downstairs. It was risky going out like this; if she were caught there would have to be endless explanations. But once having written the letter, Amy felt gay, and taking a risk made her feel gayer still.

"I'm free—I'm free!" she said to herself, once round the corner away from the house. She ran all the rest of the way to the post box, which was just down the road at the end of the drive.

"So *these* are the children," Mrs. Rockaby was saying in the drawing-room. The children had been specially brought in because Mrs. Monsoon said Amy was asleep and couldn't be disturbed, but had felt Mrs. Rockaby must be shown something; after all, she had rung up, and now she had called.

"Yes, these are my boys," George said. "Say how do you do, boys."

"George—your boots . . ." Mrs. Monsoon said.

"What? Oh, sorry," George said. He was leaving marks and bits of mud all over the drawing-room carpet.

"*What* a nice room!" Mrs. Rockaby said, "so different from our little shack. But then mine are grown-up." She smiled at the children. ("Appallingly badly brought up," she told her husband afterwards, "they just stood there and stared and said nothing.")

"And how is your sister-in-law?" she said to George.

"She's all right," George said.

"As well as can be expected, you know," Mrs. Monsoon said. Mrs. Rockaby gave her a look full of meaning. "Yes," she said, "it's a hard life being a woman, isn't it?" Mrs. Monsoon cleared her throat and glanced at the boys.

"Well, well," Mrs. Rockaby said, "and what have you two been doing? Being dreadfully naughty and dirty and happy I suppose!" The two boys continued to stare, so she turned to George and said, "So shy and sweet at that age, aren't they?"

Then Mr. Monsoon came in, and she turned her attention to him. "So frightfully sorry to hear your news," she said, "it must have been perfectly ghastly!"

He gave her a long stare.

"Mrs. Rockaby, Charlie," Mrs. Monsoon said. "You know my husband, don't you, Mrs. Rockaby."

"Good afternoon," Mr. Monsoon said, "lovely weather, isn't it?"

"You know, you really must forgive me for saying so, but you *are* a G.O.M. if ever there was one!" said Mrs. Rockaby.

Mrs. Monsoon looked rather alarmed and George frowned.

"I'm afraid I don't know what you mean," Mr. Monsoon said. He got out his handkerchief and paused for an answer before blowing his nose.

"Oh! G.O.M.—don't you know what that means? Grand Old Man!" Mrs. Rockaby said. Mr. Monsoon bowed first and then blew his nose.

Mrs. Rockaby was pleased; she saw she had got him. "Not such a bad old thing really," she told her husband on getting home, "and not frightening, really, once you get to know him. You know, Donald, in a way, shooting their daughters-in-law and so on, the Monsoons are rather fun."

Two days later Amy got a letter from Rupert, an answer to her letter. Her arm was still bound up, but she told George she was perfectly well and wanted to go to London.

"And don't say such a thing is unheard of," she said, "even wives need a holiday sometimes. You can say what you like to the family."

"You're not going to meet Rupert Tyce, Amy?" George said. Amy looked rather surprised. "Oh Amy," George said, "I'm not such a fool as all that!"

"What I do is my own business, surely," she said.

"If you are going to meet Rupert Tyce, Amy," George said, "you needn't come back!"

"You're making an ass of yourself," Amy said.

But now, either George had to eat his words, or Amy had to give in and not go, or else go, but tell lies. Amy watched

George, and George looked out of the window. They were in the nursery, where George had come to sharpen a pencil with a large, rather dangerous penknife belonging to one of the children. Amy kept it on the mantelpiece, out of reach, as she thought. It had been given to the eldest boy last Christmas by an aunt. "Not safe," Amy had said at once, and had put it away. But George was always wanting a knife for his pencils, and so, constantly, it got left about. George put it down now, on the table, and Amy picked it up and put it back on the mantelpiece.

"You heard what I said, Amy," George said. He looked firm but sad.

"I am going to London, George," Amy said in a quiet voice.

"Very well," George said.

She began walking towards the door.

"Have you thought of the children?" he said.

"Have you thought, George?" she said.

"This is your doing, not mine, Amy."

"You are a coward, George."

"And you, Amy, are an unfaithful wife."

Amy went out. The pencil still needed sharpening, so George went to the mantelpiece, took down the penknife and got on with the job. As for Amy, she didn't quite know what to do. Going to London certainly meant two days away (the journey alone, by bus and train, took over five hours), you couldn't do it in less. And she had always meant to come back. True, she had often thought of running away, but only vaguely and sadly, the way women do when unhappy, and of course because Rupert had said that she must. Now Rupert had not said that. He had written to say they must meet, which was not the same thing at all. George had issued the ultimatum. Looking at the clock, Amy suddenly got in a panic. She rushed upstairs to the box-room, found a suitcase, ran down again to her room, threw things in, changed her dress, made up her face, put a hat on over her unbrushed hair (she had packed the brush), put on a pair of high-heeled shoes and snatched her purse up. All this took less than ten minutes. This meant she had no time to think, and still in a frantic rush she ran down the stairs, out of the front door, round the corner away from the house and on down the drive. The bus stopped near by the post box out in the road. She just caught it.

Mr. Monsoon never knocked, it was his house, so he walked straight into George's room saying, "Where's Amy off to?"

George looked up from his book.

"So she said good-bye to you, did she?" he said.

"Good-bye? No! I saw her running along with a suit-case, out of the bathroom window. What *is* all this?" Mr. Monsoon said.

"She's gone, and she's not coming back. It was her choice," George said.

Mr. Monsoon closed the door with his foot. It slammed and George frowned.

"Why wasn't I told about this?" Mr. Monsoon said.

"I'm afraid, Father, you wouldn't understand," George said.

"How can I when nobody tells me anything? I insist on being told!"

"Don't shout, Father. It's no good getting angry with me. Amy has chosen to go off with Mr. Tyce. That's all," George said.

"What absolute nonsense, my dear boy! Fetch her back at once," Mr. Monsoon said.

George looked at his watch. "I'm afraid it's too late," he said. "She'll just about have caught the bus."

"Well, get the car out! What *are* you thinking of, George?"

"No, thanks, Father," George said, "this isn't one of your cowboy stories. This is real. And it happens to be my life, not yours. Leave me alone."

"You mean," Mr. Monsoon said, "you can sit there and let your wife go off with that fellow Tyce?"

"It was her choice, not mine," George said.

"But it's Amy! What have you done to Amy? Amy doesn't behave like this!"

"Well, you are wrong, Father, she does," George said. He bent down over his manuscript.

Tears came into Mr. Monsoon's eyes. "But Amy can't do this," he said. He got out his handkerchief. "It's my fault," he said, "but couldn't she see it was just an accident? Couldn't she understand? . . . But she must have! You see, George, it must have made her feel we were all against her. And she was very unhappy at the time—you realised that? You never looked after her, George. Always shut up with this blasted book. Butterflies! And what are butterflies compared to a wife?"

Someone knocked on the door.

"Come in!" Mr. Monsoon said, and then, thinking better of it, "No! wait a minute!" But it was too late, cook opened the door.

"Oh Mr. George," she said, "I can't find Mrs. George anywhere and the little boys have got the cat with a rope round its neck and they're trying to hang it! Mr. Smith's so upset. . . . But they won't listen, Mr. George, and Mrs. Stephen can't make them listen either, and she in her condition—I'm sure it's ever so bad for her—'Fetch Mrs. George,' she says, 'fetch Mrs. George at once, I feel queer . . .'"

"For God's sake, woman!" Mr. Monsoon cried, pushing her back. But George jumped up.

"I'll deal with them," he said. "From now on they are my children and no more nonsense." He brushed past cook and went off down the landing and down the stairs, fast.

"It's terrible, Sir, to think that little children . . ." cook began. But Mr. Monsoon held up his hand. "It is worse, much worse than that," he said.

Cook stared.

"You had better go back to your kitchen now," her master said.

It took Mr. Monsoon some long time to find his wife. He found her at last, after calling her name out all over the house, and then shouting and calling again in the garden—he found her at her usual morning occupation—picking, and snipping off the heads of roses. "Yes?" she said, removing her sleeve from the thorns. But she had on a jersey over her summer dress, and the thorns stuck in the wool. "Yes?" she said. The more she pulled the more the wool gave, until, jerking away impatiently, it broke.

"Now look what you've made me do," she said.

"I have something very serious to tell you," Mr. Monsoon said. He took her arm, and took the scissors and the basket full of roses from her, and led her to the bench, and then as soon as he and she were sitting down he told her about Amy. He wept, quite frankly. She frowned and shook her head and sighed. At length, he dried his eyes and sat up straight.

"Somehow, we must get her back," he said.

"No, Charlie, that is not for you to do," she said. "I must go in now. With Vivienne in her condition and Amy gone, there's rather a lot to do, you know. Whatever shall we tell the children? Poor little things. . . ."

For some time now the children's yells had filled the garden. But being used to yells, Mrs. Monsoon hadn't taken any notice. However, she now said, "Tut-tut—*what* a noise!"

"They hanged the cat. It's George giving them a beating," Mr. Monsoon said.

"Oh dear," Mrs. Monsoon said. She hurried away.

Mr. Monsoon didn't like being left alone in the rose garden. He set off to find Mr. Smith. But when he found him, Mr. Smith was so concerned about his cat (which had survived) that he couldn't talk of anything else. So Mr. Monsoon stood about in the yard watching the pigeons lead their lives high up in the stable dovecote. Some bustled in and out, some flew away to circle round and round the house, and others, already settled on their perches, cooed and cleaned themselves among the jasmine branches, out of sight.

"Damn them," he said automatically.

Cook banged on the kitchen window and then opened it. She said, "I've made a cup of tea, Sir, for you, if you want it," and looked anxious. So he said, "All right," and went in.

Mrs. Monsoon had told Vivienne the news, very quietly because of her condition, and the boys still suffered from their beating, so nobody spoke during lunch. After lunch Mr. Monsoon went off fishing, and when Stephen came home just before tea he was told the news by Vivienne. Tea was eaten in silence except for a few subdued remarks from the children and a story about some onions from Stephen which nobody listened to. But Stephen and Vivienne had plenty to say to each other in private. However, when Vivienne said Amy was nothing better than a harlot, Stephen said, "Steady, old girl—that's going a bit too far."

"But you said she was a bitch," Vivienne said.

"Not quite the same thing," he said. "Bitch is rude, but harlot is . . . well, blasphemous."

With a quite extraordinary aplomb—as though it were the most natural thing in the world—Mrs. Monsoon had taken charge of the boys after their beating. She had first of all washed their faces, and then changed their stockings and shoes. After lunch she had put them both in the drawing-room, sat them down on the sofa underneath the cherubs and handed out to one *Eric or Little by Little*, and to the other *Little Lord Fauntleroy*. Amy had never allowed such books.

"If you talk or make a noise," she had said, "you go straight to bed with no tea."

Amy had not believed in threats, nor punishments connected with food. As it happened, the children behaved very well that afternoon. After watching them for a few minutes, and then saying before she left, "You understand now, don't you?" Mrs. Monsoon had gone upstairs to turn out the children's chest of drawers—the one where their clothes were kept. She found it in such a mess that it took her till tea to get it straight. After tea, she got a pencil and paper and made out a list of all the new clothes that were needed. It was a long list, and she shook her head. "What a mother—*what* a mother!" she kept on telling herself. Later, she gave each child a bath, washing behind the ears and scrubbing hard at nails.

"There!" she said, coming down into the kitchen afterwards. "I've got them clean at last!"

Cook managed a wonderful expression—half-poker-face, half-sympathetic.

"The children's mother went off to London this morning in a hurry," Mrs. Monsoon said, looking round vaguely.

"Then we shall all have to help, Ma'am," cook said.

By evening, just as it started to rain, George suddenly made up his mind that he too must go to London. He looked up trains, but found he had missed all the good ones and the next one left at eleven.

"I shall drive then," he said to himself.

He told his mother of this decision. She was very angry indeed. "But I must get things straight," he said. "I don't know that Amy fully appreciates her position. There mustn't be any mistake."

"Go if you must," his mother said, "it's nothing to do with me. But I'm sure we don't want Amy here after the way she's behaved! No one is indispensable—don't forget that."

But when he told his father, his father said, "I'm glad, I'm very glad, my boy. Would you like me to come too?"

"No, thanks," George said. So Mr. Monsoon stood at the front door and waved and called out "Good luck to you!" as George drove away.

"It's so dreadful not knowing how one stands, where one is," Mrs. Monsoon said to Stephen.

"Bloody fools," Stephen said.

"Oh Stephen!" Vivienne said.

"Well, that's what they are. It's all a lot of nonsense. Of course it is. She's bound to come back," Stephen said.

It was Mrs. Monsoon's turn to cry now. But Mr. Monsoon went to bed in a cheerful mood. He got out *Hamlet* and read on far into the night.

CHAPTER ELEVEN

NEXT morning, just as the family had finished their breakfast, Amy came home in a taxi. After travelling all night sitting up in the train she looked pale and untidy. Meeting her in the hall, Stephen was so surprised that all he could say was "Good lord!"

"I've run out of money," said Amy, "please will you pay the taxi?" She would have walked past him but Stephen put out his hand.

"I say, old thing, you do look awful," he said. "I should have a bit of a wash or something before meeting the family. Are you all right?"

"Quite all right, thanks," said Amy.

He took hold of her arm. "Why not let George explain?" he said. "Honestly, Amy, it's none of my business of course, but there may be a scene—can you take it looking like that?"

"Oh, let me go," said Amy, "and if you want to help, pay for that taxi." She pulled herself free and walked across to the dining-room door.

"What have you done with George?" Stephen called after her. She didn't answer. So he went upstairs to find Vivienne. He was in a hurry and had been on the point of rushing off to get on with his job. As usual he had just enough money on him for petrol and lunch, but certainly not enough to squander on taxis. Half-way up he began shouting for Vivienne.

Mrs. Monsoon had suggested at breakfast that morning that as the raspberries were ripe enough now for jam the whole family could help with the picking, it would take people's minds off their worries. Mr. Monsoon had agreed. He said he would see to it that the nets were taken off. And Stephen had promised to come home early to help in the evening. Mrs. Monsoon was just thinking, over a third cup of tea, that for once the day's work had been planned, when Amy came in. Mr. Monsoon dropped *The Times*. It fell on his plate and got blobbed with marmalade. She had badly startled him.

"Mind, Charlie—your cup," Mrs. Monsoon said. He was waving his arms, unable to speak.

"Where's George?" he said finally.

"George?" Amy said.

"Obviously, Charlie, there's been some extraordinary misunderstanding," his wife said. "Have you had breakfast, Amy? Or would you care to wash first? We can talk afterwards."

"Give her a cup of tea," Mr. Monsoon said.

Mrs. Monsoon said, "Of course." She began pouring out. "Now sit down, Amy," she said. The situation was trying, but nothing was worse than an empty stomach. "And have some toast and marmalade, Amy," she said, pushing the toast-rack forward. Not wishing to cause any delay in this vital matter of filling up stomachs she had given Amy a dirty cup, hers. "You'd better drink from the right of the handle," she said. "I've rinsed it, but it isn't a clean cup."

"Oh do leave her alone," Mr. Monsoon said, and turning to Amy, "For God's sake sit down!"

Stephen came in at that moment followed by Vivienne.

"Look here, crisis or no family crisis," he said, "a man's got his work. This is up to George. I really haven't the money to spare and nor's Viv. Why can't George pay for the taxi? Where is he?"

"We shall have to find out," his mother said. "I just want Amy to have her tea."

"Well I'm blowed!" Stephen said. "What d'you mean? The old boy's gone off on his own? The old twister! Who'd have thought it?"

"Hold your tongue," Mr. Monsoon said. "Can't you see this is no laughing matter? You'll be giving the women hysterics."

"Charlie! Don't talk like that," his wife said.

"This is my house. I won't stand being contradicted."

"There's no need to shout, Charlie."

"I will shout!"

"I say," Stephen said, "I don't want to shove my oar in, but aren't people rather losing their heads? I didn't mean to poke fun at George, I just thought things looked pretty tricky and a spot of humour might help. Amy looked so down in the mouth. Well, I'll buzz off."

"Your sense of humour is odd," Mr. Monsoon said. He picked up *The Times*, noticed the marmalade, and frowned. "Damned mess," he said. "It's unthoughtful of people to disturb one at breakfast."

"But the thing is," Vivienne said, "who's going to pay for that taxi? I'm sure the man will charge for waiting."

"Taxi?" Mrs. Monsoon said. "Oh I see—Amy, I suppose you couldn't have waited for the bus? Perhaps not. No. Now have your tea, *please*, Amy."

Mr. Monsoon pushed the paper away and got up.

"Naturally, I will pay. How much is this taxi?" he said.

"I'm afraid I don't know," Amy said. She sat down and leaned her head on her hands.

"It doesn't matter," Mr. Monsoon said. He went out, pushing Stephen and Vivienne before him.

"The children were very well behaved all yesterday," Mrs. Monsoon said, left alone with Amy. Amy made no remark, so she moved the cup of tea right under her nose and continued to speak about what had happened—this and that little triviality—in a soothing newsy tone of voice. By and by Amy drank up her tea. Mrs. Monsoon picked out a nice piece of toast and placed it beside her.

Outside in the hall Vivienne was helping Stephen on with his mackintosh. It looked like rain she said.

"Well, good luck with your jam," Stephen was saying, just about to dash off, when Mr. Monsoon came in at the front door, blocking his exit.

"Stephen," Mr. Monsoon said. He paused. "Look here, my boy," he went on, "somebody's got to find George. You could hop into that taxi. . . ."

"Father, don't be ridiculous," Stephen said. "As though George couldn't look after himself! Those two have been enough nuisance. And damn it, a man has his work."

"Very well then," his father said quietly, "I'll go myself."

"No, no, Father!" Vivienne cried out. "That'll just make it one worse. Why can't somebody ring up Mr. Tyce?"

"But that would hardly be decent, would it?" said Stephen. "I mean, we don't know . . . well . . ."

"Of course we don't know! This is monstrous," Mr. Monsoon said.

"Well then, let me ask Amy," said Vivienne.

"No, Vivy," Stephen said, "you'd better keep out of this."

"But nobody's got any sense!" Vivienne shouted.

"There you are, you've made her hysterical," Mr. Monsoon said.

Mr. Smith came running along the passage. "There's a taxi outside," he said. "Does anyone know there's a taxi outside the front door?"

"Do you mean to say that taxi's *still* there?" Mrs. Monsoon said, coming out of the dining-room. No one answered, so she said, "Well, I suppose it had better come out of the house-keeping money," and went off to find her purse. Mr. Smith turned round to go back to the kitchen and bumped into his wife, who was listening.

"We could always use your van to go to the station," Mr. Monsoon said thoughtfully.

"No, thanks," Stephen said. "Now I really am off. Don't do anything rash. Best of luck." He walked out past his father.

"No feelings," Mr. Monsoon said. "The family should stick together. No sense of responsibility. I shall have to handle this all by myself."

"If you like," Vivienne said, "I'll have a quiet talk with Amy."

"You mind your own business," Mr. Monsoon said. "You go and pick raspberries."

At last, round about eleven o'clock, Mrs. Monsoon had assembled the family, and now they stood with their heads in the bushes picking raspberries. They all felt hurt. Mr. Monsoon thought having taken the nets off he had done his duty; but no, he too had to pick. Vivienne had never yet been able to have a quiet talk with Amy, and Amy didn't want to pick raspberries in the least, she wanted to sleep. To all their objections Mrs. Monsoon had replied that jam was important. Mrs. Smith was let off because someone had to cook lunch and her job was to make the jam later on. Mr. Smith was told to wait about in the hall in case the 'phone rang. (There was still no news of George.) The children had been provided with little forks to do weeding with William.

"They eat twice as much as they pick," their grand-mother said when Vivienne complained that children of their age could very well help with the picking. "And we don't want any bilious attacks just now," she had added.

No one would have guessed it, but Mrs. Monsoon herself felt hurt. It was the way George had behaved that upset her. She was very annoyed with Amy, but had always thought privately that it was no good expecting anything else except trouble from her.

"But why shouldn't I go to London, Mother?" Amy had said when questioned about events by her mother-in-law.

"Of course," Mrs. Monsoon said, "that is for you and George to decide, not I. If George agreed . . ."

"He didn't," Amy said. "But why shouldn't I? I'm not a child. Maids have their day out—why shouldn't I?"

"I'm sure you have nothing to be ashamed of, Amy," Mrs. Monsoon said, "so it isn't necessary to *defend* yourself when speaking to me. You see, my dear, George was under the impression quite definitely, that you were running away. He told me. That's why *he* went to London. It's a little unreasonable, I can't help thinking, not to have more regard for people's feelings. Men get upset so easily in any case, don't they?"

At this, Amy had cried. Mrs. Monsoon passed her a handkerchief and waited. When Amy had blown her nose she said, "Well, one must let bygones be bygones. But next time you decide you want to go to London, please let me know. Or why not go up *with* George? As you see, I can perfectly well look after the children. Just let me know, that's all."

Telling Mr. Monsoon about this conversation later she said, "I can't help feeling there's more in it than meets the eye. Why *should* George behave so stupidly if he wasn't sure something dreadful might be happening to Amy?"

"You are talking in riddles," Mr. Monsoon said. "You women are all so suspicious. Why meet trouble half-way? George has got hold of the wrong end of the stick. He's a fool that boy."

"Come along," Mrs. Monsoon had said then, "it's time we got on with our job of picking the raspberries." George was her favourite. But she had to admit to herself that his father was right; he had been fooled by his wife. Hidden among the raspberry canes, she grieved for her son.

"It's most unfortunate," she told herself. "And so undignified dashing off like that, and then coming home as he will to find out he needn't have worried at all about Amy. I suppose that's what they mean by being in love these days. Thank goodness Charlie and I were never driven to that extreme. It's sad."

Mr. Monsoon had also talked to Amy.

"Tell me, my dear," he had said, sitting down in his place at the head of the dining-room table, "is there any particular person you can think of that one could ring up? To find out about George I mean."

"No, I'm afraid not."

"You are quite sure?"

"Father, what did George tell you before he went off?"

"I'm afraid he misunderstood your intentions. We needn't speak about that."

There was a silence. Then Amy said, "I think men are impossible."

Mr. Monsoon waved aside this remark. When he didn't understand things he believed it best either to let them be, or else to illustrate facts from his own life, which life, having lasted a good long time, could be relied upon to clear up most misunderstandings. He began now, telling a story about how as a young man of twenty-eight he had been accused of embezzlement (falsely of course). It never occurred to him that Amy might not be listening.

Before going off to arrange meals with Mrs. Smith, Mrs. Monsoon had brought a letter in from the table in the hall where all letters were put by Mr. Smith when he took them from the postman first thing in the morning. "This came for you," Mrs. Monsoon had said, laying the letter beside Amy's plate. "I should finish your toast first though before you read it."

Left alone for ten minutes (this was just before her father-in-law came in for his talk) Amy opened and read the letter. It was from Rupert.

"Dearest Amy" (the letter said)—"We shall have to put off that reunion of ours for a while—here I am in France! Don't expect me to write meanwhile because I'll be travelling about. Bless you for having insisted on that car!

"I'll let you know when I'm back. Am sending this air-mail in case you took me too seriously when I said come up to London one day this week. Sorry about that, but a friend of mine gave me his ticket and I found I could get the passage for the car fixed up and I didn't want to miss the chance. I almost rang up to ask whether you couldn't make France with me, but thought better of it. After all, there's your family. It's too complicated in a hurry, isn't it. Bye-bye, my dear. Keep smiling if you can in that God-forsaken village. And my love to Mama if you see her. I'll let you know as soon as I come back. Love, Rupert."

"And here's something to think about, Amy," Mr. Monsoon was saying. "Just as my father always got me out of my scrapes, so I try to smooth the way for you children. But he died, as I said, when I most needed his good advice. Now, *I* shan't be here always. It's hard to believe that—I find it hard. And one day George will have to take over. George hasn't got my head, but he's the right sort, and when he finds himself head of the family, provided you help, he'll learn how to steer the ship I'm perfectly sure." Mr. Monsoon paused and looked down at his feet. "Yes," he said. "Now I'm going to quote a bit of poetry: 'There'll be no moaning at the bar when I put out to sea.' Tennyson. No moaning, Amy. You'll spoil your looks if you go about like this with a long face. And you are so pretty."

And now they were all outside picking raspberries.

"Amy's dreaming," Vivienne said. "Do buck up, Amy! You're holding us up."

"Well then, pass me," said Amy.

"We must all make an effort," Mrs. Monsoon said from farther down the line. They were supposed to move along as they picked, some bending to get the fruit growing low down on the canes, others standing tiptoe for the high ones, and

Vivienne, privileged because of her condition, sitting on a milking-stool. But things had got out of hand and because of the heat tempers were out of control as well. It was close with no sun and sooner or later a storm would come. "I'm afraid it is going to rain this afternoon," Mrs. Monsoon went on.

"Fruit needs rain," Mr. Monsoon said. "This jam will turn out all pips. You should have waited."

Mrs. Monsoon withdrew her head from the canes. "Wet fruit doesn't make good jam," she said.

"You could have left it another few days."

"If one waited until conditions were perfect no jam would ever get made."

"Have it your own way."

"I am only anxious that there should be jam for the family."

"Jam yesterday, jam to-morrow, but never jam today," Amy said. She laughed. No one else did.

The sky darkened early that evening; made suddenly high and vast in a flash of lightning, the dome of clouds dwindled again to hang low over the hills, caught in the flux of gathering night. Vague sounds of thunder troubled the silence. The pigeons fell quiet. The raspberries were picked. Cook made jam and Mr. Smith kept an eye on the weather. He didn't like thunder. Nor did Vivienne. She jumped at each flash of lightning, shut her eyes, and counted. Not always hearing the far-away thunder, she opened her eyes again just in time for the next flash. Mrs. Monsoon felt uneasy about her. George hadn't come home, but as Stephen said, no one in their senses could expect he would be home yet. He weighed out the raspberries for cook and made jokes about thunderstorms which got on everyone's nerves.

Amy sat at the drawing-room window. The children had been put to bed and she had made herself tidy for dinner and so had nothing to do but wait. Mr. Monsoon lay back in his chair and Mrs. Monsoon had got out her knitting and was counting the stitches.

"The swallows have been flying low all day," Amy said.

"Twenty-five, twenty-six," Mrs. Monsoon said. She nodded.

"I don't really care for swallows," Amy went on, "little sharks of the air, that's what they are. And liars because it doesn't always rain when they come down low. But this evening I think they are telling the truth. I wish that storm would come."

"Just a minute, dear," Mrs. Monsoon said, "you've got me in such a muddle. Thirty-eight plain then purl for the rest of the row. Yes, that's it. Now what were you saying?"

"The storm is coming," said Amy.

"When have you seen sharks?" Mr. Monsoon said suddenly.

"Listen!" said Amy.

A wind had got up. It blew in the curtains. The windows rattled, and the curtains fell back in place. A faint hissing sound could be heard and the sighing of leaves being lifted and tossed. Another gust of wind brought with it the smell of damp earth. Then the rain came smacking against the house.

"The storm," Mr. Monsoon said. He got up. Vivienne came in.

"I'm afraid there's going to be . . ." she began, but stopped as a brilliant flash of lightning lit up the corners of the room. "Oh!" she said. "One, two, three, four. . ." but was interrupted by the thunder.

"I think Vivienne had better go to lie down," Mrs. Monsoon said when the noise had subsided.

"I don't want to be alone upstairs," Vivienne said.

"Has anyone thought to close the upstairs windows?" Mrs. Smith called out. "I can't leave my jam."

"Send Smith up," Mr. Monsoon called back.

"Amy—your children," Mrs. Monsoon said. She had shut the drawing-room windows and was pulling the curtains across, when another flash made her jump.

"One, two, three, four," Vivienne began, but the thunder came almost at once.

"For God's sake stop doing that!" Mr. Monsoon shouted when he thought he could be heard. "This mania for counting—what's the matter with people to-night?"

"Quite a commotion," Stephen said, coming in. He made way for Amy to pass. "Going up to the kids?" he said. "Don't worry, they're tough. What's the matter with you, Viv? You look as though you'd been struck. Better go and hold hands with Smith—he's saying his prayers in the kitchen."

"You can tell him from me," said Mr. Monsoon, "that if he starts singing hymns like he did when the boiler burst I'll have him thrown out. And please look after your wife."

"It's all right," Vivienne said, "just nerves. It'll pass." Lightning showed through the curtains. "One, two, three, four," she began in a low voice, "five, six, seven—it's going away—eight . . ." but was stopped by the tearing noise thunder makes just before an ear-splitting crash. They waited. Then Mrs. Monsoon said, "Poor George."

"Very trying. Very trying," Mr. Monsoon said. "I think I'll open a bottle of port."

"Oh, not in a thunderstorm, Charlie," his wife said.

"I don't see why not."

"It'll only upset your stomach."

"I think . . . I think . . ." Vivienne said.

"Look out!" Mr. Monsoon shouted.

Vivienne was swaying. Mrs. Monsoon pushed an arm-chair forward and Stephen lowered her into it.

"Brandy, not port," Mrs. Monsoon said. "Hurry up, Charlie."

Amy sat at the foot of the stairs with a cushion on top of her head. Mr. Monsoon, distracted because of another loud clap of thunder and also because of the thought of wasting good brandy on people who fainted, walked past without noticing her. She was having a quiet bout of hysterics. Terrified of thunder and emotionally upset in. any case, she repeated over and over again to herself, "What fun this is, what absolute fun," and sobbed and laughed. The cushion fell off. She replaced it. Mrs. Smith finally rescued her. Dinner was late because the blancmange Mrs. Smith had made wouldn't set in the heat. Having kept the family waiting about, she decided at length to serve up although the blancmange was still in a semi-liquid state. Passing through the hall with some plates, she saw Amy.

"Whatever are you doing?" she said. "You did give me a fright."

"I'm going mad," said Amy.

Mrs. Smith gave her a look over the top of the plates. "Just a minute," she said. She went to put the plates down in the dining-room and came bustling back. In the interval Amy had pulled herself together a bit and had taken the cushion off her head. As Mrs. Smith stood over her, she sat on it.

"That's better," Mrs. Smith said. "Come along, you can help me serve up."

By the time the family had gathered round the table for dinner, the worst of the storm had passed. In the old days Mr. Monsoon had always said grace, but this practice had lapsed. Nevertheless they all stood by their chairs and waited till Mr. Monsoon looked ready to sit; then they all sat. No one was very hungry. They ate for the most part in silence, stony-faced, with the corseted stance of those performing their duty and, of course, keeping calm. They were very polite.

"Would you mind passing the salt, please?" Mr. Monsoon said, instead of just saying "Salt" as he generally did. Every now and then they were disturbed by distant claps of thunder. Mrs. Monsoon sipped hot water from her special glass that fitted into a silver stand and murmured, "Dear dear, what weather!" Rain beat on the window-panes. Amy shivered.

"Would you like Stephen to fetch you a wrap?" Vivienne said. She wanted it to be noticed how well she herself had recovered. ("No, no, one should never give in like that," she had said when, after her fainting fit, Mrs. Monsoon had told her she really ought to get to bed.) She toyed with the food on her plate now, eating little and trying not to feel sick.

"I'm not cold, thank you," Amy said.

"Nerves," Stephen said; and Vivienne said, "That's just it. One ought to take care of oneself in that state."

"We'll all have a glass of brandy afterwards," Mr. Monsoon said. He had very cleverly delayed opening a bottle, but now felt for some reason that he owed his family a treat.

"Not for me, thank you, Father," Vivienne said. He looked across at her. She tried to hide herself behind a vase of sweet peas.

Mrs. Smith came in with the pudding just then. As usual, Mrs. Monsoon served her husband first.

"What's this?" he said.

Mrs. Smith went out, so his wife said, "Cornflour I think." He said "Oh," but didn't appear very keen to eat it.

"So sorry," Vivienne said, "I don't think I can manage this. Mother, please will you excuse me?" She left the room rather hastily.

"Making rather a fuss that wife of yours," Mr. Monsoon said. "What's the matter with her? It's quite normal to be in her state. Unless there's something wrong. In which case she'd better see a doctor."

"It's the weather," Mrs. Monsoon said.

Amy's hand shook as she picked up a glass of water. Noticing this, Stephen said, "Don't worry, he couldn't possibly be back yet. Unless he drives like hell. He always crawls, though."

"I think if you don't mind I'll just have a look at those children," Amy said.

"They're all right. You said they were asleep. And now the storm's gone. Why must you people fuss?" Mr. Monsoon said.

But Amy excused herself and went out.

"Poor old girl," Stephen said. "She's thinking he's thrown himself in the river or something. As if George would."

"Stephen!" his mother said.

"He might let us know what he's doing," Mr. Monsoon said. "Damn it, what's a telephone for?"

During dinner Amy had suddenly thought that perhaps it was rather unwise to leave Rupert's letter lying about. She had tried to calculate how long it would take George to drive back from London, but found it difficult to make up her mind what time he could have started. The letter was in a drawer with her handkerchiefs. There was no reason why George should go straight upstairs to look in that drawer when he returned. But the thought had gradually unnerved her. "I'd better burn it in the nursery grate," she said to herself on her way up the stairs.

"Who's that?" Vivienne called out as Amy walked down the passage.

"It's me," Amy said.

"Oh do come in," Vivienne called from her bed. "I'll make cocoa and we could have a good-night chat."

"No, thanks, I'm too dead tired," Amy said. She walked on.

"If that woman's going to be stand-offish, I warn you, I shall have it out with her and speak my mind," Vivienne said, when later on Stephen came upstairs.

"Now for God's sake don't do that, Viv," Stephen said, "you don't want to kick a man when he's down. And besides we've got quite enough to put up with as it is."

"I believe you're actually sorry for her."

"I am. No one else in this house has got any imagination, that's the trouble. Just think if you were Amy . . ."

"No, thanks. Don't you remember what you were saying about her only yesterday? I am not a *loose* woman, Stephen, whatever else I may be. It makes me feel very upset all this. And you know that isn't good for me." Vivienne began to cry.

"If you go on like this I shall have grey hairs by the time the baby is born," Stephen said. He let one of his shoes drop on the boards at the end of the bed by mistake.

"Go on! Kick off the other one! You know how it startles me," Vivienne said. But he took it off and laid it down on the carpet very carefully.

"I think I shall have to be away all next week," he said. Vivienne stopped crying and picked up a book.

Later, when he had got into bed and she still went on reading, he said, "Wake me up if I snore." And ten minutes after that he was fast asleep.

Tired as she was, Amy found that she could not sleep. She listened. Every time a door shut or someone walked about she half sat up. At last, remembering that she had never said good-night to her father- and mother-in-law, she decided to put her dressing-gown on and go downstairs.

Mr. Monsoon was standing in the hall by the coat-rack trying to get his mackintosh off the hook. Someone had hung a string basket on the same hook as his mackintosh. He tugged, but the loop was held fast by the basket. He saw Amy coming down.

"My dear child, you must have ears like a fox," he said.

"The whole thing will come down if you pull like that," Amy said. "What do you mean—ears like a fox?"

"He's back."

"Back?"

"Yes! Didn't you hear him change down round the corner? George always does that. Now do come on down."

Mrs. Monsoon came into the hall just then. "Are you *sure*, Charlie . . ." she began, and then saw Amy. She hesitated.

"Well," she said. "Perhaps Amy had better see George alone—I don't know—"

"Nonsense," Mr. Monsoon said. "You let me handle this."

"But shouldn't Amy and George—"

"Amy can open the door."

"But George isn't going to *ring*, Charlie."

"Of course not. Don't be ridiculous. Amy, don't stand about on the stairs. He's coming—quick!"

Long before Amy had moved, George opened the door. He stood blinking a moment.

"Do shut the door, dear," his mother said.

"She's back, my boy, she's here," his father said. "She travelled all night and arrived home at breakfast!"

George shut the door.

"Well, really, Amy," he said.

Amy leaned on the banisters. "Hullo, George," she said.

"Come along, Charlie," Mrs. Monsoon said.

"You see, George, you have made a mistake," Mr. Monsoon said. "You owe us all an apology."

"Oh not now, Charlie, not now," Mrs. Monsoon said. She took her husband's arm and led him away.

"Well, Amy?" George said.

"Well, George?" said Amy.

"I'm damn tired."

"So am I."

"Where the hell have you been?"

"Not with Rupert, if that's what you mean."

"Of course I mean that. Don't let's argue. I went to his flat."

"Well?"

"It was empty. Or at least no one answered."

"He's in France."

"Why on earth didn't you tell me that in the first place? What's all this about anyway?"

"I can't think."

"Amy, I shall never forgive you for this. You've made a perfect fool of me."

"That's your fault. If you hadn't said when I asked . . ."

"Now don't start that. Don't let's have a row. I'm too tired. I've been travelling for forty-eight hours."

"Well, you're lucky. I had to pick raspberries."

"Raspberries?"

"For jam. Your mother insisted on picking raspberries for jam all to-day."

"I daresay she did. Now let's get to bed. I must sleep."

"George, I don't think I'm going to be able to stand very much more of this."

"I should think not. What do you mean?"

"Our life."

"Oh to hell with that, Amy. This is no time to make scenes."

"You always say that. But it was you who said that you couldn't forgive me."

"And I can't, Amy. I've put up with too much from you. This sort of thing's the end."

"That's what I mean. Now you hate me."

George took his coat off and turned round to hang it up. "As usual," he said, "somebody's been overloading the coat-rack."

"That's all you care about really—isn't it?" Amy said.

"Do stop being childish."

"All right, George. But if you don't care about me, how am I going to fit in with this life? I know I've made a mess of it, but if you are going to go on and on not forgiving me—we shan't be very *happy*—shall we?"

"Oh do what you like, Amy," George said. "You women really are devilish. Talk, talk, talk, talk—when all a man needs is sleep. I suppose you expected me to throw my arms round your neck. But you must know that's not like me. Look here, I'm glad that you're back, I'm glad that you haven't gone off with that fellow Tyce. But I don't trust you an inch. Why didn't you tell me, Amy, that you weren't going to meet him? And how did you know that he'd gone away? You'll have to explain all these things in the morning. I'm going to bed now to get some sleep. Good night." He walked past her up the stairs.

The clock struck the lengthy three-quarter chime. "Nearly twelve," Amy said to herself. She too went upstairs.

In the drawing-room Mr. Monsoon had persuaded his wife to have a last drop of brandy. He spoke of the glories of '08 port, and she knitted contentedly.

"*What* a day it has been!" she said when he paused. "*What* a day!"

"You take life too seriously. Now when I was a boy . . ." Mr. Monsoon began. But Mrs. Monsoon raised her hand. "No, no, Charlie, it's getting so late," she said. "Just you finish up your brandy. . . ."

"Oh well, pearls before swine," Mr. Monsoon said. "I was going to tell you what my own mother did when *I* misbehaved."

"That must wait for some other time, Charlie."

He went to bed first. She saw that the doors were locked, that the jam had set, that all the lights had been turned off, and then went to bed herself. Bob always slept in her bedroom now. He was getting extremely old and his legs were shaky. No one had ever suggested having Bob "put away," but sometimes Mrs. Monsoon had thought recently this would only be a kindness. So whenever he wagged his tail at her she felt guilty. He wagged his tail now as she came to bed.

"Dear Bob," she said, "I don't know what I'd do without you. You're *such* a comfort."

She got some cotton-wool and began to clean his eyes out; they watered, and the fur got clotted up if she didn't dry it. He growled but she continued patiently with his toilet, kneeling beside his basket and making soothing noises although she knew the treatment couldn't really hurt.

Afterwards, she sat up in bed for some long time finishing off a pair of bootees for Vivienne's baby. And then, turning the light off at last, she told herself, "The day isn't long enough really. So much work . . ." And fell asleep with the comforting thought that, anyway, she had done her duty.

A few weeks later Bob died after chasing a rabbit. Heart failure, the vet said. Mrs. Monsoon said she didn't want to know where the dog was buried, so Mr. Monsoon buried Bob himself. He suggested buying another pet for his wife, but she said no, not at her time of life. He was much relieved. She cried over the empty basket, and when Mrs. Smith insisted on removing it because it got in the way when she hoovered, she said, "Now *nobody* loves me."

"Well, that just isn't true, Ma'am," Mrs. Smith said. "You've got your family. . . ."

But ignoring her, Mrs. Monsoon said, "We are *all* alone always really."

"*Alone!*" Mrs. Smith said to her husband over a cup of tea, "*Alone!* We could do with a few less in this house if you ask me."

CHAPTER TWELVE

EVEN as late as nine o'clock next morning after the thunderstorm it was possible to go about with that bright-eyed early morning feeling—bustling and pink and slightly empty-headed—because after the storm everything looked so fresh and a brisk wind blew the sounds and the smells of the outdoor world into the houses. The sun shone, streams gushed from the hillsides where before no streams had been, and drenched gardens smelled like spring woods: aromatic, with a tinge of decay from old leaves through which bracken shoots up bright green curled heads.

The pleasure of opening windows to let in the fragrance of such a morning caused even Mrs. Henlow to sing. She hadn't left Mr. Swan, but was still, from her point of view, just obliging. She was biding her time. She thought as she swept the passage down that very soon now the day must come when her master would beckon her into his study to tell her, "Mrs. Henlow, I am going to be married." And she would reply, "Very well, Sir. That means I go." "Ta ra ra boom de ay," she sang. By mistake her broom bumped against the study door.

"Less noise, please," Mr. Swan called out. He was undoing a large parcel that had arrived at breakfast-time. It was his tiger skin back from the cleaners. He had missed it. It served for a rug in his study, and as he rolled it out now he was thinking how splendid it was, how fortunate, to have a rug like that tiger. He had not shot it himself. It had belonged to a friend of his, a big-game shooter, who, when Mr. Swan came home from the East, had said that he wanted to give him a present—some little token of friendship that would remind him of happy days in the past. Because he had done quite a lot for his friend one way and another, Mr. Swan had chosen the tiger skin. And now here it was. He smiled, remembering.

Just then Mrs. Henlow knocked. "Yes?" he said. "Come in."

Mrs. Henlow put her head round the door. "You've got a caller," she told him. He said, "What do you mean?" She pointed towards the french windows and grinned. Mr. Swan looked over his shoulder to see Lavinia walking along the drive. She wore trousers, which shocked him.

"Ooh!" Mrs. Henlow said suddenly. "I hope I'm not expected to hoover that thing!" She had caught sight of the rug.

"You may go," Mr. Swan said. "And please show Miss Rockaby into the drawing-room."

But Lavinia had already seen him. Instead of continuing along the drive she took the little stone-flagged path that led up to the study. Mr. Swan frowned. She tapped on the french window. He walked across to let her in.

"Good morning," he said. "I've just been dealing with my correspondence. Aren't you working this morning?"

"My day off," Lavinia said. "I thought I'd come round to give you a hand as I'm at a loose end. In the garden, you know. You sounded a little despondent about your garden in your letter."

Two days before Mr. Swan had written to Lavinia. He had said among other things, "Let us be married next year in the spring when there will be flowers in the garden to welcome us. I see no point in hurrying matters and just now the place is nothing but a wilderness—for which, I am sorry to say, I must blame my father."

"The work is far too heavy for a woman," he said now. "In any case, I prefer to manage by myself in the garden. Otherwise, you know, I would have engaged a gardener. It was a kind thought, Lavinia. But there is no need for you to distress yourself on my behalf."

"Oh, surely—even if it's only weeding—there must be something I can do," Lavinia said. "Besides, I'm used to hard work. Look, I'm dressed for it."

"I dislike seeing trousers on a woman. It's most unfeminine."

"Oh come, everyone wears slacks these days, Harold. I won't though when we're married if you dislike them. By the way, are you sure it's a good idea for us to wait till spring next year?"

"I don't feel this is quite the moment to discuss our marriage," Mr. Swan said. He looked down at the tiger rug. And following his glance, Lavinia noticed it for the first time.

"Good heavens, Harold, wherever did you get that old thing?" she said. "Fur simply breeds moths and I'd trip over its head every time I came in. So like a man to have a thing like that in his house."

"I like it. It was given to me by a very good friend," Mr. Swan said. He leaned down and stroked it.

"Sorry, Harold," Lavinia said, "I didn't know it was a present. . . ."

"You don't care for it? Neither does Mrs. Henlow. But I'm not going to have it put away in the attic!"

"Of course not. Whoever said so? What's the matter with you, Harold?"

He looked up, not at Lavinia, but somewhere beyond her into the glistening garden where the lilies stood with bowed heads after the storm. "There are some things one can't explain," he said.

"What are you trying to say, Harold?" Lavinia asked in rather a chilly voice. Mr. Swan sighed.

"When one has lived alone as long as I have in the East . . ." he began. But Lavinia stopped him.

"I do wish you wouldn't become so mysterious when you want to say something important," she said.

Mr. Swan closed his eyes and remained silent for a moment. Then he said, "I very much dislike being interrupted."

Lavinia hoisted herself on to the table. There was no chair where she could sit except the one beside Mr. Swan; but that belonged to his writing-desk and she couldn't very well sit there without permission. She swung her legs and looked down at the floor. "There's nothing very much about me that you do like, is there?" she said.

"We don't know each other very well," Mr. Swan said.

"What makes you think then that you want to marry me, Harold?"

"A man of my age needs a wife."

"Not necessarily."

"You don't think so?" Mr. Swan said, opening his eyes.

"No," Lavinia said. "It's hard though for a woman if she never gets married." She waited. But Mr. Swan said nothing, so she went on: "Yes, you know," she said, "otherwise why on earth do you think my mother ever married my father? Or why for that matter did Mrs. George marry? Certainly not for love."

"I never . . ." Mr. Swan began, but Lavinia waved her hand and said, "Oh I know, I know—you made it quite clear from the first what you thought about love. I'm not another Mrs. George, thank you."

"What do you mean by that?" Mr. Swan said.

"I mean I wouldn't trade on my husband's affections. She's carrying on with that Rupert Tyce. People think she might even go off with him. But as mother says, she knows which side her bread is buttered. Amy Monsoon is as tough as they make them. Not a nice type."

"I think you had better go," Mr. Swan said.

She looked surprised. As she didn't move, he said, "You might at least get down off that table."

"All right, all right," Lavinia said, "but what's the matter now, Harold?"

"Jealousy among women is quite despicable," Mr. Swan said.

"I'm afraid I don't understand, Harold."

"Mrs. George is extremely beautiful."

"And I'm not. Thanks."

"You should try to see these things quite impersonally. Beauty is a gift from the gods. It is not . . ."

"If there is any justice in this world she should be made to suffer for it!" Lavinia said, jumping down. "I hope she burns in hell . . . Oh Lord, I'm going to cry." She dashed out.

"Strange," Mr. Swan said, watching her disappear, "very strange. It won't do."

Lavinia ran down the garden path brushing against the laurels, which sprinkled her shoulders with cold little drops. On reaching the drive she stopped. "I've behaved like a silly woman," she said. "He'll never forgive me." She half turned round, waited a moment, and then began walking back down the path. "Pride? I have no pride," she said. She liked being cruel to herself, it made her feel honest.

There Mr. Swan was, still staring out of the window, but seated now at his desk.

"May I come in?" she called. The french windows were open, but as he said nothing she remained standing outside.

"I'm sorry," she said. "I shouldn't have behaved like that. Forgive me, Harold."

"I can't talk to you now," Mr. Swan said. "I shall write you a letter. These things can't be talked about."

"Oh, Harold, why this mystery?"

"I beg you to go."

"Very well."

Once again Mr. Swan watched Lavinia go down the path. When he couldn't see her any more he waited some time. But she didn't return. He sighed. "Now I must write that letter," he said.

Just as he reached out for his pen, Mrs. Henlow knocked on the door. "Would the young lady care for a cup of tea?" she called out.

"No!" Mr. Swan called back.

"No manners at all," Mrs. Henlow said as she shuffled off down the passage. To annoy him she sang twice as loud as before while cleaning the spoons. He didn't hear her. He was writing a very painful letter.

"Dear Lavinia" (he wrote)—"Thank you for coming this morning with your offer of help with my garden.

"I must tell you that after our conversation I find it impossible to deceive myself any longer about my feelings with regard to our intended marriage. I think you must agree yourself that we do not get on very well together. We are not suited, Lavinia.

"Therefore please believe me when I say that it is for the benefit of us both that I must reluctantly set you free from your promise. There has been no ring in our case, as when I suggested it you mocked me for my extravagance. It has proved just as well.

"You may say I wore rose-tinted spectacles, for I always had hopes of a quiet increasingly worthwhile future for us both: let us face the truth, we disagree fundamentally.

"Forgive me then any suffering I may cause you, and please release me from my promise. I deeply regret the trouble and inconvenience this letter may well cause your parents. I trust you will try to explain the circumstances which necessitated my attitude.

"You need not reply, I shall understand. Yours very sincerely, my dear Lavinia, Harold Swan."

"Yes," Mr. Swan said, reading it over. He folded the letter up, put it in an envelope and propped it against the ink-pot. Then he went out for a walk.

He found he hadn't changed his mind at all when he came back. So after taking his wet shoes off and putting on slippers he sealed and addressed the envelope and stamped it and then put the letter on the hall table for Mrs. Henlow to post when she left at one o'clock.

Mrs. Rockaby's reactions to this letter can be imagined. She said at once, "Sue him for breach of promise." But, as Mr. Rockaby pointed out, because of Mr. Swan's objection, the engagement had never yet been put in *The Times*.

"Even so," Mrs. Rockaby said, "we have a case. I'm not taking this lying down."

Lavinia remained calm. "It's not going to break up my life," she said.

"I should think not!" her mother said, "*What* a way to talk!"

As Lavinia refused absolutely to do or to say any more on the subject Mrs. Rockaby took things into her own hands and went off by bus one morning "to get some proper advice," as she said. Rather naturally, having decided to find out what the Law said in these matters, she intended consulting George's firm, who had their office in the town.

"Men are queer about giving professional advice in a friendly way," she told herself, sitting in a cramped position. It was market day in the town. The bus was full; everyone except Mrs. Rockaby carried baskets and shouted urging the driver along. How much easier the whole thing would have been, she was thinking, if, instead of having to make this ghastly journey, she could have gone up to the Grange and had a friendly talk with George one night.

Arriving at the office, she was told very politely and at length by George's partner that she hadn't a hope.

As there was no bus till after lunch, she went home in a taxi. After that, Mrs. Rockaby took to her bed for a week, saying, "This is the end." But, of course, it was not. Lavinia, who had always wanted to work with the younger children, persuaded Mrs. Hardinger to let her give lessons to junior classes. She knew how to handle young children, and young children liked her. She started to save up.

"One day," she told her father, "I'm going to get a proper training. It doesn't look as though I shall ever have any children of my own, so I may as well make it my life's work looking after other people's."

"You're a good girl. A good girl," Mr. Rockaby said. He felt more than ever guilty at being a failure and spent more and more time poring over accounts.

"Not giving the digging stunt up?" the Vicar enquired when he called. (Mr. Ashe believed in calling on families in trouble, but seldom called when things were going all right. He was known as "Old Wind Up" among his parishioners— not that he knew. This was rather unfair.)

"I've lost heart, I'm afraid," Mr. Rockaby said.

So instead of having a talk with Mrs. Rockaby, who, he had heard, was very poorly, Mr. Ashe talked with Mr. Rockaby. Putting the stuffing back into a man who had gone all flabby was the sort of job he liked best. "Now what's up? Let's have it out," he said.

"Oh, it's just that I've made a mess of my life," Mr. Rockaby said.

"I'm your friend, you can tell me," Mr. Ashe said.

And because he was very lonely, Mr. Rockaby did. It was a long story, and the Vicar listened in silence, smoking his pipe. At the end of it all he said, "You know, Rockaby, although I'm a much younger man than you, I too sometimes feel like that. A failure. I have always believed in progress—things going on—getting better; and if one approach doesn't work, well, one gives it up and tries another. For instance, my wife and I came to this village with very high hopes indeed. Rural communities, you know, compared to town folk—industrial populations—have a raw deal; they get left behind in the march of progress although their work is vital to all the rest. As I saw it, it was my job to give them a leg up. Just look at the wretched lives these people lead! No sense of community with the world outside, no culture, very little leisure—and not even a cinema anywhere near (and how I've tried to get them a bus in the evenings to take them into the town and back) and so no chance to get out of themselves and to relax. But at any suspicion of change I try to make for the better, I am opposed—always opposed. It's . . . well, it's pretty grim, old fellow. Sometimes I say to my wife, 'Oh, Helen, let's give it up and leave.' And it's a terrible grind for Helen, you know, in this little backwater. But then I think, no. Stick it out. Things must change. Life is twice as slow here as anywhere else. Have patience.' And that goes for you too, Rockaby. One needs must be, sometimes, inactive, lie fallow, wear patience like an old garment. That way one survives. You see what I mean, Rockaby? It's not a matter of letting down one's ideals, not really. Don't despair. I know you're not young, I know how this question of money gets a man down. But as you say, you have just enough to make ends meet—why worry then about your daughter and son? She's a very capable girl, and as for him, it's his job to make a life for himself. So all you have got to do is to pull yourself together, help your wife, and carry on.

This had its effect. After about a week, Mr. Rockaby was back in the organ loft, down on his hands and knees muttering and taking notes. He was not interested in the organ, but in the wall behind, where, underneath the plaster and dirt of the ages, he felt pretty sure some early wall paintings were there to be found. You could see his heart was in his work the way he got down to it: the stuffing had been put back, the Vicar had done good.

It was not so with Mrs. Rockaby. Getting up at the end of a week, as she herself said, she "just crawled about." This state of affairs went on till the end of the summer. Then, quite unexpectedly, Bertram came home. As usual, he made himself felt. He shoved the baby grand into a corner, hung all the pictures up and made a frightful mess everywhere all over the house with his sculpting. Mr. Rockaby threatened to turn him out; there were scenes, and Mrs. Rockaby had hysterics. But it was life. And by the time Bertram had had enough and gone back to Paris, his family had something new to worry about. He said he intended to marry very shortly—an American woman who believed in his Art; bags of money, but she had taste, and was quite nice.

The Monsoons also had something new to worry about. It had to do with Amy—her health this time. She was going into what in the old days would have been called a decline. She had been given liver injections and sleeping draughts by the doctor, but nothing did any good. When asked what was the matter, she always said she was trying to resign herself to life. She certainly suffered, but so did everyone else. No one liked to ask her to do things because she always said, "Very well," and sighed and performed her duties in silence. She even managed to look like a martyr while doing the hoovering. George had got to the stage of shouting "For God's sake, Amy, pull yourself together!" when she said, on being asked to mend his socks for him, "I must if I must I suppose."

"In some ways it would be better if he beat her," Stephen said to Vivienne, having witnessed the scene.

Vivienne had become increasingly possessive during these last months of her pregnancy. First she claimed the nursery from Amy. She gained it almost without a fight because Amy had become so listless. Then she said her bedroom hadn't a dressing-room attached like Amy's and there would be nowhere to put the baby. "One should *always* have a night nursery," she told Stephen.

"Steady, old girl, you can't turn George out," Stephen said. "It's his room. Always has been."

"Baby comes first, surely," Vivienne said.

By this time the cot and folding bath that Amy had used for her children had been commandeered. But Vivienne waved aside the offer of the old pram. "It's got no brake," she said, "and look at the upholstering! No, I want to have the very latest thing in prams."

She got it. There was no room for it in the garage so it had to be stored in the box-room because Vivienne said the barns were damp and it must be kept indoors. This meant that Amy's trunk had to be moved out to make room for it. For some reason this made George furious.

"That woman's trying to turn us all out," he said to his father.

"Pregnant women are the devil sometimes," Mr. Monsoon said. He was very distressed. More than anything it pained him to see Amy lose her looks, and she ate so little and hardly ever spoke and never laughed at any of his jokes. He tried to make George take action, but at length, when he saw it wasn't the slightest good, he wrote to Amy's mother himself. He said Amy looked rather washed out and needed a change.

Naturally the two families corresponded, but only at Christmas or when someone among them was ill, or when

Mrs. Monsoon felt a letter ought to be written, it was so long since they heard. Amy's mother therefore felt something must be very wrong indeed when she received Mr. Monsoon's letter. She wrote back suggesting Amy should come to stay with her at once. The children were back at school, so there was nothing to stop Amy from seizing this chance. But she made every excuse to get out of it. She told Mr. Monsoon she didn't want a holiday, and when George said, "For God's sake, woman, have a change and go away!" she said if she did she might never come back.

"You must make up your mind," he said.

It was Mr. Monsoon who finally made her go. He argued with her for nearly an hour and then when she still said "No," he banged the table and reduced her to tears and threatened to turn her out there and then if she didn't arrange at once to pay a visit to her mother. After that she went.

It was very peaceful without her. Mrs. Monsoon stopped complaining about indigestion and Vivienne gave up her campaign for more room. George relaxed, smoked his pipe in his bedroom and worked at his book until any old hour—sometimes not getting to bed until two in the morning.

The days passed. One morning Mr. Monsoon said to George at breakfast, "When's Amy coming back?"

"I don't know. I haven't heard," George said.

"But you've written?"

"I've sent her a note."

"Rather casual," Mr. Monsoon said, when alone with his wife.

"It's much better never to interfere, don't you think. More tea?" Mrs. Monsoon said.

"I'm worried about those two."

"So would I be if Vivienne wasn't going to have her baby so soon."

"I don't see that there's any connection."

"The worry. Now we've got Vivienne to worry about. She's not very young, you know, to have a first baby."

Mr. Monsoon picked up *The Times*. "Poor Amy," he said. "Ah well . . ."

Everyone noticed that George had a letter from Amy next morning. It lay on the hall table. George was last down to breakfast, so the whole of the rest of the family had had time to notice the French stamps, and of course Amy's writing, on the envelope. Nothing was said. But after dinner that night George waylaid his father on the verandah. It was a warm evening and the old man sat outside enjoying a glass of port.

"A word with you, Father," George said.

"Help yourself, my boy," said Mr. Monsoon. "Fetch a glass."

"No, thanks," George said. "About Amy. She says she's not coming back."

"Now we don't want that nonsense over again," Mr. Monsoon said. "Do sit down. And go and fetch that glass. Then we can talk."

"No, Father," George said, "there's nothing to talk about. I shall divorce her."

"Balderdash!"

"Don't talk to me like that, Father."

"But this is serious. You will bring shame down on our heads."

"You are getting more and more like Mr. Smith, Father. Soon you'll be saying, 'Vengeance is mine—'"

"I do say it."

"Well, it's no good. I must get things tidied up."

"That's your lawyer's mind. If only you'd listened to me in the first place. . . ."

"Oh for God's sake, Father, don't let's go over all that!"

"Have you thought of the children?"

"I have."

"I suppose then there is nothing more one can say."

"No."

"You had better think it over. Do nothing in haste."

George stood looking down at his father in silence.

"Well?" Mr. Monsoon said.

"This has come as no surprise to me," George said, "I have expected it for a long time. She has lost interest in us, I'm afraid. Now, doubtless, she will be able to find someone else." He walked away.

Amy hadn't mentioned anyone else in her letter, but George had always said that a woman never left a man unless it was for another man. "At least I'm not hoodwinked," he told himself.

CHAPTER THIRTEEN

VIVIENNE produced a girl in October. It was an enormous baby—nine and a half pounds at birth—and Stephen was fearfully proud and brought over some vegetable scales to weigh it, and everyone (except Vivienne) agreed that it was good for its lungs when it howled. The baby was endlessly dandled and cooed at, and didn't sleep much. At first, Mrs. Monsoon and Stephen took turns to wheel it about. But as soon as Vivienne got up she put a stop to that. She said it was utterly wrong to wheel a baby about, and had the pram wedged with two bricks and the brake on so that it was quite safe, in the shade on the verandah. So there the baby was left to sleep, alone in state. Only Mr. Monsoon didn't think much of the baby. He was annoyed anyway at being shooed off the verandah.

"The child is all right," he said to his wife, "there's nothing wrong with it. But it hasn't got delicate features like Amy's." He liked to talk about Amy. When he did, Mrs. Monsoon generally put on a rather far-away look. If he noticed this he said, "It's all right, the poor woman's not dead."

"Much better if she had been," Vivienne said once to her mother-in-law after Mr. Monsoon had gone out. But Mrs. Monsoon said, "Such remarks, Vivienne, don't sound very nice on the lips of a mother."

Hoping perhaps to effect a reconciliation, Mr. Monsoon wrote to Amy. He told her about the family, about Vivienne's child, and about her own boys. She didn't answer his letters. George had now started divorce proceedings, a fact that was never mentioned although everyone knew about it.

"I am going to divorce Amy," George had announced one day at breakfast when Mr. Monsoon had insisted on talking about her. There was a long silence. Then Mr. Monsoon said, "I don't want to hear about that. It's a disgrace. I can't stop you, you must go your own way. Never mention the subject again in my presence. I miss Amy. I always shall. It's very thoughtless of you, George, to upset me like this at breakfast."

There was some trouble over the baby's christening. Vivienne wanted the infant called Monica, but Mr. Monsoon wouldn't have it, it was an unnatural name for a baby he said. Stephen stuck up for his wife and insisted. "She won't always be a baby!" he said. So his father said, "Very well. Christen the baby without me." And he only relented at the last minute and the whole family were late at the church. During the service he said "Amen" in the wrong places and fidgeted, but the Vicar pretended he hadn't noticed. There were drinks at the Grange afterwards; a thing not approved of by Mrs. Monsoon. But as Stephen said, it was his child's christening not Mrs. Monsoon's. The house was full of relatives, and the Rockabys were there too. Mr. Swan had been invited, but never came (he wrote an apology for his absence saying "there had been a confusion about the dates"). He never went out these days, but spent all his time in his garden. And looking over the hedge, William said he had made a good job of it.

Mr. Swan wasn't exactly ostracised in the village, but people gave him a wide berth because they said he looked strange. Actually, he had taken to doing all sorts of Yogi exercises and was, more often than not, lost in meditation. Being lost like this gave his eyes a far-away look, and also, it meant that he didn't watch where he went, and he bumped into people and fell over things. But, as William had said, he made a good job of that garden—it became a wonderful sight. Mr. Monsoon, who loved gardens, although he so seldom gardened himself, often went down by the ditch and looked over the hedge; just as Mr. Swan sometimes looked over the hedge into Mr. Monsoon's garden. One day they met doing this.

"That's a fine sight, Swan," Mr. Monsoon said, pointing over the hedge with his stick.

"Yes, not bad," Mr. Swan said. "But you've got the best roses."

"I shall have to see about this ditch," Mr. Monsoon said. "Well, must be getting along. Good morning."

"Good morning," Mr. Swan said.

Strangely enough, the ditch, left untouched since the day George and William had started to dig, got done in the end. But before explaining how, I must tell you about Mrs. Tyce.

Mrs. Tyce, left alone with Smyly, stopped being Queen Victoria and took a turn for the worse. She caught the postman over the head with a stick one morning, and threw all the milk bottles—full of milk—over the hedge. Naturally the Hardingers heard about this: the milk bottles burst in their drive, scattering milk and glass all over the place. So Mr. Hardinger wrote a pretty stiff letter to the eldest Tyce, saying please come down at once. The son came with his wife. A bit later, Mrs. Tyce was removed. She was put in a home where she was properly looked after; but having endured a year of this, died. So she was brought home again and buried beside her husband in the family vault. The grass in the churchyard was specially cut, and the cats chased out. The whole village turned up for the funeral—even people like Mrs. Rockaby. And Mr. Swan was there too. Mrs. Henlow had spoken so long and so often about Mrs. Tyce's sufferings during her life and the hardship of all widow's lives and the miserable lot of women in general, that, in order to silence her, Mr. Swan had said at last, "Very well, Mrs. Henlow, I'll go." And he took a wreath too. It was the biggest funeral since the old Doctor's, and a much bigger funeral than Mr. Tyce's. (But that was mainly because the village birthrate had gone up meanwhile.) Of all the Tyce family, only Rupert was absent. From France he had gone on to Greece and nothing more had been heard since that.

The Dower House, after Mrs. Tyce's death, reverted to the rest of the Hereward Hall property and so was taken over by the school. "What a blessing!" Mrs. Hardinger said. "And just as we really needed a San!"

Afterwards, one day, the Vicar called at the school. He said, why didn't the girls use his church instead of going in to the town by bus every Sunday? Not only would this save time and money, but it would help the girls to know the village (and it was a very old place indeed)—thus perhaps throwing new light on history—such a difficult subject to teach. The bus fares were put on the bills, so as Mrs. Hardinger truthfully said, "It's not a question of *money*," (and the Vicar agreed). But the town had a Cathedral, which somehow, mentioned on the prospectus, added prestige. So it wasn't easy for Mrs. Hardinger to choose. In the end, she said "Yes." The little girls therefore went to Matins, and the bigger ones to Evensong. So ever afterwards the Vicar always had a full church.

As for Smyly, she went back to Ireland. She had been away for twenty years, but found nothing had changed. She lost all her savings gambling on horses, and, sad to say, drinking. She had caught the habit from sampling Mr. Tyce's whisky in the old days, and had gone on to brandy with Mrs.

Tyce. Then, she had minded about keeping up appearances and had always sucked mint drops; now she didn't care how much her breath smelt. But she was happy. What more can one say?

CHAPTER FOURTEEN

AND now for the ditch. George never showed his feelings, so no one knew how much he missed Amy. During the course of next summer the divorce went through. After that, Mr. Monsoon got a letter from Amy. She thanked him for all his kindness, now, and in the past; and said, please, if he didn't mind, would he continue to write to her and tell her about himself and the boys? Mr. Monsoon was touched. Of course he went on writing to her, but was rather shocked when one day George told him Amy had married again.

"Some literary fellow," George said. "I told you, Father, there was somebody else."

"Decent of him. Decent of him," Mr. Monsoon said. For however much he might love Amy, he had thought of her, after George had divorced her, as a social outcast.

Once things had settled down and George felt himself to be a free man in every sense, he got down to his book in earnest. First he removed all the jokes, and then, because the manuscript now looked a mess, he began writing it all over again. Besides this, he kept up his work in the garden, not because William was going to be sacked, but because he liked it. There had been a short consultation between William and George concerning the ditch.

"That other thing we started—I suppose we had better push on with it," George said. They had been talking about cabbages, and there had been a pause in the conversation. William was generally pretty quick, but he said now, "Beg pardon, Sir?"

Because Mr. Monsoon had really retired, not even giving advice or interfering, but just walking round and picking flowers and sunning himself in the garden, George was Sir now, not Mr. George. "The ditch," George said. "You know we started it, William. . . ."

"There's the winter coming, and the broccoli to be put in. And the ground's got to be tidied up along by the old celery beds for my seeds," William said. "If you was to *ask* me, Sir, I would turn my hand to the ditch. I'm not saying you couldn't lay out the garden for next year yourself. But it's a lot of work."

"Quite," George said. "We'll leave the ditch."

Stephen disagreed when he heard of this decision. "I *know* something about drainage, old boy—that ditch needs it," he said to George.

"Very well, do it yourself," George said. But Stephen never did.

In the course of time, round about spring of the following year, before the garden was looking its best, but when the early flowers were showing their heads, George finished writing his book. He typed with two fingers only, and the thing had to be typed, but it was a slow job on two fingers, so George wrote a note to Lavinia requesting her services. Lavinia was awfully busy these days what with her work at the school and her studies for future examinations (she hadn't saved up much yet) and Mrs. Rockaby was very exacting and trying, and insisted that Lavinia must help Mrs. Burt spring-clean, though she didn't move a finger herself. So Lavinia thought twice before answering the note. At length she compromised and sent word that she'd come at weekends—after lunch on Saturday, and the whole of Sunday if George had no objection to working on the Sabbath. George didn't mind, but Mr. Monsoon had plenty to say on the subject. However, George got his way.

The old man had been seventy-nine on his last birthday, and, as he said, "I really am old now." He behaved as old men do behave sometimes when head of the family, in a childishly dictatorial way, laying down laws, putting his foot down, and then suddenly saying when one of the women burst into tears, "But it's no good my talking—I'm only an old man. Nobody listens to what I say. Nobody tells me anything. Never mind, I'll soon be dead." Which is upsetting until you get used to it. And so the law was laid down about working on Sunday. But by this time his family were hardened and took very little notice. George was a good son, though.

"Well, I won't work Sunday mornings," he said. And after that, while the rest of the family continued to walk down to church for the morning service, George drove his father down, and then afterwards they all came back by car. It was rather a squash when Stephen was home, and Mrs. Monsoon got cross, saying she'd much rather walk there *and* back, and Vivienne said, "No, Mother, *I'll* walk," and Stephen said, "Oh come on! Do shut up." But they all got in in the end.

It took Lavinia some time to type out the book, and at length Mr. Monsoon said one Saturday afternoon—a wonderful day, bright sunshine, no wind and a cloudless sky—("the first real day of spring" as everyone said), "It's very wrong, George, to shut that girl up."

"She's not here for fun, she's doing some work," George said.

"Well, it's unjust," Mr. Monsoon said. "It's all very well for you, George, to fug. If you must write, you must. But why other people should be denied fresh air . . ."

"Father, please keep out of this," George said.

But meeting Lavinia on the stairs as she left, Mr. Monsoon stopped her and said, "Miss Rockaby, this is my house, and I should like to invite you to luncheon to-morrow. Twelve-thirty, after church." This was said in a voice of command. Lavinia accepted at once.

"Such a nuisance," Mrs. Monsoon said to George afterwards. "Who is your father going to invite next? It makes things so difficult."

Lavinia was very shy at lunch next day. "Rather a wet, isn't she?" Stephen said to Vivienne in private.

Vivienne was coping with napkins and had a safety-pin in her mouth. She made a noise like "Uh-uh" and shook her head. However, Mr. Monsoon (whose opinions still mattered) said to his wife as they walked round the garden, "That girl is rather nice." Next Sunday Lavinia was invited again, and after that, the thing became routine. Mrs. Rockaby didn't much care for it. "They never ask me!" she said. But the Rockaby family, unlike the Monsoons (and unlike everyone else in the village), didn't have roasts on Sunday—it was so bourgeois Mrs. Rockaby said. They ate out of tins. So there was no cooking to do that morning, and Lavinia wasn't missed.

Mrs. Monsoon had her own ideas about Miss Rockaby. Watching her play with the boys (this was during the holidays), she sighed. She wished that instead of being employed to type out George's book, George would employ Miss Rockaby to look after the boys. Mrs. Monsoon, too, was feeling her age, and the boys, in spite of rigorous treatment, got out of hand sometimes. George was a good father, but like so many men, he didn't have to deal with the children. He saw them and patted their heads when they were good, or smacked their bottoms if naughty, and paid for their education of course. But Mrs. Monsoon thought of all the clothes lists, the darning and patching, the endless suitable meals, the purgings, the anxiety over illnesses, the teaching of how to behave at table, the religious instruction (goodness knew what they taught them at school!)—and above all, this perpetual watching—to see that they came to no harm, to see that they didn't break things in the house, nor rushed about trampling flowers down in the garden. Mrs. Monsoon sighed again. And then, because Miss Rockaby was dealing so well with the children, she fell asleep. . . .

"How competent Miss Rockaby is," she said at tea.

"Yes she is," George said. "In another week she'll have the book ready."

"I suppose, George," Mrs. Monsoon said, "you wouldn't like to ask Miss Rockaby, would you, to come up sometimes to help with the children?"

"Help with the children?" Stephen said. "Good lord, what an expense! Vivy manages hers. But you'd help with the boys too, wouldn't you, Viv?"

"That's not quite what I meant, dear. The responsibility . . ."

"Those damn boys are getting too much for your mother," Mr. Monsoon said.

In the end, it was decided that Mrs. Monsoon should ask Miss Rockaby. It would look odd if George asked, his father said. And so Miss Rockaby was asked and she said yes, and there was peace for the rest of the holidays. And after the holidays, although the book was finished, Miss Rockaby still went up to the Grange, calling in after school hours.

"Don't desert us," George said. "You know you are always welcome here. And you can give me tips for the garden." And so Lavinia did.

Very soon Mrs. Rockaby got wind of this. Meeting George in the village, she said "Oh hullo" quite casually, and then asked him to drop in one evening for tea. He said he was rather busy, but she persisted. At length, having mentioned Friday or Saturday next week as possibilities, or if not, which day was he free—George thanked her and chose Saturday. Lavinia was there of course when he went, but as Mrs. Rockaby remarked to her husband afterwards, "Mr. Monsoon hasn't much to say for himself these days, has he?"

"I expect he was bored stiff, poor man," Mr. Rockaby said, "I know I was. What on earth possessed you, Evelyn, to ask him to tea?"

"Oh, I like having people in," Mrs. Rockaby said. She hummed a tune to herself. On the whole, she felt pleased. She had said to George as he left, "You're an old friend, you know. I wish you'd just drop in sometimes! All these invitations and things make the going so stiff—why don't you just drop in?"

And George had said, "Oh, well, thanks—yes. Right-o, Mrs. Rockaby. Thanks very much."

George never dropped in at the Rockabys', but more and more often as time went by, Lavinia dropped in at the Grange. At length, after two years of dropping in and looking after the boys in the holidays, Lavinia became Mrs. George. It had to be a Registry Office wedding because George was a divorcee, and although Mr. Ashe didn't mind, his Bishop did. This was sad for Mrs. Rockaby. Some of the village people shook their heads and there was a sharp rise in the amount of beer drunk at the pub, but most of the womenfolk in the village said it was quite right, that's how it ought to be. And as a family, the Monsoons let it be known that they were not displeased. Privately Stephen was rather annoyed. He asked George how the hell now were they going to make ends meet? But Mrs. Monsoon had just been left a small legacy by an unmarried brother "To provide for her old age," he said in his Will—a parting shot at Mr. Monsoon, who had never been liked very much by his wife's family. So things were not so desperate. And as George said, rather grandly, "There's my book now, you know. It'll soon be out." For at last, with Lavinia's help, the book had been accepted. As Stephen himself was pretty well off these days, there was nothing to worry about so long as George's new wife worked in with the rest of the family.

It was a little strange at first to see Mr. Monsoon hob-nobbing with Mrs. Rockaby. She amused him and tickled his vanity. But when she went off into fits of laughter, having said, "Just think—now one day I might be a grandmother—me a granny! Ha-ha-ha," this was too much; Mr. Monsoon drew himself up in his chair and cleared his throat.

"I hope your daughter isn't hysterical, Mrs. Rockaby," he said. "No trouble in the family like that, I hope. We come of yeomen stock. The backbone of the country."

After a honeymoon in Madeira (it couldn't be France because of Amy, Mrs. Rockaby quite understood—"It might lead to unfortunate memories," as she said—"Such a pity") the new Mrs. George settled down at the Grange and found her place.

"Now that this is your home," George said, "you must have your say, Lavinia. For instance, is there anything you think ought to be done about the garden? Just say."

And Lavinia said straight away, "Oh George, something *must* be done about that disgusting ditch."

And thus, it was done.

Mr. Monsoon lived to be eighty-four. He didn't exactly die in his boots, but very nearly. While trimming his hair one morning (he couldn't be bothered now to go to the barber more than once a month, but liked to look spruce) his hand slipped, and he cut himself on the cheek. He got some infection. They called in the doctor. Of late, Mr. Monsoon had become very difficult. He said now, even though weak, "Damn all doctors! I shall die if you send me away to hospital." And when Mrs. Monsoon brought him his pills, he said, "Chuck them out of the window. What good are pills?"

On the sixth day of his illness Mrs. Monsoon said to her sons, "Your father is going to die." And he did, in his sleep.

Death is final. Those who live on can remember, but to say Mr. Monsoon lived on is false. He did not. In time he became a legend, changed this way and that to suit his descendants; withdrawn from individual existence, but returned to a hotch-potch fund of family myth, which is itself a source of life. It is memory, not myth, that plays tricks, confusing the mind and throwing the sharpest light sometimes on far-away happenings. And just as the winter sun shines down on winter illuminating the fields, making the dark wood where one stands seem darker still, so Mrs. Monsoon would all at once remember her husband as a young man again: he throws a bunch of roses over her garden hedge, calling out as her father chases him off, "I shall come back again!" Hers had been a rather unorthodox courting. No one, however, remembers Mr. Monsoon fishing. Some of the happiest days of his life have been spent down by the river fishing, all by himself.

Perhaps Monica journeyed on with what was left of Mr. Monsoon longest; one might almost say that through her he suffered a sea-change. For Monica, aged five when he died, never forgot her grandfather: she used him in dreams. At first he appeared as a wrathful Old Testament figure, but later became a hero, a really wonderful man; no one, compared to him, stood a chance in Monica's eyes. She refused many suitable offers of marriage and was a great worry to Vivienne. In the end she ran away with a man twice her age, had identical twins—girls—and two years after, a boy. She called him Charles. Such is life.

And now it is summer again. Everyone has got over long ago what is known, when anyone thinks of it, as "Poor Mr. George's mistake"—meaning Amy. Mr. Swan, leaving the confines of his garden for once, goes out for a walk. He goes out by his garden gate, along by the fields; the ripening corn on one side, the river on the other. And suddenly he comes upon what looks like a scene of Arcadian bliss. Really it is the Monsoon family doing their duty collecting water, but not very efficiently. There is a drought. They have brought down a tremendous number of buckets, and William has just taken a couple up to the house. Where Mr. Swan is, there are no trees, but there, a little below the bridge, a

number of willow trees grow, and in the willow trees' shade
the family lazily fill their buckets and jugs, and laugh and
play. Mrs. Monsoon sits on a coat on the bank, and bending
down every so often, she catches a little water in a jug and
turns round and empties it into a bucket. Mrs. Smith wipes
her face on her apron, surveying the others, and Mr. Smith
calls out from the shade in a quivering voice, "Mrs. George,
damp your head!" George's children don't make quite such
a noise as the rest. They stand about midstream in shorts,
lordly but wet. They know how to behave. Stephen splashes
Vivienne, who shrieks, and Vivienne's daughter Monica drib-
bles into the river all by herself. She is quite old enough now
not to do this, but already a difficult child, she never does
what Vivienne says and always gets her own way. And balan-
cing on the trunk of a fallen tree which blew down in winter,
George stands directing events.

"Mind there! Hurry now! Don't play the fool. It's time we
got a bit of work done," he calls out. He is enjoying himself.

Stephen is happy too. He has filled all his buckets and is
telling everyone else what to do. Mr. Swan watches. No one
has seen him yet.

"One more load," Stephen says.

"Two more. Then we've done enough for to-day," George
shouts.

"Oh, but my back aches," Vivienne says.

"Never mind about backs," George says.

"The old Tartar," Mr. Smith says to his wife, "now if it had
been his father . . ."

"Yes," Mr. Swan says to himself, "the human family.
Yes." He stands still for a moment in contemplation with
bowed head.

George shields his eyes with both hands. "Who the devil!"
he says. Everyone looks.

"Why, it's Harold!" Lavinia says.

Mr. Swan comes to himself with a jump, murmurs "Good morning. Or rather, good afternoon to you all," and walks on.

THE END

FURROWED MIDDLEBROW

FM1. *A Footman for the Peacock* (1940) . . . . RACHEL FERGUSON

FM2. *Evenfield* (1942) . . . . RACHEL FERGUSON

FM3. *A Harp in Lowndes Square* (1936) . . . . RACHEL FERGUSON

FM4. *A Chelsea Concerto* (1959) . . . . FRANCES FAVIELL

FM5. *The Dancing Bear* (1954) . . . . FRANCES FAVIELL

FM6. *A House on the Rhine* (1955) . . . . FRANCES FAVIELL

FM7. *Thalia* (1957) . . . . FRANCES FAVIELL

FM8. *The Fledgeling* (1958) . . . . FRANCES FAVIELL

FM9. *Bewildering Cares* (1940) . . . . WINIFRED PECK

FM10. *Tom Tiddler's Ground* (1941) . . . . URSULA ORANGE

FM11. *Begin Again* (1936) . . . . URSULA ORANGE

FM12. *Company in the Evening* (1944) . . . . URSULA ORANGE

FM13. *The Late Mrs. Prioleau* (1946) . . . . MONICA TINDALL

FM14. *Bramton Wick* (1952) . . . . ELIZABETH FAIR

FM15. *Landscape in Sunlight* (1953) . . . . ELIZABETH FAIR

FM16. *The Native Heath* (1954) . . . . ELIZABETH FAIR

FM17. *Seaview House* (1955) . . . . ELIZABETH FAIR

FM18. *A Winter Away* (1957) . . . . ELIZABETH FAIR

FM19. *The Mingham Air* (1960) . . . . ELIZABETH FAIR

FM20. *The Lark* (1922) . . . . E. NESBIT

FM21. *Smouldering Fire* (1935) . . . . D.E. STEVENSON

FM22. *Spring Magic* (1942) . . . . D.E. STEVENSON

FM23. *Mrs. Tim Carries On* (1941) . . . . D.E. STEVENSON

FM24. *Mrs. Tim Gets a Job* (1947) . . . . D.E. STEVENSON

FM25. *Mrs. Tim Flies Home* (1952) . . . . D.E. STEVENSON

FM26. *Alice* (1949) . . . . ELIZABETH ELIOT

FM27. *Henry* (1950) . . . . ELIZABETH ELIOT

FM28. *Mrs. Martell* (1953) . . . . ELIZABETH ELIOT

FM29. *Cecil* (1962) . . . . ELIZABETH ELIOT

FM30. *Nothing to Report* (1940) . . . . CAROLA OMAN

FM31. *Somewhere in England* (1943) . . . . CAROLA OMAN

FM32. *Spam Tomorrow* (1956) . . . . VERILY ANDERSON

FM33. *Peace, Perfect Peace* (1947) . . . . JOSEPHINE KAMM

FM34. *Beneath the Visiting Moon* (1940) . . . . ROMILLY CAVAN
FM35. *Table Two* (1942) . . . . MARJORIE WILENSKI
FM36. *The House Opposite* (1943) . . . . BARBARA NOBLE
FM37. *Miss Carter and the Ifrit* (1945) . . . . SUSAN ALICE KERBY
FM38. *Wine of Honour* (1945) . . . . BARBARA BEAUCHAMP
FM39. *A Game of Snakes and Ladders* (1938, 1955) . . . .
. . . . DORIS LANGLEY MOORE
FM40. *Not at Home* (1948) . . . . DORIS LANGLEY MOORE
FM41. *All Done by Kindness* (1951) . . . . DORIS LANGLEY MOORE
FM42. *My Caravaggio Style* (1959) . . . . DORIS LANGLEY MOORE
FM43. *Vittoria Cottage* (1949) . . . . D.E. STEVENSON
FM44. *Music in the Hills* (1950) . . . . D.E. STEVENSON
FM45. *Winter and Rough Weather* (1951) . . . . . . D.E. STEVENSON
FM46. *Fresh from the Country* (1960) . . . . MISS READ
FM47. *Miss Mole* (1930) . . . . E.H. YOUNG
FM48. *A House in the Country* (1957) . . . . RUTH ADAM
FM49. *Much Dithering* (1937) . . . . DOROTHY LAMBERT
FM50. *Miss Plum and Miss Penny* (1959) . DOROTHY EVELYN SMITH
FM51. *Village Story* (1951) . . . . CELIA BUCKMASTER
FM52. *Family Ties* (1952) . . . . CELIA BUCKMASTER

CPSIA information can be obtained
at www.ICGtesting.com
Printed in the USA
LVHW111559030820
662257LV00001B/231